Mr. Beautiful

By R.K. Lilley

Mr. Beautiful

Copyright © 2014 R.K. Lilley

All rights reserved.

ISBN-10: 1628780177
ISBN-13: 978-1-62878-017-8

DEDICATION

This book is dedicated to my husband. Yes, another one. I know, I know, bear with me here. He deserves it.

Christopher, thank you for being my biggest supporter and having *endless* faith in me. It is humbling. You bring out my best. You always have. We both know it. I'm a better me because of *you*. Don't think for a moment that I take it for granted. You're my rock, boo.

R.K. LILLEY

BOOKS BY R.K. LILLEY

THE WILD SIDE SERIES

THE WILD SIDE

IRIS

DAIR

TYRANT - COMING SOON

THE OTHER MAN - COMING SOON

THE UP IN THE AIR SERIES

IN FLIGHT

MILE HIGH

GROUNDED

MR. BEAUTIFUL

LANA (AN UP IN THE AIR COMPANION NOVELLA)

AUTHORITY - COMING SOON

THE TRISTAN & DANIKA SERIES

BAD THINGS

ROCK BOTTOM

LOVELY TRIGGER

THE HERETIC DAUGHTERS SERIES

BREATHING FIRE

CROSSING FIRE - COMING SOON

TEXT LILLEY + YOUR EMAIL ADDRESS TO 16782493375 TO JOIN MY EMAIL NEWSLETTER.

Visit my website: www.rklilley.com for news and new releases here.

Mr. Beautiful

By R.K. Lilley

PROLOGUE

MY REMAKING

PRESENT

JAMES

I've been remade four times in my life.

It is a distinct feeling. Impossible to mistake. The very marked sensation of being unraveled and reknit into a new thing, a new person. It can be good or bad, helpful or harmful, but above all, it is unstoppable.

I was remade when my parents died, went from a happy childhood, into navigating a very dark world, with endless responsibilities, surrounded by enemies and despairingly alone.

It happened again at the hands of a cowardly predator. I'd become angrier with that one, more cynical, and it undoubtedly turned me into the kinky fuck I was today.

The third happened swiftly. One day I looked up into a pair of pale blue eyes and saw the other half of my soul. Checkmate.

I went from a completely controlled existence, a life where I made every decision with cold calculation to a man overcome with feelings and emotions that were foreign but somehow wonderful.

And all too soon after that cataclysmic change was this fourth one, this one where I begged a God I'd never entertained to spare the life of a woman that I could not live without.

CHAPTER ONE

MY SUFFERING

Four days.

Ninety-six hours.

Five thousand, seven hundred and sixty minutes I waited for her to wake up.

And every second of those long minutes I *suffered*.

There was no numbness to be had. Not one merciful second of disconnect. I felt each one of those days, those hours, those minutes, those torturous seconds, with no anesthesia.

Bloody visions filled my head.

All of those bodies strewn out across the ground like some terrible Greek tragedy. They ran on repeat, those vile visions, burned into my mind, branded there for the duration.

And when my head wasn't filled with gory visions, it was filled with the most torturous, bittersweet memories.

CHAPTER TWO

MY ENNUI

PAST

JAMES

My phone chimed a message at me as the gate agent let me onto the jet bridge. This flying commercial business, even if it *was* a private charter, was more hassle than I was used to.

"Mr. Walker is running a few minutes behind, but he will be joining you shortly," the gate agent told my back.

I just nodded, thanking her for letting me know. *What were a few more minutes, when I'd already wasted forty-five minutes just getting to the plane?*

I checked my phone, my mouth twisting into a grimace when I saw that the text was from Jolene. She managed to beg to see me again, *and* beg for money in one short text. Usually she tried to separate those two requests, but I kind of appreciated her brevity. It made me feel less like a cad for occasionally fucking women that I couldn't stand when they proved to want money out of the exchange. I far preferred to give her money as opposed to my time.

James: I'm otherwise engaged for the foreseeable future, but contact Ben K for the money. The usual routine. Just tell him how much you need.

Jolene: Thx! Can't wait to see you again. Last night was incredible. Love u xoxo

I nearly rolled my eyes. Last night had been tolerable, and I hated it when she threw out the *L* word. All we'd ever shared was a predilection for rough and kinky fucking. And she knew very well that I wouldn't be contacting her anytime soon, if ever. More and more, hooking up with her just wore on me. Which was sad, considering how seldom it ever even happened. *How could you get sick of a person that you saw twice a year, and only for sex?*

I tucked my phone away as I approached the entrance into the aircraft. There was no one to greet me at the door, but it didn't matter. I knew that there was supposed to be a few passengers in coach, and that Bram Walker and I would be the only ones in first class, which wasn't hard to find.

I turned left, glancing down at my watch as I stepped into the first class cabin.

I looked up, and froze.

A tall blonde flight attendant nearly ran into me, but stopped just short, her chin tilting up to look at me. Her eyes widened, and she froze. She was lovely, with the palest blue eyes I'd ever seen and soft pink lips that formed a small O of surprise as she looked at me. A very attractive pink blush colored her cheeks. It made no sense at all, but we just stood there, frozen in place, staring at each other for a solid five minutes.

I studied her, instantly attracted, though that was an understatement. I was enthralled. There was something so irresistible in her eyes. They were so pale they struck me as a hint translucent. Pale blue eyes often came across as cold, but not hers. Hers were clear as water, so clear I felt like I was seeing something impossible, some hint of a kindred soul peeking out, or perhaps, of a person who would complement my own proclivities.

I doubted she was a sub; the chances were just too slim, but I was certain she was suited to be one. I felt as though I was holding her in place with just my force of will, and I loved that feeling.

My whole body felt alive, excitement pulsing through me. It made me realize suddenly just how clinical sex had become to me—nothing more than the methodical scratching of a biological itch.

How long had this ennui had such a hold on me? I had no idea. I hadn't realized that I'd been suffering from it at all until just that moment.

Like waking up from a nightmare, when you hadn't known you were dreaming.

I wasn't feeling it now, though. Not with this one.

I felt suddenly awake, suddenly alive.

This one seemed too perfect. I couldn't remember the last time I'd felt desire like this. *How long had I just been going through the motions?* I couldn't have said, but I had a moment of absolute clarity as I stood staring at her. I had been disinterested in way too many personal aspects of my life for far too long. I couldn't bring myself to be upset about that, because I wasn't disinterested *now*. On the contrary, I was fascinated at a glance.

Neither of us moved until I heard Bram's damned voice booming at me all the way from the jet bridge. "James Cavendish!"

Bram was a bit obnoxious. He was an old-time CEO at heart; from back in the day when being in charge meant you could do whatever the hell you wanted. Nowadays it was just the opposite. Being in charge meant that you had to be professional around your employees at all times, but Bram had never gotten that memo. I knew he'd be drunk before we took off, even though this was a business meeting. I would tolerate him, though and hear him out.

I could remember when he would come over to our house for dinner when I was a kid, before my parents had died. He and my father had been close. Because of their bond and those memories of my father laughing at his loud jokes, I'd always humor the obnoxious old bastard.

The loud voice of her boss galvanized the lovely woman into action, and it was only as she shifted that I realized she'd been holding a dripping bag of ice for our entire stare-down. There was a tiny puddle of water between us. I watched as two more drops gathered on the bottom of the bag and then fell to hit the ground.

I grinned. At least I wasn't the only one who'd forgotten that the rest of the world existed.

"Excuse me, Mr. Cavendish," she murmured in a soft voice.

I shifted to the side, then turned to watch her as she made her way to the back of the plane. She was just handing the bag of ice off to another flight attendant when Bram moved in to block my view of her.

He grinned at me, waving his arm for me to take a seat. I could tell just from glancing at him that he was already well into his cups. It was going to be a very long flight.

I felt like I'd just had a lobotomy as I made my way into the nearest seat. I couldn't think straight—couldn't focus at all, not on one solidified thought, let alone whatever Bram was going on about as he followed me.

I sat near the aisle, making Bram nearly stumble over my

long legs to get to the window seat.

I nodded at whatever the hell he was saying, trying not to crane my head around to see what that woman was doing. I thought of her soft voice and how she'd called me Mr. Cavendish.

She'd sealed her fate with that alone . . .

She was wringing her hands when she approached our seats. Other than that small tell, though, she seemed to have regained her composure. I didn't like that. I wanted to ruffle that composure again.

"Welcome aboard, Mr. Walker, Mr. Cavendish. What can I get you to drink?"

"Crown Royal on the rocks, sweetheart," Bram told her with a big smile.

"Just a bottle of water," I told her, not liking Bram's greasy smile.

"May I take your jackets?" she asked.

We both shook our heads no. I watched her walk away, admiring the view.

"I see you're enjoying my airline," Bram said with a chuckle.

I gave him an arch, and not entirely friendly, look. "It wasn't your airline I was enjoying."

He shrugged. "Same thing. I have a whole fleet of girls like Bianca."

Bianca, I thought. I had a name. It was a start.

My mouth twisted. "Not possible. You show me one more girl in her league, and I'll give you a million dollars."

His eyes narrowed on me. He suddenly reminded me of a shark scenting blood in the water. "Actually, I was getting to that. I'm glad you brought it up. I need a bit more than a million, son."

I sighed heavily as he went into the expected spiel about his airline. I tried to listen, but in actuality I was focusing on the galley at the front of the cabin, catching glimpses of Bianca as she worked.

I cursed myself for the bad seating choice and studied the cabin to find a better one.

Another flight attendant passed by our seat, heading toward Bianca. It was a brunette, and Bianca towered over the shorter woman. They had a brief, friendly-looking exchange. I only caught small snippets of what they were saying.

"Sure, take one," I heard Bianca saying in breaks from Bram's long dialogue. "I only have the two up here. I'm more than stocked."

"Thanks, Bianca," the other woman said, sounding relieved. "It's always so nice when the first class galley has their shit together. Half of them hoard the carts whether they need them or not."

"No problem. I'll help you take it back," Bianca told the woman, and I caught a glimpse of her smile. It was a small smile, just a slight upturning at the corners of her mouth. It was meant to reassure because the other woman was obviously stressed out.

I tried to put my finger on why I was so affected by that little smile. *It's her eyes*, I thought. They got to me. They held such a mixture of kindness, tragedy, and reserve. They were soul stealing.

You didn't get eyes like that without hardship. You didn't get eyes like that without anguish. She was a stunningly beautiful woman, but that was just the surface. I was so certain there was depth there and that intrigued me.

She served us, and every time she glanced at me, a lovely blush touched her cheeks.

I was making plans to pursue her before the plane had even taken off.

Her jump seat was just out of my view as she sat down for take-off. I made a note to sit in 2D the next time I took one of her flights. I would have had an unobstructed view of her seat from there.

It was a solid hour into the flight before I was able to approach her in the galley. She was bent down, stacking plates onto a silver, three-tiered cart.

"Do you really need to take a cart out for just the two of us?" I asked from behind her.

She visibly started, turning and standing to stare at me, gifting me with that becoming blush. "Mr. Cavendish," she said, looking stunned.

I smiled. "Bianca. Do you really need that cart for just the two of us?" I asked again.

She gave me a small but gratifying smile. "I tend to try to follow service procedures precisely when I'm serving the CEO of the airline."

I loved the sound of her voice. It was soft but steady. And I adored that little smile. "What's your usual route? Is Las Vegas to New York the normal routine?"

She looked a little surprised by the question, but she answered quickly enough. "Yes, it is, actually. Layovers in New York, and turns to DC."

"Turns?" I asked her, unfamiliar with the term.

She bit her lip. "Sorry," she said. "Airline lingo. A turn is when we fly somewhere, then turn around and fly back the same day."

"What days do you usually go to New York?" I asked her, studying her face steadily.

She opened her mouth, so close to answering, when fucking Bram interrupted, shouting my name, and distracting her.

"Excuse me, Mr. Cavendish, I have to get back to work. Did you need something?"

You. Under me. For fucking days.

I gave her a neutral smile. "I'm fine. I guess I'll leave you to it."

She nodded. "Please ring your call button if you need

anything at all."

You. Spread out, restrained, open, helpless before me, purposed absolutely for my use.

She turned away before she could see my nostrils flare, eyes and mind gone *wild*.

I didn't get another opportunity to approach her. Bram kept me occupied for the rest of the flight. I listened, feeling an obligation to at least hear him out for my father's sake, but I was ready to throttle him as the plane began to descend, and I hadn't been able to approach her again.

"You know I can't give you that kind of funding if you don't give me some control over the airline," I told him for at least the tenth time.

He smiled at me. It was a con man's smile. I wasn't impressed. "You know you can trust me to keep this ship afloat by doing things my way," he said.

I didn't know that. What I did know was that if he kept running things 'his way,' the airline would be bankrupt in a hurry, and grounded soon after that. I couldn't invest in it, not even for the sake of nostalgic childhood memories. The man ran his company like it was a game, throwing money around like he was getting his gambling fix. If he wouldn't give up control, I would just be prolonging the inevitable, burning pointlessly through millions in the process.

"Will the flight crew be staying in New York?" I asked him, changing the subject. I was sick of talking in circles.

"No. They all turn around and go back to Las Vegas. Why?"

I shrugged. "Just curious." I'd considered getting Bianca's number from him, or even her schedule, but I knew he wouldn't cooperate. He'd just see it as something he could use as leverage. I'd find another way.

I didn't even get a moment alone with her as we deplaned, though I tried. Fucking Bram lingered, though, so I just nodded at her. "A pleasure, Bianca," I told her on my way out, my mind coming up with the numerous ways that I planned to pleasure her in the very near future.

It was a graphic visual.

"A pleasure, Mr. Cavendish," she repeated back politely.

Not yet, I thought, *but it will be.*

I parted ways with Bram as soon as I could, striding swiftly towards where I knew Clark would have a car waiting at the curb.

I nodded at him as I slid into the backseat.

"To the hotel?" he asked with a raised brow.

"To the apartment," I said. I could tell he was surprised by that answer. I rarely quit working this early in the day. I knew it was useless to even try to work just then, though. I couldn't concentrate on a damn thing. My mind was stuck on that woman . . .

Clark began to drive, but he kept shooting me questioning looks in the rearview. "You meeting a woman, sir?" he asked.

It was a nosy question, but I was used to it. The man was so good at his job, and had been working for me for so long, that he'd gone beyond the role of employee to that of a friend, and we both knew he could say whatever he wanted and I wouldn't be offended. "No, Clark."

"Maybe you should. You look like you could use one."

I shot him a sardonic look. It was disconcerting how well he could read me. "No, but I need you to find one for me, actually. Her name is Bianca."

"No last name?" he asked without missing a beat. It wasn't as though I asked him to find women for me often. He was just an unflappable kind of guy.

"No. She's a flight attendant, and her name is Bianca. That's all I know."

"Walker's airline?"

"Yes."

"Physical description."

"Tall, blonde . . . beautiful. She looks like a model. I need her schedule ASAP. I could also use a number, address, anything you can get your hands on, really."

He sighed. "I'll see what I can do. It'll be a pain in my ass."

"I'll be eternally grateful."

"I know."

I felt a little lost when I walked into my apartment. I'd taken the afternoon off. *But to do what?* If I weren't acting like a besotted fool over a stranger, I'd have called one of the five women I knew that were in the city who could cater to my specific needs. I had no desire to, though, and that was the problem.

I felt dazed as I walked directly to the master bathroom, stripped down, and got into the shower. I didn't use cold water, but steaming hot. I closed my eyes and leaned against the tiled wall, picturing those devouring blue eyes of hers again. They'd been steady, but so submissive, as though she knew just what I needed from her.

Needed, I thought. *Yes*, that was the word.

I soaped my hand, stroked my throbbing cock and remembered how she'd blushed for me, and her little smile, and of course, those mesmerizing eyes.

Fuck, I thought in shock, coming in a few short strokes. And worse, that release wasn't enough. I was jerking myself off again within a few short moments. I felt like a teenager again, jacking myself off repeatedly in the shower.

I didn't even consider finding a woman to ease myself with. That was the worst of it. I knew I would find more satisfaction just *thinking* about *her*, than actually having another woman.

Bianca was trouble for me, I knew it, and still, I didn't give a fuck. I was going to have her.

I brought myself to another orgasm, gripping my length tightly, then began stroking again before I'd even finished, in danger of rubbing my own cock raw, thinking about a woman that I'd never even seen naked.

I thought about her body that time, about that neat little dress suit covering delectably round breasts, slender hips, and the best pair of legs I'd ever seen. I stroked my cock harder.

I remembered the delicate wrist I'd studied as she'd served me. I pictured tying those wrists to my bed as I jerked hard on my aching cock and came again with a rough groan.

It was early, but that didn't stop me from drying off and going straight to bed. I dreamed that night about silky blonde hair and pale blue eyes that I could lose myself in.

I'd only met her once. Why did it feel like I'd wanted her forever?

CHAPTER THREE

MY PURGATORY

PRESENT

"What will I do if she doesn't make it through this? How is it possible that I could find something, someone like this, and then lose it? What's the point of it all?"

And what about Stephan? He was in worse shape. What would I do if he didn't make it? How would I tell her a thing like that?

She was in surgery, and they weren't giving me nearly enough information to cope. I knew she was getting the best care possible, but it didn't help alleviate the purgatory I was experiencing as I waited to see if it would be enough.

Tristan's eyes were sympathetic in a way that let me know he'd been through hell and back, too. He existed every day in a purgatory of his own, I knew.

The poor bastard.

"First of all, she's going to pull through this," he said quietly.

"I know it. The fact that she's still breathing, after everything that happened tells us that. But also, James. About the how, and the why. A love like that makes you better, even if you lose it all, even if it was for one precious *moment* in your life, you can't be sorry that you had it. Trust me on this."

CHAPTER FOUR

MY RITUAL

PAST

I checked my watch again, then took it off impatiently, tossing it into a drawer.

She was supposed to be here in fifteen minutes, but I'd been ready for her for hours. I was too preoccupied to work, instead putting my efforts into grueling workouts and dinner prep.

I began to pace.

I was antsy, distracted, and restless in a way that was foreign to me.

I'd dismissed my staff halfway through the day, needing total solitude in this strange mood of mine.

For the first time that I could remember, I wasn't sure how the evening was supposed to play out or the best way to handle things. This sort of meeting usually only went one way for me. It didn't start with dinner, and it didn't end with a sleepover.

I didn't know what she wanted from me, or what she

expected, and that was the whole problem, because I wanted many things from her. Things she didn't seem remotely interested in.

It was safe to say I'd never run into this problem before.

Taking off my watch was no help, as I was checking the time again a scant two minutes later.

Where was she? Would she really cut it this close?

With a curse, I sought out a phone and called her.

"Hello," Bianca answered breathlessly.

It had me on instant alert, my entire body stiffening. "Where are you?" I heard myself asking, voice unwillingly harsh.

"I was just about to head out," she said, tone so strange that I found myself dissecting every word, looking for a clue to what it was about it that had my jaw clenching.

"I'll be there in about twenty minutes," she continued, "if I don't make any wrong turns."

"What's going on? You sound strange. And you're going to be late. This is one of many reasons why I wanted to send a driver."

"I'll be right there." Her voice broke on that sentence, and that's when I knew what I heard in her voice.

Desire. *Need.*

"What are you doing?" I purred, eyes closing in pleasure. If she was in this state now, I knew just how to control the situation, and the shift in power gave me instant relief. Reaching down, I pinched the tip of my erect cock hard. "Why do you sound so breathless?"

There was a long pause on the other end, but finally she answered, "Nothing."

A lie.

My jaw clenched, and I pinched myself harder. "Are you touching yourself?" I bit out.

"No," she lied again.

"Do you remember what I said I'd do to you if you lied to me?" I asked her, in equal parts turned on and infuriated by her defiance. "I believe that's three times now. Don't make yourself come. Your cunt is mine, and so is your pleasure. You're not allowed to come unless I say so."

She moaned, and I just about came in my hand.

"If you don't get into your car this second, I'm coming there, and then I won't let you come for hours," I barked, hanging up on her.

I went into the one of the property's control rooms, waiting impatiently for her vehicle, my mind filled with the ways I would own her in a few short minutes.

It was her first time, but I didn't want to take it slow or easy on her, didn't know if I was capable of it. Was she a true masochist? Would she find some enjoyment even in *that* sort of pain?

I was beyond impatient, yearning, longing to find out.

I opened the gate as soon as I finally saw a car approach, shrugging out of my shirt and heading to the entrance hall to watch for her.

I swung the front door wide as she reached the bottom of the small set of stairs that led up to the entrance, taking her in with gimlet-eyed satisfaction.

She paused there, and we stared at each other for a long time.

The lust in the air just then was so thick I felt like I could reach out and touch it with my hand. Could stick out my tongue and *taste* it. It was heady, drugging.

All-consuming.

She wore a sheer black dress with flowers painted across it.

It was flimsy, revealing her figure even in the near dark.

Even delivered to my doorstep, clearly dressed for sex, she looked cool and untouchable.

I would make her touchable. I knew it and she knew it, and it drove me *wild*.

"Get in here," I told her, wondering how I was even going to last from here to the bedroom.

She obeyed without a word, her expression stoic.

I was taking up most of the open doorway, which forced her to brush very close to me.

I sucked in a breath.

Just how out of line would it be to take her virginity on the floor of my entryway? How uncouth and unforgivable? I wondered. Because it was about a second away from happening.

"I had dinner ready, but that's going to have to wait," I informed her, my tone clipped, patience shot. "You're a little minx, you know that?"

She shook her head, looking nonchalant as she glanced around.

Her silence made my jaw clench. I didn't know what to do with it.

"I gave my entire staff the night off, so we're quite alone," I explained to her, to reassure her of our privacy in the event that I did, in fact, take her where she stood.

I held onto my control by the *thinnest* thread. I'd had my fingers inside of her, had felt the barrier of her hymen, and been obsessed with it ever since. I'd had time to dwell on just why it consumed my thoughts and came to the conclusion that it was the ownership it gave me. It was mine to take, to claim, to break, and in the breaking, I'd own a part of her that no one else had ever touched.

She ignored me as though I hadn't spoken, moving to run her hand along the heavy rail of the stairway that ran to the second floor.

I couldn't take it. I moved behind her, a breath away from touching her, a heartbeat away from losing it.

"Where's your bedroom?" she asked, her tone damn near casual.

A deep, primitive hunger rocked through my body. I shuddered in pleasure, my hand gripping her nape. I squeezed, then began to rub.

She leaned into the contact.

I grabbed her hair, making it into a handle at her nape, and began to lead her upstairs.

If she was going to refrain from all artifice, all teasing, I could restrain myself for at least the time I took to get near my bed.

I led her like that to my bedroom, stopping just inside of the door to let her take it in.

I'd arranged things just how I liked them, not pulling any punches. I wanted no misunderstanding here.

Restraints hung from the latticed top of the bed, others strewn at the posters. It was spelled out in barbaric letters all over the room. This was where I would take her body, claim ownership of it.

"Are those ropes?" she finally asked breathlessly.

"Yes," I answered, watching her.

"Is that a riding crop?"

If I'd been capable of idle chat, I'd have asked her then if she liked riding, if she knew how, but I was not. My vision had gone into tunnel vision just then, with only one thing on my mind.

"Yes," I said, moving to nudge her forward with my hand in

her hair until she was only steps from the bed. "I have more toys that I want to use on you, but I didn't want to intimidate you by laying them all out."

She laughed, and it was a touch hysterical.

That only made my heart pound harder. "You need to pick a safe word," I told her.

I watched her heavy breasts move as she took a deep breath. "I assume you know I've never done any of this before?" It was a question.

That got to me, because I did know it. It had become the single biggest obsession of my life these past days.

"Yes," I breathed, voice thick and intense.

She paused before finally answering, "Sotnos."

"Sotnos?" I questioned, rolling the word around in my mouth, like she had.

"Yes," she said shortly. Nothing else.

Infuriating woman.

I pulled on her hair hard, tilting her head back and to the side until she looked at me. "There are rules here," I explained harshly. "I become your Master in here, and I will punish you when you defy me. I will read your reactions, and try not to go too far, but if I do, or if there's something you just can't handle, that's the word you use."

She didn't seem the least intimidated, in fact her chin had lifted defiantly at my words. "What about outside of here? Didn't you say you would punish me for lying to you? But we weren't in here when I lied to you."

I smiled. I enjoyed her spirit. "There are exceptions. I will never lie to you, and I expect you to learn to do the same. Tell me what your safe word means."

She shook her head, jaw set stubbornly. "No."

I drew in a steadying breath. "Would you rather take more lashes than just tell me what that means?"

She didn't hesitate to nod. "Yes." She sounded confident.

I studied her. "How about an exchange?" I cajoled. "Is there something I could give you in exchange for that information? Something you want to know about me? Something you want in general?"

Again, she didn't hesitate, shaking that stubborn head of hers.

I gripped her hair harder. "You're driving me crazy," I told her softly, maneuvering her towards the bed. "We need to talk. We need to figure out this arrangement. But I can't wait any more for this. Nothing has ever made me feel this wild before. I need to mark you. I need to own you. I need to punish you. I need to open you up and strip every detail out of you. And I will get you to tell me what that word means to you."

There was a pregnant pause, where she neither agreed nor protested.

"Lift your arms," I told her when I'd moved her very close to the bed.

She did, and I peeled her dress off her swiftly, sucking in a breath at the sight that greeted me.

I was feverish with want. I needed everything at once. To touch her, to taste her mouth. To take out my cock, make her suck it, climb inside of her bare.

I restrained myself. Barely.

Instead, I circled, eyes devouring every sweet inch of her. She wore nothing but a bra and thong now, her big breasts heavy and swelling out of the thin material of her joke of a bra, the coral tips pebbled into tight, hard peaks. Best rack I'd seen in my life, bar none.

I bent down swiftly and bit her through her bra. Hard.

She made a delicious little noise, and I straightened, continuing to circle her.

I snapped her tiny little thong as I passed her hip. She was shapelier than I'd realized, her torso more hourglass than straight, rounding into soft hips that were just perfect for gripping.

"You are too much," I told her as I studied her shapely little ass. "A virgin with the sexiest body I've ever seen in my life. Too fucking perfect."

I knelt behind her, leaned forward and bit one pert cheek *hard*.

She sobbed in a breath and glanced back at me.

I kissed the mark I'd left there, looking up to meet her eyes.

She turned to face forward again, her breathing agitated.

I fingered the tiny scrap of material at her hip. "I want to cut all of your clothes off, but I love everything I see you wear, and I have no idea where you got any of it, so I don't know how to replace it."

"The thongs are from Victoria's Secret. So is the bra."

I smiled at her approvingly, then slapped her ass.

"Don't move," I ordered, moving to grab a knife.

The look on her face made me laugh. "It's just for cutting clothes. I would never cut your skin. The thought is abhorrent to me. I just want to blister it a little."

I moved to her, grabbing the front of her bra, pulling it out, and cutting it cleanly in one motion, taking the cups apart.

I watched her nipples tighten, pinching them several times, each time harder than the next. "How sensitive are they? Did you like the first touch better, or the last?" I pinched harder, until she moaned, and had to stifle my own moan. "Or the fourth time?"

She swallowed hard but answered quickly. "The fourth."

"Good. I have something for you." I went back to the nightstand drawer, put the knife away, and grabbed a pair of nipple clamps I'd picked out earlier.

The clamps were peach colored, with a silver chain connected between them. I wrapped the chain around the back of her neck, fastening it there.

She took it well when I pinched them onto each hard peak.

"Nipple clamps," I explained. "Are they too tight?"

She shook her head, studying them.

They looked perfect on her. In fact, I couldn't decide if I even wanted to pierce her, they looked so right.

Next, I cut off her thong, watching her face to gauge her reaction.

"Climb on the bed," I ordered, voice gone hoarse.

She obeyed.

"Climb over to that ramp until your knees are touching it. Yes, right there."

I climbed up behind her, pushing her face down onto the ramp I'd arranged in the middle of the bed, which pushed her ass up just where I wanted it.

Her cheek was touching the riding crop, and she was trembling. It was almost too much.

"This isn't your knee," she told me.

That surprised a laugh out of me. "It is not. My lap isn't a safe place for you at the moment. We'll get to that, though, I promise."

I slipped a rope over her ankle, then drew it taut.

"The more you struggle, the more these will chafe. Keep that in mind." I secured her other ankle, then moved to her wrists, binding her quickly.

I moved behind her again, leaning over her until I was flush against her back, my erection digging into her ass.

She wiggled, and I swatted one cheek lightly.

"Hold still," I ordered and slid the crop out from under her cheek.

I moved off her.

She moaned in protest, and I lightly spanked her again.

My heart tried to beat its way out of my chest as I just studied her for a long time, almost nervous to start.

She looked so beautiful like that. So perfect, tied up, bound for my use.

This was my poetry, my art, her body my canvas.

I felt giddy for what was to come.

"Do you have anything to say before I begin?" I asked her.

"I'm sorry, Mr. Cavendish," she said, arching her back.

I hummed, deep in my throat, and let the crop fly.

I started lightly, only hitting harder when I saw her reaction.

She moaned and wriggled, and I could see how wet this was making her.

I made myself stop, panting at the effort. I didn't want to overdo it, when I was still so unsure of her limits.

She arched and muttered a protest, rubbing her chest against the ramp.

I felt dizzy. I held my hand out in front of me, and it was shaking.

I'd never jumped into something so fast or carelessly before. My instincts told me she wasn't a liar, but instincts could be wrong, and for all I knew, she wasn't even on the pill.

I'd been scrupulous about protection from the time I'd become sexually active. Getting some random woman pregnant simply wasn't an option for me, as plenty of fortune hunters would have loved nothing more than to take advantage of a careless moment.

None of this had slipped my mind. It wasn't a matter of oversight. Not at all.

It was a change of heart.

My MO was evolving rapidly into something even I didn't recognize or completely understand. But I did understand something. I'd be coming inside of her bare. The thought of getting her pregnant wasn't even that alarming to me. In fact, if I was honest with myself, the idea of tying her to me in such a way was more than a little appealing.

I glanced down at my heavy erection. It was swollen to the point of painful, turning red, thick veins apparent along my shaft. I twitched, pre-cum dribbling out from my tip.

I'd never been so aroused in my life.

"I need to stop there," I told her gruffly. "I don't want you too sore to lie on your back when I take you."

More of that silence from her that I had no notion what to do with.

My attention caught on her creamy white flesh. "Fuck. I can see the liquid running down your legs." I fingered the trail of moisture on her thigh.

"We need to do a few things before I fuck you. I have a health exam on the table over there. I've been tested. All the results are clean. Do you want to see it? It's available for you. I want to bury my cock in you bare, if you'll allow. You said you're on the pill, right?"

She nodded. "I am. I'll take your word for it. If I thought you'd lie about something like that, I wouldn't be letting you tie me up and pound the V-card out of me, now would I?"

I laughed and bent to kiss her cheek.

I pushed the ramp out from under her, letting her fall to the bed.

I freed her ankles. I gripped them, pushing her up higher on the bed. I flipped her over with just that contact, surprising the breath out of her.

This twisted her arms above her head and allowed me to spread her legs wide. I tied them like that, devouring the sight.

She was so lusciously blonde. Everywhere. She was breathtaking, her ripe body with all of its perfect alabaster skin, trembling before me.

Mine.

I claimed her with my mouth first, beginning with a chaste kiss to her lips that was nothing so much as an assertion of my will, then moving south to stake my claim on every inch of her untouched skin.

Next, I took her body with mine. I did it with ruthless skill, and the closest I'd ever come to wild abandon. I broke through her barrier and became frenzied to the point of madness.

I heard my own low, guttural moans as I took her. I'd never been loud, had always controlled my noises, but now, *now*, I just couldn't hold things like that back.

I never took my gaze off hers. Those pale eyes of hers both devoured me and fed me.

They swallowed me whole and kept me intact.

I felt her around me, felt her tender flesh clench, and I went insane.

I cursed silently, groaned aloud, tensed, then started heaving like a madman, hurting her I was sure, because she wasn't accustomed to an invasion like this.

And thinking of that had me losing my mind even more.

She was sobbing out her pleasure at the end, begging for release.

I kept going, rutting in her uncontrollably, driven like a fiend.

Finally, when I reached my limit, I took her to the edge. I started rubbing her clit relentlessly as I pounded in and out. "Come, Bianca," I commanded, my eyes eating up every detail of her passion-slackened face.

Incredibly, she obeyed. Like she was an instrument already tuned to my touch. Like she was made for me.

Because she was.

Mine.

Irreversibly. Irrevocably.

I jarred into her hard with one last brutal thrust and emptied my seed deep inside of her.

I couldn't stop kissing her as I came down from that giddy high. Her lips were lush, but that wasn't why I couldn't stop obsessing about them. It was their softness, their malleable, pulpy, trembling silkiness that had me craving, needing more.

Afterward I drew a bath, my mind reeling, racing, reconfiguring my life as I knew it.

I moved back to the bed when the bath was ready, studying her limp, sated form with vivid pleasure.

I tried to place what I was feeling. It was beyond satisfaction. More like something akin to fierce pride. She couldn't know it yet, but this beautiful creature had sealed her fate in that bed.

I wasn't letting her go. She was skittish, but I wouldn't let that daunt me.

It wasn't a question of *if* anymore, not after that. I'd be keeping her. Now it was just a question of *how.*

I carried her to the bath and washed her clean with my dirty hands.

In spite of my thoughts, my desires, I could tell I said something wrong when she tried to leave before dinner and only barely cajoled her into staying for a meal.

I lost all of my usual finesse with this woman; the charm I counted on seemed to have no effect.

She was close-lipped and distant, but I managed to wrestle small bits of information out of her.

She didn't trust me, or expect much from me, but I meant to change that.

I had her again, taking her on the table with dessert.

I shouldn't have. I knew it. I'd used her roughly her first time, but she swore she wasn't too sore, and I didn't have the self-control to keep from slaking my thirst with her luscious body a second time.

I kissed the rope marks on her wrists. "I love seeing this on you," I spoke against her skin, voice thick with something far stronger than mere desire.

I pushed her back flat against the surface of the table, spreading her legs wide.

I moved between her legs, my cock a whisper from her entrance.

"Look at me," I commanded. When her eyes met mine, I continued, "Watch me. I'll punish you every time you look away from me when I'm inside of you."

She nodded, lips trembling, pale eyes steady and relentless, claiming pieces of my soul with but a look.

"Ask me for it," I ordered, stroking myself.

"Please, Mr. Cavendish, fuck me."

I obliged, pushing into her roughly.

I couldn't contain a deep groan as I began to thrust in earnest.

"Does it hurt?" I asked without slowing.

"It's perfect," she moaned.

Even after we'd finished, I stayed inside of her, carrying her up to my room while I bounced her on my insatiable cock.

"Let me know if you reach your limit," I told her roughly when I'd carried her back to my room. I still held her, still buried deep. "You should be sore and tender after your first time. I should be considerate and let your body recover."

"Please, don't."

That nearly undid me, combined with her needy tone.

"You want me to finish you like this, standing up and impaled on my cock?" I asked, anchoring her to me as I worked her up and down my stiff length.

"Y-yes please. Oh, yes."

She was on the edge, and I was right there with her when I clipped, "Come, Bianca."

She fell apart, and I fell with her.

I stayed up all night.

I'd worn her out, and she slept like a baby. I'd worn myself out, and somehow it wasn't enough. I wanted, needed more.

I left the bathroom light on, door open, and left the room illuminated enough to watch her, touch her, and stare at the ceiling, wondering what the hell I was going to do.

This, *this* was what my agnostic mind pictured the spiritual mind feeling when it attended confession. A leaking out of all that was bad and a flowing back in, a joyful inhalation, of the most substantial life-sustaining nourishment.

So much of this ritual had become a habit; one that I knew was designed in part to avoid intimacy. If our bodies were temples, the things I did to my subs were meant as sacrilege.

This was not that.

31

This was beyond the ritual, beyond the habit. I had wallowed in her, basking, reveling, and in my revelry, I had slaked *beyond* my physical thirst and delved into another need entirely.

This was different.

This was intimacy. This was sacred.

I couldn't get enough. I couldn't stop, even when I knew it should be enough, that I was overusing her unused body.

Somehow, I knew, *just knew*, deep in my gut, where certainties held the most sway, that I would never have enough of her.

I was lost. I was found.

I, James Cavendish, unrepentant dominant, sexual deviant, and prolific slut for more years than I cared to count, was in love.

I'd taken her virgin body, but just as surely, she'd taken my virgin heart.

CHAPTER FIVE

MY DESPAIR

PRESENT

To believe in that perfect love, and your whole life know that it isn't for you, that what you've been shaped into makes it fundamentally impossible, then one day you blink, and there it is, someone so perfectly formed to complement your own complicated needs.

It was heady, a rush like nothing else.

And like all highs, the low was more than its match, a despair so harsh, the teeth it sunk in me so jagged and sharp it had my breath dragging in and out like it was a physical affliction that ailed me.

I bent over her sleeping form, waiting for her to wake up.

Even I couldn't have said at first if I was merely holding vigil or outright praying, but it was a fact that that is exactly what it turned into.

It brought to mind something Tristan had said to me once,

just after his rehab days, as he'd been coming to terms with the things he'd lost, and I hadn't been able to hide my surprise about his newfound need for spirituality.

'I get that it's not for everybody, but it's helping *me*,' he'd explained. 'God doesn't need us, James. You don't have to believe in him to keep him relevant. That's not the issue. *We* need *him*. Listen, I'm not saying I have all of the answers, but I have enough to take it a day at a time.

I have lost *so much*, and I have only myself to blame for it. I could *destroy* myself with the guilt of that. Trust me, I have that inside of me. But by some miracle, I did not do that, instead, I opened my heart and my arms and begged for help, and that's when I realized: God doesn't need us, but when we need him, no matter what we've done, how far we've fallen, or how long it takes us to find him, he's still there for us.'

At thirty, bent over with the weight of my heavy burdens, more exhausted and weary than I'd ever been, taking up residence on an uncomfortable chair in a Vegas hospital, for the first time in my life, feeling wretched and despairing, I opened my heart and arms and found some small bit of peace as I waited through the hardest hours of my life.

CHAPTER SIX

MY MADNESS

PAST

I felt so stripped of every normal, rational part of me with her that it was almost unpleasant at first.

Like air on a fresh wound.

I had so little control of myself where she was concerned. It was madness like I'd never known. Trembling urgency. Crippling desperation. Undiluted frenzy. Savage abandon.

It was an alien feeling, and I wondered sometimes why I didn't fight it. Why I didn't withdraw from it, why I never even considered staying away.

I couldn't quite believe how much I'd lost it, couldn't understand this total upheaval of who I was, this assault on my peace of mind, and most of all, couldn't comprehend how I could love it, crave it, need it so.

"**H**ello," I answered my phone.

"Who's your best friend in the world?" Frankie's voice called out gleefully to me, on the other end of the line.

I smiled. "You are, of course. What's got you sounding so tickled, my dear?"

"If you liked me before, you're going to love me after you meet this new sub I found for you. She's perfect, James. Right up your alley, and you know I know your type."

I stiffened, blinking slowly.

It wasn't so unusual. Frankie had introduced me to girls before. She was more involved in the scene that accompanied our lifestyle than I was. But the timing was off.

In fact, after what had happened last night, it was horrible.

She kept talking, not noticing right away the significance of my utter silence. "Dark hair, gorgeous hazel eyes. Twenty-six and trained by the best. Body to die for. She's smart and sweet, too. It'll be a nice change for you."

She went on about this mystery woman's many apparent virtues, and my mind wandered for a bit, across the country, on a flight with my reticent lover of the night before.

Finally, I interrupted her. "I met someone," I said shortly.

She was quiet for a beat, then, "Oh. Is it . . . serious?"

I could tell from her tone just how unlikely she thought that was. I searched for the words to explain that it was more than serious. It was *necessary.*

"She's the one."

Heavy silence on the other end let me know that she was

processing the information properly.

"Wow," she finally spoke, sounding equal parts elated and disbelieving. "That's wonderful! How is this the first I'm hearing of it, and have you set a date yet?"

"It just happened, and I wouldn't mark your calendar yet. I finally fell for a girl, but, and you're gonna love this, she's not sure she's that into me."

"Huh?"

"I'm not sure yet if she likes me."

"What?"

"She's doesn't know what to make of me."

"Excuse me?" Her tone was somehow more incredulous with each question.

I sighed. "She thinks I'm an asshole with too much money, and it might take a miracle to get her to come around. Does that clear it up for you?"

Her voice dripped with her utter delight. "I need to meet this girl. I can already tell I'll LOVE her."

She paused for a moment, then delicately, "So, are you going to do some demonstrations with her?"

I blanched. "No. No. No. Never."

"Will you be bringing her to the fetish parties?"

"No. Those days are over for me. What I have with Bianca . . . it's not something I can share. I have to keep it private. Anything else would drive me mad."

"I get it. Totally understandable. I'm so happy for you."

I was smiling when we ended the call.

CHAPTER SEVEN

MY HELPLESSNESS

PRESENT

Finally, after agonizing, waiting, remembering, Bianca came to with a violent jerk, her eyes snapping open.

A great shudder rocked through my body, and I had to look down at our joined hands for a moment to stay composed. It wouldn't do to break down in front of her just then.

A relief like nothing I'd ever known flowed through me, top to bottom, like cold water, raising every hair on my body.

She was awake. She was alive. We were actually going to survive this.

All those hours, and she hadn't even been resting.

She'd been waiting, it seemed, her own bloody visions keeping hold of her, because the second she spoke, she said, "Stephan?" A world of pain and fear in her voice.

I gasped when I finally found the courage, the composure to look at her again. Into those beloved eyes I never thought would look at me again.

She knew. She knew he was grievously injured. That fast, and she remembered.

"He's recovering from surgery."

She processed that for just a moment before asking, "How badly was he hurt?" It sounded like she was talking around a mouth full of marbles. I flinched, imagining the damage that had been done to the inside of her mouth. "Will he be okay? I need to see him now."

Unbelievably, her words were accompanied by her trying to sit up.

I chose my words carefully, wondering how to get her to stop moving so much. It couldn't be good for her. "He's in the ICU. He was badly hurt. No one can see him—"

My body seized up in shock as her hand shot to her arm and brutally ripped out her IV.

I started shaking. I couldn't seem to breathe. How could I stop her from hurting *herself*? I could only watch her, feeling helpless and futile.

She sat up. "I need to see him *now*," she said vehemently.

Two nurses had been hovering near enough to hear what was going on, and they snapped into action, wrestling her back down, two more nurses and a doctor joining in before they could get her IV back in.

She met my eyes as the nurse worked on her arm. "Please, James. I have to see him."

Eventually I nodded, not knowing what else to do. "Please don't do that again. I'll arrange for you to see him, but you must stay in your bed."

She nodded, shutting her eyes, her tense body finally relaxing back into the hospital bed.

Arrangements were made, and I walked with her as they wheeled her bed to his.

She calmed after she saw him, though he was still unconscious.

But sure enough, less than two hours later, he roused for the first time since the shooting.

I told her the second she woke up. His vitals were improving. They were both going to live.

Miracle on miracle. After all that had happened, I couldn't believe our good fortune.

I made a vow then and there never to take even one single *second* of our life together for granted.

"**H**ave they buried my father?" she asked the next day.

"Not yet, I don't believe," I answered, studying her face, trying to figure out why she wanted to know. "They will in the next day or so. Is there anything you'd like me to do?"

"Could you please get me a pen and paper?"

I had it fetched, watching in puzzlement as she scribbled a few sentences on the paper, then folded it carefully and handed it to me.

"Could you please have that buried with him?"

"Yes of course." I recalled a rather important detail. "He's actually being cremated, unless you object."

"No, that's fine. Have it burned with him please."

I agreed, still watching her blank face. "May I read it?"

"Go ahead." No hesitation in her answer.

I opened the neatly folded letter, brows rising as I read the brief scrawl.

To the monster,

Fuck you. You can't hurt us anymore. Oblivion is too good for you. Enjoy the fire. You've earned it.

Your daughter

I looked up, caught her eye.

She gave me a rueful smile. "It's therapeutic."

I smiled wryly, refolding the paper. "Indeed it is. Do you have any desire to . . . go to his funeral?"

She shot me a look. "No. *Never.* It's bad luck to spit on someone's grave, and I'm not sure I could stop myself."

CHAPTER EIGHT

WORST NIGHTMARE

PRESENT

STEPHAN

I awoke to bright lights and hospital sounds. And pain. Agony shooting through me with every breath.

It all came back to me in a flood.

The blood. The bodies. The unmitigated horror of it.

Bianca.

Bianca going limp, crumpling to the ground, blood in her hair, blood on her face.

My worst nightmare come to life.

Bianca.

I'd seen her shot, seen her fall.

No. No. No. *No.* I couldn't lose her. It was inconceivable.

"Bianca," I wheezed, my chest burning like it was on fire with that one word.

CHAPTER NINE

I'M OKAY, YOU'RE OKAY, WE'RE

OKAY

PAST

STEPHAN

We didn't shake hands or touch gloves. Not that we got to wear gloves.

It wasn't that kind of a fight. Some underground clubs had rules. Some of them even operated under a code. This wasn't one of those. That kind of ring wouldn't take an under-aged street kid into the mix, no matter how good he was at hurting people.

We nodded at each other across the small space allotted us for this desperate bout of violence. I made the mistake of meeting his eyes.

They were dead. He already thought he'd lost everything.

He was about to lose more.

I wanted to tell him just to fall with the first blow, that I never lost, so he shouldn't make me hurt him more than I had to, to get paid.

I wanted to tell them all that. I didn't want to do more damage than I had to, but sometimes I couldn't help it.

I *never* wanted to reach the place where I couldn't help it.

I took a deep breath, letting my eyes move through the crowd to find the only face in the world that reassured me.

Bianca's serene eyes met mine, and I felt instantly better.

The place was packed, but there was an invisible barrier around her that no one dared to encroach on, thanks to me and my temper.

Everyone here knew what I'd do if someone so much as bumped into her. It was a rough crowd, and I'd made a point of educating them with a few bloody examples.

"Love you," she mouthed, looking utterly composed amidst this chaos. It was just what I needed. Her calm was the anchor that kept me grounded, always. I did the fighting, but she was the one that kept me safe and alive. I'd have lost the will to live a long time ago, if I hadn't found her.

"Love you," I mouthed back.

Of course, everyone assumed we were young lovers. We always let them assume. It was just easier than explaining that, though she'd never be my girlfriend, she was as essential to me as air, and I'd die before I'd let anyone hurt her.

I focused back on the task at hand, my will renewed. I hated fighting, hated it more than just about anything, but it was a necessary evil, at the moment.

And hate it or not, I was very good at it. Undefeated, in fact. Defending myself against someone four times my body weight from an early age was my training. And it was good training.

The bell rang, and I went to work. He started dancing my way, light on his feet for such a big guy, and trained to box, I guessed.

It wouldn't be enough.

I was trained to *survive*, to fight dirty, no matter the means.

I dodged his first quick blows, observing his moves before I made my own. He was quick, but I knew I was quicker. And more desperate. I didn't just have myself to win for.

I stopped his fancy footwork with one brutal blow to the gut, followed through instantly with a vicious fist to his temple.

He went down, but unfortunately, I hadn't knocked him out.

He came at me again, and I blocked each of his blows easily. The blow to the head had made him slower, and I could see each hit coming.

I clenched my jaw, cursed myself, and attacked, landing three quick-fire, savage punches, two to his midsection that I knew would leave him coughing up blood for days, the third an uppercut into his chin.

He went down, and when he got back up, his eyes were dazed, feet stumbling. I'd messed him up good, and I wasn't done.

He managed to clip me on the shoulder before I laid into him again, but it was nothing, certainly not compared to the damage I did to him that round.

He just kept getting up. He'd barely managed to land a blow, but he wouldn't stay down. Either he had a death wish, or he didn't understand.

We got a breather after a time, and I went to check on Bianca while the poor bastard went and licked his wounds in the corner.

"You okay?" she asked, wiping my brow, her eyes as steady

as her hands.

I nodded. "I'm fine, but *he* won't be, if we keep this up. Guy doesn't know when to quit."

"Be careful. He strikes me as desperate."

I let her see the bleakness in my eyes. "We all are."

She nodded. "I know, but I don't trust him. Just be extra careful, okay?"

I agreed and kissed her on the forehead.

She leaned into me, unmindful of the sweat, uncaring of the filth and blood on me.

It was what I needed. It was all I'd ever needed.

Acceptance.

Such a simple concept, but I needed it like I needed air to breathe, and only one person had ever given it to me.

I hugged her into my chest and breathed it in. It was more than salve to a wound.

It was life-sustaining.

I soaked up as much as I could before heading back into the ring.

My girl had impeccable instincts.

The guy pulled a knife on me for that round, jabbing me with it before I saw his intent.

It wasn't serious, just a flesh wound, but it set me off.

My vision went red, and so did the room.

I took his legs out from under him with a vicious kick to the front of his knee and a hard shove. I followed him down, pummeling his face.

Someone tried to pull me off him, several someones, but it was useless.

And then I heard her. Calling my name. Snapping me out of it.

I shook my head, stilling. I lifted my bloody fists up, staring at them. They were trembling badly. As I saw this, I realized my whole body had begun to shake.

I looked down at the mess of a man underneath me.

By the state of him, I'd been at it for some time.

I cringed, and retching, I scrambled off him.

It was his face that really got to me. It was a bloody pulp, unrecognizable, pounded into just so much misshapen meat.

And he was so still.

I was barely clear of him when I emptied out the contents of my stomach on the ground.

Soft hands were stroking my shoulders from behind, Bianca saying something that I couldn't hear over the crowd.

I couldn't hear them, but I felt the words, knew them by heart, and tried to believe them now.

The room had gone wild with noise, cheers, and applause. They loved the raw, brutal violence of what I'd done. It's why they came, why I made money at this.

I wanted to curl into a ball and disappear. This was the worst one yet.

Had I killed him? I wondered, praying that I hadn't, though it seemed that I was grasping at straws. No one was trying to move him, as though they didn't think it was worthwhile to even try.

I felt slender arms hug me from behind, soft kisses on my temple, and then her voice in my ear, "You're okay. He's okay. I'm okay. We're okay," she chanted soothingly, over and over.

It helped. Even if it wasn't entirely true. It helped. She always knew how to take care of me.

She always had.

Always understanding, always accepting, always loving,

from the very start.

Things got out of hand in the ring sometimes. I'd done my fair share of damage, but so far, I'd never killed anyone in one of these fights. I found I was having a very hard time coming to terms with it.

I *had* killed before. When I'd stopped that old man from raping Bianca I'd beaten his head so hard against the pavement that I'd felt when his skull caved in.

No. This wouldn't be the first time I'd killed, but that didn't make it any easier to stomach.

Who had he been? Who would miss him? Why was my life worth more than his?

It wasn't. I knew it wasn't. But *hers* was worth more, and she needed me. The thought galvanized me, as it always did. I would do what I needed to for her. I'd do anything for her. Because it was a fact that *she* was worth it, and that certainty had gotten me through many o' rough thing.

Who I assumed was a doctor was finally kneeling by the other fighter, tending to him. He didn't pronounce him dead right away, and I took that as some small sign of hope.

Bianca pulled me gently away from the mess I'd made on the floor, and I blindly followed her.

Old Sam, the bastard that organized these things, came to stand in front of me, a sick grin on his face.

He waved a wad of cash in front of me.

I grabbed it, glaring at him.

He was the source of my livelihood at the moment, but I still hated him. He was the worst kind of opportunist and had no qualms about preying on the weak and desperate.

"Good job, son," he told me with a good-natured chuckle.

"Don't call me son," I told him, my voice gravelly from all of the retching.

He shrugged. "You always get touchy after these things, but you're a natural, my boy. We're going to do great things together."

I opened my mouth to say something scathing, but Bianca beat me to it.

"Just go away. Leave him alone," she told the man in her coldest voice. "Give him space."

The man lifted his hands, as though to show he meant no harm, and still smiling, walked away.

"He's a *parasite*," she said vehemently when he'd left. "If we never set eyes on him again, it'll be too soon."

I couldn't have agreed more.

We stayed in the room long enough to ascertain that the other fighter was definitely still alive, and there was a chance he'd stay that way.

When the doctor pronounced this to the crowd, there were more boos than cheers.

I thought I might be ill again.

I went on autopilot as Bianca led me away to a dimly lit bathroom in the back of the building.

She lifted off my shirt, washed me, and tended to me like I was a child, fussing over the cut in my side, and I let her.

She left, snagged some supplies from the doctor's bag, and came back quickly. She cleaned the cut, worrying over it.

I soaked in her loving ministrations.

"The doctor said he'd come back here to check you out after he finishes with the other guy."

I just nodded, feeling disconnected.

She'd taken the money from me and counted it to make sure it was all there.

"Four hundred dollars. Let's get a room tonight, okay? You

need to take a nice hot shower and sleep in a soft bed."

I didn't argue. This was the usual pattern after a fight, one of the few things that made it worthwhile to hurt people for money.

Four hundred dollars, I thought. I was willing to do that to a man for four hundred dollars, to beat him beyond recognition.

I swallowed hard, taking deep breaths to keep from gagging.

I had no notion of how much time might have passed before the doctor came to check on me.

He didn't do much, or didn't take long, but it seemed to reassure Bianca to let him tend to the scrape of a knife wound.

"Will he live?" I croaked at him. I'd been working up the courage to ask him since he'd walked in.

"Yes. He won't be pretty, but he'll live."

I breathed easier, but only a little. I nodded and thanked him.

There was a weekly budget rental place within walking distance, and I stayed outside while she went into the office and got us a room for the night. It was one of the few places that took cash and didn't ask for ID.

I stiffened when I saw who was behind the reception desk, but Bianca was already heading back to me, key in hand.

"Don't *ever* talk to that guy," I told her, my voice harsh with fear. "Stay away from him."

She studied me, her tragic eyes seeing everything. "Oh Stephan, what did you do?"

I flinched. "Don't. Please."

She moved into me, wrapping her arm around my waist and leading me. "He wouldn't take any money. Said you'd settled up the last time we were here."

Her tone held not an ounce of judgement, but instead a

world of pity and grief.

"Please. Don't," I said again, suddenly wanting to cry.

"I love you," she said calmly. "More than my own life, *I love you.*"

I didn't respond, too occupied blinking away tears.

"What did he make you do?" she asked when we'd stepped into our room.

I looked around, avoiding her eyes now. At least it was clean. Mostly.

"It doesn't matter," I told her.

She wasn't innocent. She'd seen too much for that. But she was pure, and I wouldn't corrupt her ears or mind with the filthy thing I'd done to pay for our room the last time we were here.

"Oh Stephan," she uttered softly, her tone undoing me.

I shook my head, swallowing hard. "I'm going to shower."

She let me go.

I didn't hurry, but I didn't linger either. I needed to get clean, but it would take more than hot water and soap for that.

I crawled into bed still damp and waited, trembling, while she took her own shower, and joined me.

I wrapped myself around her, burying my face in her clean wet hair. Just a few deep breaths and I already felt better.

"Did he hurt you?" she finally asked, voice muffled into my chest. "Can you talk about it?"

I couldn't. What could I say? She knew what I'd done, or at least enough. Explaining that letting him suck my dick, instead of the reverse, had made it palatable enough for me to accept was hardly going to make me feel better.

My long silence told her everything. Her voice was clogged with tears when she spoke again. "Don't ever do that again. Please. Promise me. I can't bear the things you put yourself through."

I couldn't refuse her when she pleaded with me like that. "I won't," my voice was thick and full of anguish. "I promise."

We were silent for a very long time, but that was fine. The contact was what I needed.

I did eventually recover enough to talk about it. "I hate that part of me. *Hate it.* All I want is to keep you safe and never have to hurt anyone again."

Her chest moved against mine as she took a very deep breath. "I know. I'm so sorry."

"Don't be sorry. This isn't on you. It never was. I just . . . wish I wasn't like my dad."

"You're not. This violence is not who you are. It does not define you."

I let that penetrate, let it comfort me, as it was meant to.

"This is all temporary," she told me, her tone wistful. "Remember our little houses."

I smiled. This was a popular fantasy of ours.

"Side by side," I added.

"Neighbors," she agreed.

"I want grass in my yard."

"I want nothing but rocks and maybe a cactus." I could hear the smile in her voice.

"You'll get to keep all of the pictures you make."

"And give some to you."

Eventually I was comforted enough to drift off into sleep, her soothing chant calming me, as it always did—*I'm okay, you're okay, we're okay.*

We were having breakfast at a diner the next morning (a rare treat, and one courtesy of my fight money) when she became very serious, making me look across the table and directly into her soulful eyes.

"No more," she said, resolve inundating each word until it felt like she was raising her voice, though she spoke softly. "We'll try foster care again, but I can't watch you do this to yourself anymore. Not *any* of it."

I started shaking my head.

She kept nodding. "It won't be for long. As soon as you turn eighteen, we'll have more options."

"No. It's too risky. He'll find you again. I can do this."

"There are no good choices for us right now, but we need to do our best to take the safest ones."

I nodded in agreement. I knew she was right, but I wasn't sure how to follow through on it.

She knew me too well. She gave me a look.

"*This* isn't safe," she continued. "Don't you see? We weren't meant to be anything but *statistics*. We have no safety net. No one cares what happens to us except for *us*. If we don't make the right decisions, one bad night will be our last. I just know it. We have to get out of this and away from these people."

I knew she was right. We *were* statistics. Worse than runaways.

Throwaways.

We weren't even the faces you saw on a milk cartons. Those kids had people looking for them. All we had on this earth was each other.

If we wanted to survive this, we had to make it happen ourselves, because no one else would.

CHAPTER TEN

WOULDN'T EVEN BE ME

PRESENT

STEPHAN

A warm, firm hand clutched mine. I swung my eyes to meet watery black ones.

Javier cried my name, looking equal parts terrified and relieved.

I let out a sob, making agony course through my chest. I tried to hold it back, to stop the pain, but it took a long time before I was coherent enough to say again, "Bianca?"

I had to know. She had to be okay.

The alternative was unthinkable.

It was a fact that I would not be okay without her. I wouldn't even be *me* without her. I'd be someone else, someone with important pieces missing, pieces I couldn't get back.

He seemed to snap out it, leaning closer to me. "She's okay.

She's recovering, but okay. She's in better shape than you, actually."

I studied him, wondering if I'd heard him right, wondering if I was dreaming. "She—she survived that?"

What I'd seen had looked like a headshot wound. How had she survived that, and in better shape than me?

He nodded emphatically.

I was so worn out that I was already going back under, but at least I knew she was alive.

She was alive.

I woke up again still remembering that. This time when Javier and I looked at each other, we smiled, though there were plenty more tears, as well.

CHAPTER ELEVEN

SHE SAVED MY SOUL

STEPHAN

Growing up, I'd had a cloud of guilt that followed me around. Even before my uncle had started molesting me, I'd been plagued by nightmares. An overzealous Sunday school teacher told my class one week that those of us not paying tithing would burn when the world caught fire, during the imminent second coming, and my young mind had taken it very literally.

I was eight at the time, and over the summer I'd earned a whopping ten dollars of chore money, and blown it all on candy during a trip to the grocery store. I hadn't even thought of paying tithing for it. No one had told me.

I'd felt horrible guilt and fear about it, even when I'd earned more money, just to pay it back.

I was a wicked boy for so many reasons, the largest of which were my thoughts. I doubted, I feared, I resented, and in my resentment summoned up some pretty horrible opinions about my strict, mean father especially.

Mostly, I kept those opinions to myself, but occasionally, I'd snap back at him, and he always, always made me regret it.

Even after I ran away, that guilt followed me relentlessly. It chased me down, no matter how far I went to get away from it.

And then I met her.

Bianca put it all in perspective. She needed me. I protected her, she accepted me, and we became inseparable.

I saved her life. She saved my soul.

By the time I was in my early twenties, I thought I'd mostly left that heavy guilt behind me, but it still lingered in deceptive but destructive ways.

I couldn't be myself, or at least, I felt it was necessary, even proper, to hide parts of myself from the world. This self-destructive instinct was so strong, and so knit into the fiber of who I was, that it nearly cost me the love of my life.

CHAPTER TWELVE

WAS IT ME?

PAST

STEPHAN

He was much older than me. I was seventeen, and he had to be pushing thirty. I knew that was bad, but he had so many other things going for him.

He was handsome. He had a great smile. He was even-tempered, and just as vehement as I was about staying in the closet.

I met him at the bookstore. We were both looking for the same book. It was so romantic. The kind of story you could tell later and share intimate smiles about.

We hooked up the third time we went out.

We were getting cleaned up when his phone chimed.

His expression didn't change as he moved to check it, but his brow furrowed as he continued to study the screen of his phone.

"Everything okay?" I asked him, shrugging into my shirt.

He looked up, his eyes gone somewhere else. He had to blink a few times to come back to the here and now. "What? Oh that? Yeah, it's fine. My wife is just being a nosy bitch. Nothing new there."

My whole body froze, even my lungs, to the point that I could barely breathe, let alone talk.

Was it me? Was I cursed, or doomed, to only pick out guys that would hurt me at the first opportunity?

"Your *wife*?" I finally managed to get out.

He didn't roll his eyes, but he may as well have, with the look he gave me. "Now don't get all touchy about this."

"You told me you were gay. Not bi. Not *married to a woman*. Gay."

I was careful to keep my voice down, though it was a struggle, because Bianca was asleep in the next room.

It dawned on me suddenly why he'd insisted on coming to my place.

This time he did roll his eyes. "I am. I'm only attracted to men, but that doesn't mean I want to live that lifestyle. That's why I'm in the closet. Like you."

"You're married. You're nothing like me. You're a *liar*."

"Everybody's a liar. Being in the closet is a lie. It's something you'll figure out around the time you grow up, kid."

"Get out."

"Excuse me?"

"Leave," I said through my teeth, hoping he would listen, because I was about a second away from hitting him.

Luckily, he went. I never heard from him again.

CHAPTER THIRTEEN

DO ME A FAVOR

PRESENT

STEPHAN

It wasn't until the next day that I got Javier's other reaction. The delayed one, that came after the relieved one.

"What were you doing?" he burst out with suddenly. "What were you even thinking, going back there, getting yourself shot?"

I'd known this was coming.

"I had to," I said calmly, though it hurt to speak. "She was in danger. I had to do something."

"You had to take a bullet for her?"

"Yes."

"Do you know how fucked up that is? Who does something like that?"

"It's not fucked up. It's who I am."

"How? Why?"

"This is how I love, Javier."

"It's how you love *her*."

"Yes. And it's how I love you. I'd do the same for you."

"You'd take a bullet for me?"

"In a heartbeat."

He laughed mid-sob. "Do me a favor. Please don't *ever* take a bullet again. Not for anyone. Not even me."

"Deal. And you do me a favor."

"Anything."

"Marry me."

CHAPTER FOURTEEN

BUT THEN I MET HIM

PAST

STEPHAN

I heard every story there was to hear about Javier before I ever laid eyes on him. He was slutty. He was a snob. He loved drama, and it followed him everywhere. He couldn't keep a secret.

There was more dirt flying around about him than I could keep up with, and though I tended to shy away from gossip, I had every reason to believe most of it, based on the fact that there was just so *much* of it.

But then I met him. No one had told me he was drop dead gorgeous. Just beautiful in a way that spoke to me. Every part of him was defined and perfect, from his lips to his hands. Elegant and devastating.

No one told me that he had the thickest eyelashes on the

planet, or that his calm dark eyes sparkled when he smiled.

I was wildly attracted to him the instant I set eyes on him, but even so, I didn't *like* him. He had a shitty reputation, and he was *not* my type. Not at all.

My unruly body and my stupid heart couldn't seem to keep that straight.

We met at the crew headquarters. He was our fifth flight attendant, not a part of the regular crew, which meant he was on-call and had likely had to rush to work with only an hour's notice. He didn't look it. He looked very well put together, his tie straight, his hair perfect. He looked calm and relaxed, and good enough to eat.

Everyone was there, including the pilots, so we did the crew briefing as we waited for the bus that would take us to the plane.

It was a short briefing, because almost all of us had been working together for a full month, and Bianca and I always worked together in first class. I sent her a brief smile, and that was all, before addressing Javier, whose eyes I'd felt on me since the moment we'd been introduced.

He was brazen, that one.

"Jessa has the galley," I told him, "and Julie is our usual third this month, so that makes you fifth. You'll be doing the count and helping the girls between their carts."

He just nodded, giving me his full attention in a way that unnerved me. He didn't know I was gay. Very few of the people we worked with did. I never dated anyone from work, and only our closest friends had any inkling of the truth. Most thought Bianca was my girlfriend, and that suited us both fine. But the way he looked at me felt like a come-on, and I felt myself both infuriated and fascinated by that. There was no way he could know. I didn't believe in that gaydar crap.

I held Bianca's hand as we sat together on the crew bus. This was in no way unusual for us. We were close to the point of inseparable and had never felt the need to hide it, not from anyone. Still, somehow, with Javier's stare boring into me across the aisle, I felt defensive about the handholding, and I wasn't sure if that was because I wanted to explain it to him, or use it to warn him off. It rankled that I even had to think about it. I didn't owe explanations about any part of my life to anyone, I told myself firmly, let alone some little troublemaker I'd just met.

The plane was boarding through the second door at this jet bridge, so the passengers were entering the plane between the front of coach and the back of first class. This had Javier at the door with me, side by side, as we waited for the passengers to board.

"You and Bianca make a beautiful couple," Javier said quietly beside me.

This had me raising my brows and looking directly at him. He was smiling, a brow arched playfully.

Was he messing with me? Did he really think she and I were a couple, or was he mocking me?

I honestly couldn't tell.

"Thank you," I replied, my tone very neutral.

"Like Barbie and Ken."

That almost had me laughing. "Don't tell *her* that. She hates it when people call her Barbie. We've gotten that comparison a lot."

"I don't know why she'd hate that. Most girls would kill to look like a Barbie doll."

"Well, not Bianca. My advice would be to stay on her good side, and rule one to doing that is not to call her Barbie."

"Got it. Have any rules for staying on *your* good side?"

64

"To always be on Bianca's good side."

"So it's like that . . . interesting."

I studied him, almost positive that he was mocking me. "We're a package deal."

"Noted. I always wanted a best friend like that. You two are lucky."

"We're more than just best friends," I told him firmly, wanting to set up clear boundaries.

He smirked at me, and I knew, just *knew*, that he had guessed my secret. "Sure. Okay. More. I get the hint. You two have any plans for the layover?"

I shrugged. We were headed to Miami with a twenty-four hour layover. "Probably just hanging out at the beach or the pool. Nothing big."

"Would you mind if I tag along, or do you two need to be alone?"

I glared at him, wondering why he felt the need to be so sarcastic. "Tag away. This is a friendly crew. They'll probably all be out there."

"Thanks. I hate it when I get the crews that stay in their rooms all day."

"No problem. It's Miami, and the weather is supposed to be beautiful. It would be a pity to stay inside."

"You going to hit the gym?"

I chewed on my lip, considering my answer.

I wanted to avoid working out with him, if that was what he was getting at. I couldn't explain it, but I felt like I needed to avoid him altogether. "I'm not sure."

The first wave of passengers began to board, which was a relief, because even chatting with him unnerved me.

Boarding, takeoff, and our redeye service went smoothly and

quickly. I didn't even see Javier again until the flight was half done.

I was drinking coffee in the front galley alone. Bianca was in the back, chatting with Jessa, so I was manning the front of the plane, wondering if I should call them up to the front.

I didn't like to be alone. Not ever.

I jumped a little as a smiling Javier burst through the curtain, nearly making me spill my coffee.

"Hey," he said, moving to stand way too close to me. "I thought you might be lonely up here, with all the girls chatting in back and all of the passengers sleeping."

I made a noncommittal noise, staring at him. One black curl had fallen onto his forehead, bringing out his thick lashes and his dark eyes. He really was just a striking man.

"So about the workout tomorrow. I like to hit the gym. I'm not ripped like you, but I try to keep fit. I hate going alone though."

"I'm not sure," I said, trying hard to take exception to the way he was staring at me. He was just *so* brazen.

I should call him out on that, I thought, but I didn't.

I watched his hand move to my arm, gripping as though to test my muscle. "What are you doing?" I asked him, my voice hard with tension.

"You don't get arms like this by skipping the gym. I think you're going to go, but you just don't want to go with *me*. What have you heard about me?" As he spoke, his hand moved to my abs, skimming over the taut ridges under my shirt.

I didn't react right away, genuinely shocked at his nerve.

Finally, my free hand shot to his, gripping it hard enough to make his eyes water with pain.

"What have you heard about *me* that makes you think I want

you touching me?" Each word came through my clenched teeth.

"Nothing," he said, pulling on his hand.

I let it go, and he shook it, as though to shake away the pain. "I've only heard how hot you are and that you're with that girl."

"Bianca."

"Yeah. Her."

"Why did you touch my stomach?"

"I was just making conversation. I . . . wanted to feel your six pack, since I could tell that you had one. You can't tell me you aren't working out tomorrow. I won't believe you. I was just trying to prove my point."

"You shouldn't grab people like that without their permission. What the hell is wrong with you?"

Javier didn't answer, his gaze arrested, pointed at my crotch. I'd grown hard at his first touch, and I couldn't hide it, even in my work slacks.

He swallowed hard, staring. And staring.

Great, I thought, *this one is sure to tell the world my secret.* And on the tail of that thought: *Well, now that he knows, the harm is already done . . .*

That was a dangerous line of thought.

As though he hadn't heard my last sentence, as though my anger scared him not at all, he reached for me, stroking me through my pants.

My free hand gripped the counter behind me for support.

"Stop that," I told him gruffly, but there was no heat in it.

All of my heat had pooled below my waist.

"Let me take care of this. You don't have to do anything for me. I just want to suck you off." His lovely black eyes looked up at me so sweetly that I felt captured by them.

I shook my head, but could not find the will to make it

convincing.

He moved until his chest touched mine, still working me with his hand. I hadn't had anyone touch me like this in so long. It was hard not to let it cloud my senses.

He kissed me, his mouth coaxing mine open.

I set my coffee down very carefully, before grabbing his hair, pulling his face away from mine.

"What are you doing?"

"Kissing you. I've wanted to kiss you since the moment I laid eyes on you. Please, let me kiss you."

"I don't do this. I don't do this casual thing. I'm not like you."

"What am I like?"

"Easy. Promiscuous. I don't do sex unless I have feelings for a person."

He smiled huge. "You are a different one, aren't you? So have feelings for me, and kiss me."

"Don't make fun of me. I don't find this funny at all."

"I wasn't. I meant it. I'm putting myself out here for your enjoyment. What do I need to do to be with you? Because that's what I want."

I didn't believe him, but I kissed him for that, for the way his words made my heart race and my breath catch. We didn't pull back for a very long time, and when we did, I felt out of control.

"Come to the bathroom with me. Fuck my mouth, Stephan. I want you to do whatever you want to me with this big cock of yours. Anything."

"You never get to fuck me, you understand?" I growled at him, gripping his hair to the point of pain. "I don't do that. Not ever. I won't even consider it."

"That's fine. That's fine."

He sounded like he meant it, and I let him tug me into the bathroom.

I had a brief moment of lucid thought, as he sat on the closed toilet in the tiny confined space, frantically undoing my pants, that in all my life I'd never done a thing so sordid, even when I'd traded my body for shelter. But I quickly lost all lucidity as I sprang into his eager hands, and he went to work on me with his mouth.

I hadn't had a lot of partners, and I'd never had a blow job like the one Javier performed on me.

He deep-throated me, sucking until my vision blurred.

I didn't last thirty seconds.

I bit my lip not to shout as I came, my tip deep in his throat. I felt his muscles work as he swallowed every drop.

Perhaps there is some advantage to hooking up with a slut, I thought.

He was talented.

He stood up to kiss me when he'd sucked out every drop, still stroking me with his hand.

I flushed hotly when he pulled back. "I usually last longer than that."

He just smiled, looking happy to the point of joyful. "It was a BJ. You aren't supposed to last long, if I'm doing it right."

I raised my hand to stroke his lower lip. "You're very good at that. How often do you find yourself sucking off strangers in airplane bathrooms?"

All of the joy died from his eyes, and I was instantly sorry. Most slutty gay men weren't sensitive about being slutty, but I'd clearly put my foot in my mouth. "That came out wrong."

"I don't know what you've heard about me, but I haven't slept around in a very long time. I just . . . liked you."

"I'm sorry. I didn't mean to be insulting."

"Will you workout with me in the morning?"

"Okay," I agreed, since he clearly wasn't going to let it go.

"I want you to fuck me," he said, pulling back to stare at my cock, which was starting to swell again in his stroking hand.

I swallowed hard. "God, you're forward."

"Not always. Not usually. Touch me. Please."

I reached down, gripping him, stroking him through his pants. It was the first contact I'd had with that part of him. I loved the feel of him in my hands, hard and straining. He was more elegantly made than I was, though still a good size.

"Come to my room and fuck me tonight. I don't even care if you get me off. I just want you to take me."

"This is moving too fast," I told him. "We haven't even been on a date yet."

He blinked up at me, slow, hypnotizing blinks. "You want to date me?"

I didn't think I actually did. I still didn't know anything about him. We hadn't even had any real conversation yet. But his tone had been so hopeful, so unabashedly delighted, and flattered, that I found myself saying, "Isn't that the way this usually works?"

He hugged me. "Not for me. Not with guys like you."

Maybe I did want to, I found myself thinking.

He was much sweeter than he let on. Sweet could soften my heart like nothing else.

"How about tomorrow night?" I said slowly, working it out in my head. "I'll take you to dinner, maybe a movie?"

He squeezed me tighter. "I'd love that. Just the two of us?"

I laughed. "It is a date. Do you usually go on dates with more than two people?"

He pulled back to look at me, kissing my chin, and then my

mouth, just pecks. "Will Bianca be okay with it?"

"She never minds staying in to read, and I'll bring her some takeout."

"So she is just a friend . . . right?"

"More than that. She's my family. My whole world."

"But not your lover?"

"No, not that."

"Good," he said, then pushed up to kiss me.

I gripped his hair and kissed him back. I was fully hard again when I tore my mouth away. I was still hanging out of my pants, and I glanced down as I started to grind against his own constrained bulge.

With a moan, he pulled my mouth back to his. He was the sweetest kisser, his lips soft but hesitant, not for lack of finesse, but almost a timid restraint, as though to communicate with the give of his mouth how he wanted me to proceed. How he wanted me to take over. That was more than fine with me.

CHAPTER FIFTEEN

DON'T GET HURT

Bianca was ecstatic when I told her I had a date.

She was less thrilled when I told her whom it was with, but still supportive.

Bianca was not a romantic, but she knew that I was, and so worried about my love life.

I worried about hers more. I knew that all of the trauma she'd suffered as a kid had left parts of her cold. Untouchable.

She didn't go out with guys. They asked, but I'd never seen her so much as consider it. The only person she let in was me. And who could blame her, after all she'd been through?

It made me sad, but I didn't know what I could do to change it.

"So he asked you out on the flight . . . or vice versa? This all came out of nowhere." Her tone was curious more than anything else.

I flushed. "I guess he hit on me first, but I'm the one that asked him out."

"Oh. Well, you must have hit it off. You don't usually work so fast."

The flush turned into an outright blush. She'd as good as asked, and I couldn't keep anything from her for long, even things that embarrassed me. "We hooked up in the first class bathroom."

Her eyes widened, mouth falling open. It was hard to shock her like this, and it made me smile a little to see her usually composed face react like that.

"Wow. Just wow. How did *that* happen?"

I bit my lip and tried to give it to her straight. "I hardly know him, but I'm really attracted to him. He made a pass at me, and I just . . . couldn't, or didn't want to, tell him no. Now we're going out because I guess I just want to see if it's more than chemistry."

She nodded, face serious and studying mine now. "Okay. Well, good luck. Don't get hurt."

I kissed her forehead on my way out. "I'll try my best. I'll bring you back takeout."

"You don't have to do that. I can find my own food."

"I want to. I'm taking him to that Cuban place we love."

"Oh, well then, I'll take you up on that."

"Your usual?"

She nodded and smiled, giving me a thumbs up.

I took him to a movie first. An action flick that had been out for several weeks. The theatre was deserted without another soul in sight, and he seemed more interested in touching me than watching the movie.

I didn't know what to make of that. This was supposed to be a first date, not an excuse to get off in public again.

That being said, I wanted to get off again. I wasn't proud of it, but my resolve was weakening with every touch.

"Don't you like the movie?" I asked.

He was plastered to my side, kissing my neck, his hand teasing my thigh. "I don't know. I can't pay attention."

"Are you bored?"

He was panting in my ear. "Bored?" His hand found my aching cock. "Does this feel bored to you?"

I swallowed, my hand finally sliding off my knee onto his. "This is supposed to be a first date. I don't hook up on first dates."

"Let's have our first date another time then. Let's call this something else, something where this ends with you fucking me, or me giving you a hand job in a movie theatre."

I shook my head, trying not to smile, not to encourage his audacity.

I grabbed his hand, pulling it off me, then linking our fingers together.

He seemed okay, even content, with that, squeezing my hand and shooting me happy smiles.

I didn't know what to make of that. Did he think I'd only been asking him out to hookup?

Things were going well up until the short walk from the theatre to the restaurant, when he grabbed my hand where anyone could see.

I shook him off, shooting him a look. "Knock it off! Not in public, okay?"

He looked baffled. "What does it matter?"

"We could run into someone we know. We're only a ten minute walk from the crew hotel."

That shut him up for a while. The silence was more than awkward. It was full of questions I didn't want to answer, but that I knew he'd be asking and soon.

Finally, he pressed the issue. "So you're not out. Not at all. You're hiding it."

I hated the way he said it, like I was doing something wrong. I felt instantly defensive. "It's no one's business but mine. I like my privacy, okay?"

He went quiet again, for the rest of the walk, and I hated it.

We'd ordered our food and were one drink into the meal when he came out of it.

"I'm sorry," he said softly, his lovely black eyes warm. "I'm being a jerk. You have a right to your privacy. I won't say anything. I mean, we can keep this under wraps as long as you need."

I just nodded, not knowing what to say. I couldn't reassure him in any way. No matter how this went, be it one date or one hundred, I wasn't planning to make it or us common knowledge. I'd been too fiercely secretive about my preferences for too long to change it on a whim.

"You know you can trust me, right?" he questioned, looking earnest. "I'm sure you've heard awful things about me but . . . they aren't true. I'm not a liar, and I don't spread gossip."

"I do trust you," I said simply. And I found that I did. I didn't know him well yet, but I knew enough.

He gave me the sweetest smile I'd ever seen. "Thank you. You—you're everything I wanted you to be, you know that?"

I couldn't hold back a grin. "I'm not sure what to make of that."

"I've seen you before, though you didn't notice me. I've watched you, and heard about you . . . fantasized about you. I was hoping you were this great guy, and well, you are. It makes me really happy."

That made me pretty happy, too. He had a way of softening

me, right from the start.

I wanted to, but I didn't last three dates before hooking up with him again. Not even close.

I dropped off Bianca's takeout and walked him to his room.

Things got out of hand after that.

I meant just to kiss him goodnight on the cheek. He turned his head and didn't catch my mouth so much as put his in my path.

Once we started kissing, I was done for.

I had one brief moment of almost sanity when I saw that he'd been prepared for this, that he'd planned for it, everything laid out, and I almost held back.

"I was hoping," he told me with a sweet smile and a sweeter kiss. "I wasn't expecting. Just hoping."

I nodded curtly and let him roll the condom on, my hands running over him, gripping into his hair, kneading at his flesh. More than anything, I just wanted to touch him, to have full contact, skin on skin, but my control failed me in the face of his sweet, giving submission.

I backed him into his room and had him. I bent him over a chair, jerking him off with my hand while I fucked him from behind.

"I'm sorry," I breathed into his back when I'd buried myself to the hilt. "I know I'm big. I'm trying not to be rough."

His response was to moan and grind back against me.

I started moving, great heavy thrusts that he met beat for beat.

I let myself get rough with it when I saw that he could

handle it, jamming into him at full strength, brutal jackhammer thrusts that made him hold on for dear life and cry out loudly.

I bit down at the straining tendon between his neck and shoulder as I kept up a punishing rhythm, hammering into him.

His cock jerked in my hand, and he cried out.

I outlasted him, but not by much. He was still spurting in my hand when I let myself go, ramming hard into him one last time as I came deep inside of him.

After, I peeled off the condom and tossed it in the trash, far from done.

I pushed him on his back on the bed and started kissing him, my hand still on his cock, pumping at him, enjoying the feel of him, even soft.

I wasn't soft. I was ready to go again way too quickly, grinding myself between his legs, jabbing my tip against his sac as I thrust my tongue into his mouth.

"Oh God," he cried out, panting, his arms holding me to him like I was the answer to a prayer.

I couldn't get enough of him. His sweet acceptance undid me.

I sat him up, pulled his thighs over mine, and lined our shafts up together, using his hand and mine to stroke us both into a frenzy, rubbing, stroking leisurely, then urgently, until we were spilling on each other, coming together. I looked up to find him watching my face at the end, a look of rapt adoration on his.

I still hadn't had enough, and started kissing him again mid-ejaculation, rubbing myself against him as I devoured his mouth with mine.

I pulled back only long enough to catch my breath and started kissing his perfect body. He was lean, but muscular; his skin a pale olive that I thought looked perfect under my sun browned hands.

He whimpered when I caught his growing erection in my mouth and started sucking. I didn't stop, instead clamping down with my lips and going harder, crawling over his body until my own hardening length was pushing against his mouth.

I pushed my fingers into his back entrance while we sucked each other off.

I lay on my back and pulled him over my chest when we'd finished, stroking a hand over his soft hair, kissing his forehead, sated but with a stomach still alive with butterflies.

"Wow, just wow," he breathed, running his hands over me, turning his head to kiss my chest repeatedly. "I've never . . . I never, um, that was amazing."

I smiled, my eyes closing, a feeling of utter contentment blooming to life, sheer delight working its way through me. "Yes, it was."

I didn't even ask. I just stayed the night in his room.

I noticed with the crew the next day that he changed in front of other people, became more stiff, less open.

It was like this with everyone, I would learn.

He was so different with me. He gave me something distinctly unique from what he gave the rest of the world. With me, he didn't hold back a thing. He was more open, more honest, sweeter, better.

I fell for him. Hard and fast. As though I was too naive to know better, as though I was innocent instead of tarnished, I dove in headfirst.

He made me feel good about myself, like I was the missing piece of his puzzle, the one that made him fit right in his own skin.

In a perfect world, when you found the person that did that, that was it. End of story. Happily ever after.

But this wasn't a perfect world, and even though I fell for him deeply, I knew it couldn't last.

He was always on the offense about his sexuality. I, on the other hand, was firmly stuck in my defensive stance.

He was insulted that I continued to insist on hiding our relationship.

I was resentful that he didn't understand or respect my need for privacy.

My pigheaded stubborn pride had doomed us from the start.

CHAPTER SIXTEEN

THE SWEETEST MONTH

We were joined at the hip after that. Every second of our free time was spent together.

I was anxious at first about what Bianca would think of it all, but I shouldn't have worried. She was ecstatic about it, so happy for me she was bursting with it. She pushed me in his direction at every opportunity.

"Go," she'd say. "I'll just be painting all day, anyway. This works out perfectly."

It only lasted a month, but it was the sweetest month.

He was on-call, and good friends with the girl who ran scheduling, so he managed to snag the fifth position on nearly all of our flights.

I was on cloud nine. I'd always been a romantic, but even so, I'd never been *in love*. Not like this. It was a brand new, heady, wonderful experience.

Of course, it all just made the quick plummet of our breakup that much harder to bear. It didn't seem to matter that we'd had such a short time together, because that time had been spent earnestly making bittersweet memories that I would dwell on in all of my troubled, lonely reflections after.

But that was after. During . . . during was another thing entirely.

The making of the sweet memories before they turned bitter.

We loved to go hiking. There was this little private spot at Red Rock that we hit every chance we got. We'd hold hands and talk for hours there.

It was maybe the fifth time we'd gone, and we had just reached the peak at the top of our hike when he shot me his best smile. "Pinch me. I feel like I'm dreaming here."

"Why's that?"

"*You* is why. I never thought you'd ever even talk to me, let alone give me the time of day."

"Why?"

"You're out of my league, if you haven't noticed. And you're so nice. A fairytale prince that came to rescue a loser like me."

I melted. Every hard thing inside of me went soft for this man.

If it'd just been us, we would have been fine, I figured.

It was the rest of the world that was the problem.

It wasn't the long walks that ended us, or any of the time in private.

It was the parties, the active social scene that went along with our line of work that sealed our fate.

Javier had been respectful about my ban on PDA from the first time I'd mentioned it, but there were times when I could tell it bothered him. Many times.

One time in particular was the last straw for him.

We were at a house party for our friend Damien's birthday.

I was standing with Javier and a group of pilots and flight attendants, but I was watching Bianca across the room. She'd been cornered by Damien, who everyone knew had had a thing for her since the first time he'd seen her.

A lot of people thought this was juicy gossip, since they assumed she was with me, and they knew we were all friends.

That wasn't why I was staring. I was watching only to see if she needed me to run interference.

She liked Damien and was trying to be nice, but I could tell he was making her uncomfortable.

Damien was one of our closer friends, and one of the few that knew Bianca and me weren't *together*. Sometimes I wished he'd never caught on. Bianca was never going to care about him the way he wanted. She just didn't feel that way about him, and if she could have used me as an excuse to keep him at bay, I knew she would have.

"I don't know why you put up with that shit, Stephan," one of the pilots said loudly. His name was Allen, I was pretty sure.

I glanced at him with a raised brow. He was an overweight guy, in his early thirties, I guessed. A first officer, I recalled, and one that had a reputation for being difficult to work with. I barely knew the guy, but he sounded like he had a very strong opinion about my life. Of course, he wasn't exactly sober at the moment.

"Excuse me?" I asked, hoping to politely deflect him.

He was red in the face, his brown hair messy and falling in his eyes. He waved a hand toward Bianca and Damien. "He's after your girl. Everyone knows it. And he's supposed to be your friend? It's none of my business, but I don't know why you put up with it."

I gave him a bland smile. "You're right. It is none of your

business."

"You need to put a ring on that one," he said, tone snide, "before Captain Dimples snatches her on up."

He was getting on my nerves in a major way, but I still made a mental note to harass Damien about that nickname as soon as I could.

"I'm not worried about it, so I don't know why you are," I told him pointedly. Though I did know. I recalled there was some kind of beef between him and Damien, something involving a woman that preferred Damien more, though I didn't know all the details.

Apparently he thought that could be solved by egging me into fighting him.

"What kind of a guy isn't worried about someone else hitting on his girl?" Allen asked, tone snide.

I gave him another bland smile, though this one was harder to fake. "Listen, it's Allen, right?"

He nodded.

I continued, "I know you and Damien have some beef between you, but don't drag me into it. I'm guessing you've heard that I can handle myself in a fight, you probably heard the rumor that I used to be a cage fighter by the way you're acting, but listen carefully to this part: Nothing you can say is going to get me to go over there and do your dirty work for you, and we all know if you tried to kick his ass yourself, he'd clobber you."

He tried to respond, looking angry, but I spoke over him. "Now you, *you* aren't a close friend of mine, and you're starting to piss me off, so you I could be convinced to fight, but not him, and not by you. So move along before you find out firsthand if I did really used to fight pro."

That had its desired effect, and he left with a few grumbling complaints about me being a prick.

That was fine with me. I was smiling when he left, thinking I'd defused the situation well enough.

A look at Javier's face told me otherwise.

I sighed. I didn't know what, but something about that exchange had deeply bothered him.

He'd been playful and engaged before that, enjoying the crowd we were hanging with. He became withdrawn and stiff after.

There was no good way to get it out of him there, no subtle way to get him alone that wouldn't look suspicious, so it wasn't until later, post-party, that I got him to talk.

"What's bothering you?"

We were getting ready for bed, brushing our teeth side by side in the mirror. I saw his mouth tighten.

He set his toothbrush down and met my eyes. "You really don't know?" he asked quietly, but something in his tone was very loud, so loud it was screaming at me, trying to tell me something that I wasn't ready to hear.

I shook my head. "I know you got upset after I threatened Allen. You don't think the way I handled that was appropriate?"

He grunted. That was it. Just grunted and went to bed.

I followed him, a kernel of annoyance moving through me. I was plainspoken, and sometimes I really wished that he were too.

"I don't speak fluent grunt," I told him as I got into bed. "Want to tell me what yours meant?"

He didn't even crack a smile. "I think it bothers me the most that you don't even understand how screwed up that all was."

I sighed. I hated arguments like this, so full of riddles and land mines. "I guess I don't. Explain, please."

"You were so willing, happy even, to get into a *real* fight over a *fake* relationship. You weren't bluffing. You would have followed through, kicked Allen's ass if he kept it up."

"The guy was being a jerk, talking that way about Bianca, trying to stir shit up with me and Damien. And he never would have fought me, so it *was* a bluff. I'm twice that guy's size."

He grunted again, and this time I could interpret it into a noise of utter frustration. "You don't get it!"

"Explain it to me then," I muttered sullenly, wanting nothing more than to get off this subject.

He was in my face suddenly, eyes wide, passionate. "You're so scared to show the world who you are that you would cripple your life for it! Why?! What are you so scared of? The world is not your sick dad. Half the guys we work with are gay. Do you see the straight ones stringing any of them up? This isn't the fifties. We don't have to hide anymore!"

My jaw clenched, and I just stared at him, refusing to talk about this.

He cupped my face in his hands, eyes imploring. "There's nothing wrong with you, Stephan. Nothing at all. You are who you are, and even if you wanted to, you couldn't change it. No matter how you hide it, you can't run from yourself, and you shouldn't want to, because there's *nothing wrong with you.*"

I didn't cave one single inch, staring him down with cold eyes, letting him talk, giving him nothing.

One sad tear ran down his face. "You're perfect, Stephan. Perfect. I love you. I'm in love with you, but what are you even doing? How long can you live with this farce? How long do I have to pretend to be your bro, your bud, in public, lovers only in private?"

Nothing. I gave him nothing. No part of me was willing to cave to this. I would not do it, not even for him.

He was getting more desperate by the second, eyes wild, lips trembling. "You know what terrifies me? That you're so willing to risk us, to risk this, just to keep up the front."

Nothing. I gave him nothing but cold, resolute eyes.

He got the message, shaking his head back and forth as he looked into them with sad eyes. "It's not even a dilemma for you, is it? If I made you choose, go public or lose me, you wouldn't even hesitate, would you?"

My breath caught. That one got to me. "Don't," I said quietly, a plea in my voice.

He backed away, his jaw hardening. "No. I need to know. If you care about me, you'll choose me. Choose me, Stephan. Please."

"Don't do this. It's not fair. It is manipulative. I have a right to be a private person. You shouldn't want to force me to live other than how I choose to."

"Tell me one thing, do you think you need more time, or will it ever be an option? Do you plan to spend your *whole life* living a lie?"

"Stop. Just stop. This went too far."

"I notice you didn't answer, and I'm not surprised. I can't do that, can't live a lie, Stephan. Tell me which you choose. The lie or me. Which one is more important to you?"

I was suddenly furious, so angry at him, at his impatience, his inability to see my side of it, that I wanted him gone. Wanted it enough to say, my tone glacial, "I choose to be *me*, and I *refuse* to be manipulated by you into living my life as *you* see fit. We don't all have to march in the Gay Pride Parade, Javier. That's never going to be who I am. So if you're looking for an excuse to leave, there's the fucking door." I waved my arm at it.

He gasped, face going slack, like I'd slapped him. "This isn't about gay pride, but do you even realize, even comprehend, how ashamed you are of being gay?"

I didn't like that. It definitely hit me in a place I wasn't comfortable exploring. I made him sorry he'd said it. "We're done here. Get off your soapbox and leave. *Now*."

His face crumpled.

I'd been mean to him, when I was never mean. I was on a roll, though, and I wasn't done. "I mean it. *Done*. This thing has run its course anyway."

I was numb for a while after he'd left, but the numbness didn't last long.

When the pain hit me, I crawled into bed with Bianca, moving like a wounded animal.

She welcomed me with open arms, and it helped, as it always did.

CHAPTER SEVENTEEN

HOT BUTTON

Javier didn't budge, and neither did I.

Unlike me, though, he wasn't interested in or willing to be civil. If I entered a room, he left it. If he was assigned to work one of my flights, he called out sick.

It was an awful breakup, and we'd only been together for a month.

Maybe it was for the best that it'd ended so abruptly, no matter how senseless that ending might have felt, because I couldn't imagine how much worse it could have gotten, the breakup, if we'd been together a substantial amount of time.

It was a while before he even said one word to me, and I quickly found I preferred the frigid silence.

We were at a Valentine's party. Murphy was throwing it, so even though I wasn't really in the mood to celebrate Valentine's Day, we wound up going.

Javier was there, I saw right away, hanging out in the

backyard with some of his friends.

I really hadn't wanted to see him today of all days.

I preempted his usual snub and just avoided him. Or tried to.

It was a few hours in, and I myself was about three drinks deep.

Javier was at least six. Not good.

I was in the kitchen, hanging out with Murphy and a group of pilots, distractedly trying to follow their conversation, which was about building a proper beer pong table.

Javier came walking in unsteadily, drink in hand, bitter eyes all for me.

Oh Lord, I thought resignedly.

"How's your Valentine's Day, Stephan?" he drawled, moving to stand in front of me.

I saw where this was going, and I shifted away from the group, ushering Javier to a quiet corner in the dining room.

It didn't matter. Javier was in no mood to be quiet, wherever the setting.

"I asked you how your Valentine's Day is," he said insolently.

I stared at his angry face, the tense set of his features, and all I wanted to do was touch him.

Why did it have to be like this? Was there any way that I could fix it? Would he ever see my side of it?

My mind awhirl with questions, I answered his, "It's not great, Javier. How about yours?"

His lip curled up, his eyes filling.

I had to look away.

"How is your *Valentine*? Have you proposed to her yet?" His voice was loud and mocking.

I sent him a warning look. "You leave her out of it. I mean

it."

"Or what?" he hissed, more quietly at least. "You'll dump me, and go back to her, go back to your comfortable lie of a life?"

He swayed on his feet, and without thinking, I reached out and caught his shoulders, holding him steady.

With a cry, he launched himself into my chest.

I caught him there for one brief moment before I remembered where we were, that we had no privacy, and I stepped back, thrusting him away from me like he was on fire. Like he was unwanted, despite the fact that I wanted him badly.

That, of course, didn't make anything better.

He cussed me out, loudly, calling me just about every name in the book, but not outing me.

I took it in silence, watching him, hating myself.

Bianca showed up in the middle of it, looking ready to do battle, and so I knew it was time to end it.

"Enough," I told him quietly.

He had one last salvo to throw at me as a parting shot. It was a good one.

He leaned in close, his sorrowful eyes just killing me, and whispered, "You were the only guy I've loved who ever made me feel like I was worth anything. Anything at all. I guess the joke was on me, huh?"

Boy did that get to me. Feeling worthless was my own personal hot button.

"I'm sorry," I mouthed, having no reassurances for him. I couldn't even reassure myself. I could never be what he wanted.

CHAPTER EIGHTEEN

TO PROTECT HER

PRESENT

STEPHAN

James came to see me on his own one afternoon. He looked at me solemnly for the longest time before he spoke, "Thank you."

I started shaking my head. "You don't have to thank me. She's my family."

"She's my family too, now. And you saved her. Thank you."

I nodded solemnly, studying him.

"You were the one that stopped him. The shot that killed him. Did you know that?"

"Yeah," I said, wondering if I was supposed to feel something other than relief that the monster was finally dead. "I remember."

He shifted uncomfortably in the chair beside my bed. "Let me know if you need any sort of counseling for that. I don't know from personal experience, but I understand that it can take a toll on you, no matter how justified."

"I'll be fine." I took a deep breath. "This wasn't the first time I've killed for her. To protect her. It happened once before."

His eyes went wide, his body still. I'd managed to shock him.

I grimaced. "The first time we met, the man that was attacking her. I caved his skull in. I felt it. That took some time to cope with. I didn't know him, didn't know what drove him. What if he was just crazy? What if the right meds would have fixed him? Looking back at it now, I'm adjusted to it, but it was hard at the time, because I was a kid."

I'm not sure why I felt the need to tell him, but it had always been easy to pour my heart out to him. Too easy to talk to him, even when it had felt like a conflict of loyalties.

"You did nothing wrong."

I just nodded. "What I'm trying to say is, back then, I could have used some perspective, some counseling, to deal with what I'd done, but not this time. This time, I only wish I'd done it the first time I had the chance."

CHAPTER NINETEEN

THE MONSTER

PAST

STEPHAN

Bianca and I had been doing quite well for a while. Longer than usual in the system without any problems. In foster care, both going to the same public school. We'd managed to stay together, which was the important part. We had a roof over our heads and food.

We were staying with a couple that owned a small restaurant, and we both worked there after school. They weren't supposed to make us work, we were too young, but they were keeping us together, so we didn't mind. I bussed tables, did dishes, and Bianca served food.

Neither of us had a problem with the arrangement, usually. Both of us had had to endure so much worse, in the past.

I was a little annoyed with the situation today, though. I'd had to stay after school for a project and wanted Bianca to stay with me.

We didn't like to be apart. Not ever.

But our foster caregivers had needed her to work right after school, so she'd left without me.

It made me antsy, for more reasons than I could name, one of which being that it just felt wrong.

I got out of there as fast as I could manage, hurrying to the restaurant. I went my normal route, using an alley, and cutting directly to the back entrance.

I heard before I saw.

All the times I'd ever fought, all the reasons I'd done it for, I'd never experienced the blind, all-consuming rage I did when I realized what was going on. Not even close.

And it was a fact I had a horrible temper.

I heard some grunts of noise up ahead, folded around a corner, out of sight.

They sounded off. I didn't like them right away. They came from *him*, I'd piece together later.

If it'd come from her, I would have known instantly, and acted accordingly.

Another noise I didn't like followed quickly, the sound of something punching flesh, a hard hit on a soft target.

I winced. Someone was fighting, and I wondered if I'd have to become involved. It would really just depend on the situation, I mused.

A growl came next, and then a curse from a low, hard, accented voice.

I quickened my step. Something I'd heard had jarred the edge of a memory, enough so that I was starting to react before I processed. To panic before I *knew*.

And then I heard it, just before I turned the corner. Heard *her*. Her cry. Her cry *of pain*.

I broke into a run, making my way around the bend with a few quick strides.

And saw them. Bianca on the ground, her hair trailing into her face as she curled into a ball to protect herself from the next vicious kick. A brute of a blond man standing over her. A monster. *The* monster. I'd heard enough of a description and saw enough of a resemblance to know it right away.

Her father, come to hurt her.

He never landed that kick

I roared like a maniac and charged.

I hit him in the midsection and took him down. Hard. We fell away from Bianca, clearing her of harm, which had been the point.

I reared back to punch, but his fist met my face first.

He wasn't going to take this lying down, and he was a huge motherfucker.

I wasn't daunted. Hatred fueled me, and hate was impervious to intimidation.

He'd put hands on her. I couldn't stand the thought. All I knew for sure was I'd make him pay. I'd make him hurt. I'd make him regret it.

I tucked my head down and started punching, fast vicious jabs to his gut that were designed to do the most damage. I'd tenderize his insides until he pissed blood for a month.

A meaty fist caught the side of my head, but I just kept hitting and hitting, curses spewing from me. He was huge, and strong, but not fast. I was all of those things and feeling no pain at the moment, to boot.

I'd demolish him, or die trying, I swore then and there.

His next hit caught me in the temple, and I saw stars, but it didn't slow me down. Instead, it set me off.

I took a cheap shot, punching him in the groin.

He yelped like a wounded animal.

I did it again, and again, then went for his face. I held myself up on one arm and did as much damage to it as I could before he managed to stumble away, staggering up to his feet.

I rose to join him. I spat a mouthful of blood on the ground, shrugged my shoulders to loosen them up, and smiled at the bastard.

He shot me an assessing look that held more than an ounce of approval in it. The man respected a good fighter. It was likely the only thing he respected, the piece of shit.

"That's my daughter," he told me, his voice deep and scratchy, his accent thick. "This is family business. You do not need to interfere."

I saw red, and with a roar, charged again.

"She's *my* family, you bastard!" I cursed him, shoving him up against the wall of the building. "I'll kill you if you ever lay a hand on her again! *I'll kill you*, you bastard. I swear it!" I was screaming by the end, spittle flying, hands going for his throat and squeezing.

He was turning blue before he managed to dislodge me. Another blow to the head that I'd feel later.

Later. But not now.

Now I caught his face with four knuckles with enough force to knock out some teeth.

"You her boyfriend?" he asked me, gasping it out.

"I'm her family," I shouted, moving in close to start in on his stomach. It was my most vicious move, usually a last resort, but always effective.

I started working at him again, same spot as before, with a mind for doing some permanent damage. I grunted with the force of the quick fire blows, just wailing on him.

He growled, grabbed my hair, and started punching the side of my head.

I had to retreat. Too many more hits like that, and he'd knock me out. That was not an option.

I looked around, searching for something to bludgeon him with. I wasn't trying to fight fair. I wanted to destroy the bastard, by any means necessary.

There was a jagged wooden plank sitting on top of a dumpster, thin enough to grab and swing. Perfect. I went for it, grabbing it and swinging it around just before he hit me, taking me back and slamming me into the wall.

I dropped the plank, throwing my arms up to protect my head.

I'd gone into defense mode, and I wasn't happy about it. With a roar, I head butted him, shoving as hard as I could.

He sprawled out on the ground a few feet away, and I went for the board.

I swung with all my might, catching him hard on the shoulder as he rose, my body rocking off balance with the force of it.

He tried to wrest the makeshift weapon away from me, but I held on tight, twisting until I had it free of him, then circling to swing again.

I landed three more punishing blows before he started to move away, trying to run.

I went after him. I needed him to hurt bad enough to remember the pain, and remember why he wanted to avoid going near her again. Pain had a short-term memory, so I needed to make an impression that would last.

I needed to break some things. Specifically, some of his bones.

I whacked him in the back of the head, and when he was down, I crunched his knee, catching the front of it with the board.

He turned into an enraged bear after that, coming at me again, nearly knocking me out with the first hit.

Fuck. I blinked several times, fighting to stay conscious.

I kicked out at his hurt leg, making him scream, and went at him again with the plank.

I knocked him down with a heavy blow to the head, and he lay still for just long enough to make me think he was out.

I stood over him, honestly contemplating taking his life. He could *never* hurt her again, if he were dead. It was more than a little tempting.

The moment passed as Bianca called out my name.

I ran to her.

She was sitting up; those tragic eyes of hers wide as they sized me up.

"Are you okay?" she asked.

If I weren't so out of breath, I'd have laughed. "That's what I should be asking you. Are *you* okay?"

She nodded, looking far from it. She looked rattled and terrified. Face ashen, tone shaky. I'd kill him.

"We can't stay here anymore," she told me. "We need to disappear again."

I helped her stand, pulling her into my chest. "Why?"

"That's how he found me. A caseworker told him. Gave him the location. We can't trust anyone."

I took a few deep, steadying breaths. "Okay. We'll figure it out. We'll be okay. We just need to go back to the house, grab a few things, but we can be off the radar by morning."

As I spoke, I turned and glanced back at where I'd left him, out cold on the ground.

He was gone.

CHAPTER TWENTY

SAME DAMAGED ROOT

PRESENT

STEPHAN

James sat at my right, giving me very serious eyes. "I know you've been in a tough position with me, from the start. With your need to protect her, and having no way of knowing whether or not she'd need protection from *me*. That's all past now, though. We don't ever need to make things hard for each other. I want you to know that I won't ever try to come between you. I know how necessary you are to each other."

That was good. Anything else wouldn't have worked. You couldn't separate the inseparable.

Still, he was a good man for trying his best to understand us.

I tried my best to explain it to him.

"We were throwaway kids," I told him quietly. "It's a tough thing to be, though at least we had each other. Looking back at it,

I can tell you right now, I know for a *certainty*, neither of us would have made it, if we hadn't found the other.

We are fundamentally connected. We met when we were broken seeds, when we were still being formed into something. We had to grow together to survive. Some part of us will always be like that, connected, growing together. We're different flowers, but we were nurtured from the same damaged root."

CHAPTER TWENTY-ONE

MY PROMISE TO YOU

PAST

STEPHAN

I stepped out of the shower, briskly toweled myself dry, and pulled on fresh boxers and shorts.

Some asshole at the club had barfed on the dance floor, spraying half the crowd, but luckily I'd been close enough to the hotel to run back and change.

I was still shirtless, toweling my hair dry and wondering where I'd left my phone, when I heard Bianca's voice in the adjoining room.

"Ste-Stephan?" she called out haltingly.

I came out of the bathroom, surprised that she was back, and so early. "Hey, Buttercup. Some knucklehead got barf on my shirt, so I had to come back to change." As I spoke, I moved toward her.

The room was dimly lit, but as I got close to her, I caught a clear look at her face.

And went cold, then hot, my heart pounding as I pulled her into my arms.

I knew, just knew, that something was horribly wrong. She looked so lost.

"Oh, Bee, what is it?"

She started sobbing. My heart seized up in my chest, and I began to shake and cry myself.

My strong, stoic angel breaking. It was too much. I couldn't stand it.

What had happened? I was afraid to ask.

I was afraid of what I would do when I found out what had brought her to this state.

"Shh, it will be okay," I soothed. "We will survive it, Bianca. Whatever it is, we'll survive it together."

Someone started pounding at the door to her room.

"Bianca, open the door," James shouted, his voice filled with desperation.

I stopped breathing, my vision going red, head filling with a great, vile, black rage.

"We need to talk," he continued. "Don't lock me out. Open the door. Now."

I held her to me, trying to get a handle on myself, on my temper.

He just kept pounding at the door.

We tried to wait him out.

It became too much for her, and suddenly and violently, she ripped out of my arms, flinging herself onto the floor on the far side of the bed.

She folded her legs up to her chest, leaned her head forward, visibly trembling, and began to rock herself.

I nearly lost my mind.

I was at the door flinging it open to glare at James between one breath and the next.

"Don't do that," I bit out. "She doesn't want to see you. Just look at her!"

James tried to move past me, to her, and I met him head on, shoving my shoulder against his hard enough to bruise us both.

"What have you done?" I panted, trying to shove him out the door.

The bastard was strong, though, and I had to settle for pinning him up against the wall.

He stopped pushing at me, as though he'd given up, and I involuntarily let up on him.

He jerked, trying to get out of my hold.

I contained him again, barely.

He made no move to hurt me, instead trying frantically to get to her.

But that wasn't happening. No way.

I'd been avoiding looking at his eyes, and when I finally met them, they were imploring.

"Just let me see her," he pleaded through his teeth. "I just want to make it better. I'm not here to hurt her, Stephan."

That set me off. "You've already done that! Look at her! What did you do?"

No wait. I didn't need to know, shouldn't know, before he left. I'd really lose it then. *"You need to leave!"*

"I see her," he said, sounding as tortured as I felt. "Bianca," he called out to her. "Just hear me out. That woman was just a friend."

I felt ill, and so enraged I couldn't contain it. I reared back, then forward, driving my fist into his stomach. I'd have kept going, but now I wanted answers, and a few more hits like that would render him unable to give them. "What woman?" I growled, panting into his face.

"Please, just let me go to her. I can't see her hurting like that. It's killing me."

"So leave. You made her like that, and you need to leave. If she wants to talk to you, she has your number."

"Bianca," he tried again, voice breaking.

I slammed him hard into the wall, putting my elbow to his throat. I knew this left my stomach and sides unprotected, but he didn't take the opening. In fact, he made no move at all to hurt me back, only struggling to get around me.

Over my dead body.

"Just say you'll hear me out, Bianca," he told her. "If not now, then later. But promise me you won't just shut me out completely. Promise me, and I'll leave. If that's what you want."

"I give you my word," she said, her broken voice like daggers on my heart, "Just like you did, when you said we were exclusive."

"Fucker!" I roared, landing another vicious blow to his stomach.

The fucker kept trying. "We were," he gasped. "We are. I never lied to you. I tell you the truth about everything, even when it hurts, because I want you to trust me."

"You said you didn't date," she shot back, a new knot entering her voice, finally some anger to accompany the pain. "That was a lie, since I met your date for tonight."

I cursed, slamming him into the wall. "You bastard," I panted in his face. "You swore to me that you wouldn't hurt her, but I haven't seen her this hurt since the last time her dad got his hands on her."

James went still, then limp, the fight gone out of him. I didn't care. I kept pushing.

The bastard. I'd been so happy to see her finally falling for a guy that I'd pushed her towards it. Towards *this*.

I wanted to hurt him. *I wanted to make him to bleed.* I knew I was just one degree away from losing it completely.

"Bianca, please, you can't just leave me. Just agree to talk to me again, when you feel up to it. I'll let you pick the time and place, but I can't just let you go without a fight."

"Fine, if you'll answer one question for me first." Her voice was stronger now, though the tonelessness of it was worrisome in its own right.

"Anything," he agreed without hesitating.

"First, agree not to come near me, so Stephan can let you go."

"If that's what you want."

I didn't want to let him go. In fact, I wanted to put my hands around his neck and start squeezing, but that desire let me know just how necessary it was for me to get away from him.

Abruptly, I let him go, and began to pace, one wary eye still on him, in case he tried to go near her.

With every step away from him, I realized how far I'd gone. I felt sick. I hated violence, but I couldn't seem to escape it; I was a violent man.

"You can come to my house Monday afternoon, at five. We can speak then." Her voice was firm and steady now. And the more she calmed, the more I regretted losing my temper.

"Sooner, please," James had the nerve to press his advantage. "Waiting until Monday will be pure torture."

She shook her head. "No. Monday. Now answer my question."

He nodded, shoving his hands in his pockets, looking as helpless as I felt.

"Have you fucked Jules?"

"Yes," he answered.

My hands clenched into fists, and I nearly charged him again.

"But it's been a long time," he added.

"When?" Bianca prodded.

"A year, at least. I'm not sure exactly how long."

"Was it just the one time?" Her tone was pointed now.

He shut his eyes. "No. But it never meant anything, I swear."

"So you've been sleeping with her for years, and you were going on a date with her after I left tonight, and it didn't mean anything?" she questioned.

"I know it sounds bad, but it's not like that. I've known her since high school, and our families have ties that go far back. Her brother, Parker, is a close friend of mine. And she is only a friend to me. I swear it."

"But you obviously fuck your friends." Her voice had gone flat, and I knew she was shutting him out. At this point, she was just building up her case against him.

"Not anymore. Anything I had with her means nothing. It never did."

"And you've only known me for a week," she shot back. "What does that say about us?"

She was done with him, I could tell. I only worried what it had cost her to write him off so quickly.

He wasn't done trying to change her mind. He didn't know her like I did. It was a lost cause now.

"Please don't do that," he implored. "It's different. We're

different."

She turned her back on him. "Please go. I'll talk to you on Monday. And please don't be on any of my flights. If you are, I'll work in coach to get away from you."

He stared at her for the longest time, looking so desolate that I almost felt bad for him.

When he finally left, I went to her. I bent down and cradled her into my arms, carrying her to bed. I held her tight, feeling helpless.

When she started crying again, I couldn't stand it, I broke down with her.

But as she sobbed, I realized something. She hadn't completely frozen him out yet. She wouldn't be crying like her heart was breaking, if that were the case.

I didn't know what to think, what to hope for. I couldn't tell from the conversation just how far James's betrayal had gone, and how much of it was a misunderstanding.

I felt disloyal for even questioning it, but I'd had such high hopes for them, for her, that it was hard to just let it go.

She didn't want to talk about it, and I didn't press the issue.

In fact, we barely spoke at all, but on the edge of sleep, when all of the energy had been sobbed out of both of us, I heard her quietly chanting, "You're okay, I'm okay, we're okay."

It broke my heart all over again. I hadn't heard her fall back on that in years.

She was better the next morning, though still not talking about it.

I didn't pry, and I had to run interference several times on the smitten Captain Damien.

He was a good friend, and he knew Bianca well enough to see something was wrong as soon as he set eyes on her the next morning.

He shot me a look. I shook my head at him.

"I can tell she's upset. Did she break up with that guy?" he asked me, first chance he caught me without her.

I sighed. "It's not a good time, man. I'd just let it go, if I were you."

I knew he sought her out anyway, tried to offer comfort. I hoped he succeeded, but doubted it was possible.

James had already texted me several times before we even took off that morning.

JAMES: I'm so sorry.

JAMES: Is she okay this morning? Has she said anything?

JAMES: Thank you for taking care of her. For being there for her.

JAMES: Words can't express how much I regret how things went last night.

JAMES: Please believe me when I say that I care for her deeply, and I understand why you'd be upset with me. Things look much different than they are, and I don't blame you

for wanting to protect her. I'm sorry it came to that.

JAMES: I'd like to talk to you, when you get a chance.

JAMES: Can I call you?

JAMES: My men tell me she looks pale and drawn. Is she all right? Is she eating? Please make sure she takes care of herself.

When I checked my phone again, after we landed, I saw that he'd tried to call me several times during the flight. I wasn't at all surprised.

I felt torn. I believed him, believed he cared for her deeply, believed he had her best interests at heart.

It felt disloyal, and I debated even speaking to him, but Bianca told me that I should handle him however I saw fit.

She went and crashed for hours after the trip, but I stayed up, looking at my phone and agonizing about what was the right thing to do.

"Will you let me explain my side of what happened last night?" was the first thing he said when I finally took his call.

This was just the thing I'd been worried about. "I'll hear you out, but you need to understand that I won't take anything you say to her. She doesn't want to hear it, not even from me, if that is your angle."

"It's not. I know what you are to her, and I need you to understand what *I'm* trying to be to her. I respect your role in her life, and I'd like to begin to earn my own place there, as well, because I'm not planning to go anywhere. You and I should not be at odds."

I let out an agitated sigh. He sounded so sincere. Either he was an exceptional actor, or he meant what he said, meant it earnestly. And what reason did he have to lie? Why would he bother?

"Tell me who that other woman was last night," I said grudgingly. "The one Bianca seems to think you're with."

"I'm not! She's an old acquaintance, and that is *all*. We had a long-standing social engagement for a charity event that happened to fall on last night. I—Stephan you have to understand that I have a past, a sordid one, but it is my *past*. I've promised Bianca exclusivity, and I will stay faithful to that. She's . . . very special to me. I want to create something lasting with her. That's *all* that I want."

Fuck. I believed him, and that only made everything more complicated.

"I don't know what to tell you," I said, feeling torn.

"There's no conflict here, Stephan. Talking to me is not disloyal to her. We want the same things for her, you and me."

"You have to know I can't just take you on your word on that."

"I understand. All I want is a chance. An opportunity to earn your trust back, and hers." There was a long sigh on the other end, and then, "I'm in love with her. Completely. Absolutely. I mean to marry her."

My eyes tried to bug out of my head. "She'll run the other way if she hears you talking like that, you know."

"I know. She's skittish. I understand that. Things have happened too fast for her, when I should have taken it slow, but my feelings are real. They aren't going anywhere, and neither am I."

"Why did you tell her you didn't want to date then? Why were you hiding your relationship with her?"

"Every woman I'm seen with undergoes a destructive amount of scrutiny. The press makes things up. They print things about the women that date me, things I'm not sure I can stand to have said about her. I'm protective of her too, Stephan. This is what that was about. Protecting her."

"You've done a shitty job of it."

"Yes, I know. I can do better though. I just need another chance."

"What exactly is it that you think I can do? My loyalty is to her, always; and it's her you need to convince."

"I intend to. But I can see how this works, and I need your blessing here. We both know it."

"Fuck, James. What a mess. I can't give you anything, not as things stand, not until you make it right with her. You hurt her, and you need to fix it."

"Always. I'll *always* fix it, Stephan. That is my promise to you."

CHAPTER TWENTY-TWO

COMING OUT

PAST

I was in the hospital when I got the text. It was from a strange number, and so I didn't even look at it at first.

James and I were taking turns sitting vigil with Bianca, who'd been brutally attacked just days before.

Sometimes we flanked her, each taking a hand, because neither of us could stand to be far from her when she was so obviously in need, but a lot of times, like now, the nurse needed to check in on her, and one of us had to move out of the way so she could.

This time, I had stepped away from her. It was hard to do, but I knew it was necessary. I had to learn to share her now, as much as that went against the grain of the complexity that was my relationship with Bianca.

I was in a bad place, though not because of that. It was the attack that had me in a dark state—the fact that someone had hurt

Bianca.

The last few days were an awful blur. The nightmare of finding her sprawled out on her floor, beaten unconscious. I'd called an ambulance, and just as I was getting in my car to follow it to the hospital, James had pulled up, looking distraught as he saw her being pulled away.

We'd ridden together, followed her here, gone through the ordeal of uncovering all the damage that'd been done to her together. It was a toss-up which one of us was more messed up about it.

I couldn't believe what had happened, and how I had failed to protect her. I'd been just minutes too late.

I knew James felt the same. We were bonding, in a way, over it—a shared, impotent self-loathing over how this impossible thing never should have happened.

I checked my phone again as I paced outside her room, more to pass the time than anything else. I went through all of my other texts before I checked the one from the unknown number.

It's Javier. New number. I just wanted to make sure u r ok. I heard about Bianca. Is she ok?

That had my heart pumping faster. I programmed his new number into my phone.

He hadn't contacted me in so long. And here he was, actually being nice to me, actually asking how I was.

I tried not to let that make me too hopeful.

STEPHAN: I'm ok. She's in rough shape, but she's going to be fine.

His response was near instant.

JAVIER: Thank God! Ty for getting back to me. I've been so worried. I can't believe she was attacked. Sending prayers and much <3 your way.

That warmed my chest considerably.

STEPHAN: Ty. It's really nice to hear from you. Ty.

JAVIER: Let me know if you need anything, or if you ever just want to talk. I'm here for you. I'm off until Wed, so I can meet up even, if you want.

STEPHAN: Ty. I'd like that. It would do me good to see you.

JAVIER: Can I visit at the hospital? If it's not ok, I'll understand.

STEPHAN: No, that's great. I'd love that. Visit any time. I'll be here until they discharge her, which won't be for a few more days.

JAVIER: Is now a bad time?

That had escalated quickly, I thought, not at all upset about it. Just the opposite.

STEPHAN: Now is perfect. I could use the company.

It only took him twenty minutes to get there, but for some strange reason, it felt like forever.

I'd closed myself off from him a long time ago, but I found that, letting him back in, in even the smallest way, had my feelings for him coming back in great waves. In that time between the texts and direct contact, the anticipation of seeing him again was nearly overwhelming, so much so that, every one of my pores had opened up to let the flood in, as though it were making up for lost time.

I missed him.

I hadn't let myself even think that before, but I let myself think and feel it now.

I missed him.

Why had I let him go? Had it really been necessary?

It had certainly felt necessary at the time, as though I'd been forced into it.

But why?

Had it been stubborn pride or self-loathing that fueled that breakup? I'd always assumed it was one of the two.

Even now, with over a year under my belt to think about it, I wasn't certain.

Perhaps it was neither.

The scared, rejected kid that still existed somewhere inside of me, the one who knew he was so unworthy he hadn't even been guaranteed food and shelter, that boy thought it was panic, just sheer irrational panic at the idea of living my secret out in the open. Of showing the way I loved to the world.

That kid scared the shit out of me, so much so, I rarely gave him a say in things, but sometimes he was right.

Bianca was still sleeping; James camped out beside her, looking awful. I gave him a heads up and went out to the parking lot to greet Javier.

I met Javier just outside the doors. He was carrying a large bouquet of sunflowers, enough to fill his arms.

"For Bianca," he told me, when I just stared at him.

He looked good. So good I wanted to do something completely insane, like kiss him.

"Thank you," I said, the words coming out low and hoarse.

He stared right back for just as long, uncertainty in his eyes. He'd come for support, but I could see that all he'd thought he'd find here was a polite rejection.

Jesus, I didn't know what to do with him. What to do with myself.

For now, I settled for walking him inside.

We didn't say much as we brought the flowers to her room. They were already in a vase, so we just found the perfect spot to put them.

I introduced Javier to a despondent James. Bianca was still out, so Javier and I went back out into the hallway to talk.

"You look good," I finally said, to break the ice, and because it was true.

A corner of his mouth kicked up in a crooked smile. "Thanks. You look good too. Sad and tired, but good."

I grimaced. "It's been a rough couple days."

"I can't even imagine. What crazy person would attack Bianca, of all people? Don't they know you're going to rip them apart with your bare hands now?"

"Who indeed," I said, not wanting to elaborate.

He studied my face. "If you're worried I'll tell anyone anything about it, don't. You can trust me not to say anything, if you wanted to talk about it."

I nodded shortly. "Thanks. I don't really want to now, but I might . . . some other time."

We walked down the hallway, and I led us back outside. I needed some air. I hated hospitals.

We found a bench outside and just sat there in silence. He didn't sit close to me. We were both being very cautious.

I don't think either of us knew what was happening.

"Thank you for checking up on me and for coming by," I said, feeling like I was repeating myself, but I didn't know what else to say. No topic was safe for us.

"Of course. I texted the second I heard. But . . . did you say that because you're ready for me to leave?"

"No! That's not what I meant by that at all. I like having you here. I hope you can stay for a bit?"

"I can," he said simply.

Another silence swallowed us. It was full of things I was scared to say.

Finally, I said it. The thing I needed to say, the thing I should have said a long time ago.

"I'm sorry for the way things ended with us," I told him quietly.

I heard his gasp and reached blindly for his hand. He clasped mine warmly, with no hesitation.

"I didn't want it to end," I added. "I wasn't ready for the things you were asking me to do, but I wish I had been."

His voice was thick when he replied, "No, *I'm* sorry. I was such a jerk to you. I really regret it. I was just so hurt."

"I'm sorry for that. I was hurting too. And you were right. I just wasn't ready to hear it yet."

"No, I wasn't right. You were. You have a right to your privacy, to dictate how you want to run your life."

I took a very deep breath and sent him my most honest smile. I knew it was a broken one, but it was mine, and it was real. "I'd like to be with you again. I'm in no rush. We can take it slow, but eventually I'd like to try to make it work between us. I never did get over you."

He was suddenly pressed hard to my side, face buried in my neck. "Yes, yes, yes," he said against my skin. "I want that very much. So much. That's what I've always wanted."

I turned my face and kissed him, just a quick press of lips before I pulled back.

He was breathless when he said, "You don't have to make a big production out of it. You don't have to throw a party or anything. In fact, you don't have to say a word to anyone. Just stop hiding, stop lying about it."

He was right. He was so right, and I was finally ready to see it. I was letting the past have too much power over the way I lived my life. I had been for a long time.

"Coming out is not as painful as you think," Javier told me, his tone playful, teasing. "You'll barely feel it. Trust me."

"I did come out once," I confessed, watching his face, pulling slightly away, taking my hand out of his. "To my parents, when I was fourteen."

That had swept the rug out from under him, going by the stunned look on his face. "You did?" he asked.

I nodded. "I know you love your parents, and you've told me how supportive they've been of you, but you've got to know that's not typical."

"I know. My mother is the best. I can't wait for you to meet her."

"My parents were not like that. I knew they wouldn't be, but I told them anyway. You know why?"

He shook his head, solemn eyes carefully scanning my face.

I clenched my jaw, clenched my fists. "Because I was hurting. Physically. Mentally. I was conflicted and surrounded by people that would not, could not ever accept what I was. Who I was. I've told you that my dad was abusive. Well, I thought he might kill me when I told him, in fact a part of me, a big part of me, expected him to." I cleared my throat. "Not even expected. I *wanted* him to."

He was blinking his eyes rapidly, and I looked away before continuing. "So I told him, laid it all out. We beat the shit out of each other. I couldn't help it. I fought back. No matter how much I've ever hated myself, I've always had that instinct to defend. To survive.

"I don't know how long we fought. I remember it was light when it started and dark when I lost consciousness. I guess my mom finally got fed up waiting for him to overpower me, because she clocked me on the back of the head with a frying pan."

Javier was crying. He reached for my hand, and I let him take it.

My eyes were dry. "I woke up in his work shed, in the backyard. He'd tied me to a chair and tied the chair to a wooden beam. I couldn't budge it. Couldn't move my arms or my legs.

"There was just one dim light in the shed, but I could see him when I woke up. He was just sitting there staring at me, hate in his eyes. Disgust. So much disgust. Like I was everything he hated and feared in life, sharing air with him, his own flesh and blood.

"*God*, he hated me. I swear, to this day, I can *taste* that hate, chew on it until bile rises up in my throat to gag me. It was what he felt for me, but it was so strong, I think he projected some of it *into* me. It's hard to have your own father feel that way toward you and not feel some of it yourself. Not hate yourself at least a little."

I took a few deep breaths, trying to ignore the awful noises Javier was making on my behalf. "Did I tell you my dad was an electrician?" I asked him.

He was sobbing nearly too hard to answer, but I finally made out a sobbing, "No."

"Well, he was. Not a very good one, I don't think. Or at least, not good at making a living out of it. His brother often had to help him pay his bills. But he was good enough, I guess, to rig up this *thing*. This grid looking contraption. He had it all set up in the shed, hooked up to my temples, and," I waved at my torso, "some stuff stuck to my chest."

"Oh, God," he gasped in horror.

My mouth twisted unhappily. "His own homemade version of electroshock therapy, I guess. You see, he knew before I'd told him. He'd been doing some research, heard you could cure a person with the right brand of pain. Well, okay, I know that's not the science behind it, but that's how it felt at the time. What he did just felt like torture. My dad was no scientist."

"It *was* torture," Javier sobbed. "He *tortured* you." He said it like he couldn't believe, like it was too horrible to actually have happened to someone he knew. Someone he cared about.

Story of my life. Not many people could relate to the things I'd been through.

"Yeah, well, he called it curing me. It didn't work, obviously. I don't think even he believed that it would. I've since read up on it, and he wasn't even trying to use the usual methods. He just shocked me, over and over, and said awful things to me. He did it until I passed out again."

"I don't know who untied me, but when I woke up I was laying on the floor. I went inside the house, packed a bag. My dad tried to keep me from leaving. We fought again as I walked out the front door, but he finally got fed up and told me to leave and never come back. I left. I was on my own after that. A homeless runaway. Alone, until I met Bianca."

"I'm so sorry," Javier said, burrowing into me like he wanted us to merge. "I'm so sorry. I never should have pressured you. I didn't know. I didn't know."

I held him to me, let him comfort me, comforted him.

It was some time later when I spoke again. "The good news is, coming out this time has *got* to go better than the first time."

He didn't find that very funny.

CHAPTER TWENTY-THREE

MY PRIVILEGE

PRESENT

JAMES

I woke with a violent start.

A desperate sort of anxiety had a very firm hold of me. I tamped it down as much as I could, but it simmered, always, just beneath the surface.

I was alone in bed, when I shouldn't have been.

I had the foresight to throw on some loose athletic shorts before I headed into the courtyard. There were no security personnel inside the house at night, but there were several on the property, keeping a close eye on the grounds at all hours.

I stormed to the closest guard station, but a dressed down Clark met me before I reached it. He lived in a large guesthouse situated near the back of the estate. It was his home, but it also held the largest guard post on the property. I caught a glimpse of someone behind him whose presence and state of undress surprised me, but I made a point not to stare.

"She's with him," he said shortly.

I nodded, and taking a deep, steadying breath, I turned on my heel and changed directions.

I only knocked once on the door before Javier opened it.

"She's fine," he told me instantly. "They're both fine. I was just about to call you."

"Where?" I asked, still agitated from waking up alone and to a panic that I doubted would ever leave me completely.

"Our bedroom."

I moved past him, headed there.

It didn't even occur to me to ask permission.

Where Bianca was I had a right to be. This was the order of the universe.

Calm, the first I'd felt of it since waking up alone, filled me at the sight I found in their bedroom.

We found them curled together in a heap, Bianca burrowed into Stephan's naked chest, his face buried in her soft hair.

They were beautiful together like that. It made my gut wrench to see it.

What was one's normal reaction to finding the love of your life in bed with another man? Well, I had no trouble picturing what it would have been, if that other man had been anyone else. But Stephan was, of course, the exception to all rules and boundaries.

"It's what we signed on for," Javier said quietly, eyes glued to them. "They're a package deal. There's no way we can claim we didn't have fair warning. And I'm not sad about it."

"Bianca wouldn't be Bianca without Stephan," I said softly, my voice succinct.

Javier nodded solemnly. "And clearly, he'd rather die than lose *her*."

"I owe him *everything*." It was debt that was so integral to my being now that I felt it deep, a part of me that resided in the very marrow of my bones.

"He doesn't see it that way."

This was a rare moment for us to talk. "I hope you know that anything I have is yours. *Anything*, any want or need that either of you have, anything on this earth, know it's yours."

"We know. Thank you."

"Those aren't just words. I mean them literally."

He smiled wide. "Oh I know. We're living in a mansion that you bought us. Doesn't get more literal than that. Aside from this, though, we're simple people. We don't need much to enjoy our lives."

"Well, never hesitate to come to me if you require anything."

He nodded, eyes back on them. "They need each other. I've never seen anything like it, but I know, for a certainty, that if one of them had died in that shooting, the other wouldn't have survived it. They met when they were broken and fixed each other. The things it took to fix them formed them together into something that can't, and shouldn't, be taken apart."

"Perhaps you guys should stay at the house for a bit longer," I said wryly.

They'd been staying at our house since the shooting. This was the first night they'd left our house for theirs. Clearly, that had been a premature development.

"You see, I can't be without her, either," I said softly. "There has to be a peaceful way to share, and her leaving my bed for his is *not* it."

Javier chuckled softly. "Yes, I can see that. So how should

we do this? Shall we move back in tonight?"

I glanced at him briefly before my eyes returned to my woman, locked in another man's arms. I couldn't stand the thought of disturbing her rest. She needed it.

Javier sighed. "We can't just watch them all night. And that bed isn't big enough for four."

I didn't point out that there were lots of other beds. I was pretty sure Javier hated sleeping without his injured Stephan as much as I despised the idea of my bed without Bianca in it.

I was resolute, but not bitter or upset, not about this. I'd made the grievous mistake at the beginning, thinking that patience, and Stephan, were my lesson, the price to be close to her.

Tolerating their closeness was something to be born, to be endured, is what I'd been foolish enough to think.

They were not.

They were my privilege.

I tried to be reasonable and had settled on sleeping at their house, camping out in the closest guest room.

That lasted for about an hour before I took up residence outside their door, back against the wall, arms folded over the top of my knees.

I leaned my head back and closed my eyes, sleeping in fits and starts for a few more hours.

I went back into the room when I heard their voices.

They were still huddled together on the bed, speaking in low-pitched tones, faces close.

They stopped when they noticed me looming over the bed.

"James," Bianca said softly, rolling onto her back. "I'm sorry. Did I disturb your sleep when I left?"

I shot her an exasperated look, turning my attention to Stephan. "We're heading back over to our house. You and Javier are coming with. Clearly we separated you guys too soon."

He just nodded.

I reached down and snatched Bianca out of his arms and up into mine.

I nodded at him once, kissing the top of her head tenderly before I started to carry her back.

"Are you upset?" she asked as I moved.

"Yes, but not at either of you. It was an upsetting way to wake up, but I'll live."

"I'm sorry. I just woke up, remembered, realized he wasn't in the house, and I had to see him, had to touch him, to reassure myself."

"Trust me, I know the feeling."

Our extensive security had come out in force with all the activity. We'd had to hire several extra people, all carefully chosen by Clark, and I was still getting used to the new faces. It was not an easy adjustment, especially now, as they all lined the path from Stephan's house to ours, a scantily clad Bianca in my arms.

She wore nothing but a thin slip with a whisper of a thong underneath. I almost chastised her for it, with all of the security we had on the property, but I bit my tongue. She hadn't been thinking, she'd been reacting, and I could certainly sympathize with that.

"Is she okay, sir?" one of them asked.

My eyes swung to the young man that had said it. He sounded legitimately worried, as though he cared beyond the job.

It raised my hackles a bit, but I smoothed them back down.

I knew more than anyone did just how unreasonably jealous I could be when it came to Bianca. I was working on it, as it was a condition that was both bad for my relationship and my well-being.

I told myself that the man was just doing his job, though a part of me didn't believe it.

Joseph was his name, I recalled. Twenty-five, clean cut. Blond and handsome, in a nondescript kind of way. A blank slate of a man, exactly the kind I felt most threatened by.

"She's fine. Give us some privacy."

They dispersed like a silent cloud, and I tried to shake off my dark thoughts.

I carried her up to our room, settling her in bed.

"Can I get you anything? Are you hurting?"

She was in considerable pain, she admitted, and I brought her pills and water. She downed them and lay down.

I lowered myself carefully beside her, taking her gingerly into my arms.

She (not gingerly) burrowed into me, plastering her lush body to my clenched one. It was as torturous as it was pleasurable.

"I want you," she said into my neck, her hand snaking down.

I stifled a groan and caught her hand, jaw clenched, body throbbing. "No. It's too soon, love. You need to rest. And heal."

She must have agreed, because she fell asleep between one breath and the next.

I, unfortunately, did not, though this arrangement was a marked improvement over the earlier one.

It was the next morning, over breakfast, that I mentioned, "I think Clark and Blake are sleeping together."

"I already guessed," Bianca said, without batting an eye. "They're totally in love. Just mad for each other."

"How long has that been going on?"

"Since the shooting, I think. Nothing like almost losing someone to show you how you really feel about them."

No kidding, I thought.

CHAPTER TWENTY-FOUR

MY RAVENOUS SELF

It was some endless span of time later, after the shooting.

Weeks that felt like ages. Time I'd spent agonizing and worrying.

I'd adjusted almost completely to working from home, as I wouldn't even consider leaving her side while she recovered. My businesses suffered through some minor hiccups for this, but nothing catastrophic. All of it had become rather relative, besides.

So what if a few other people helped me run things, and I lost control over some of the minute details that used to consume me? I couldn't even recall why it was so important to manage it all myself anymore.

What was the worst that could be happen? I'd become slightly less filthy rich?

We were dining privately, and Bianca was being very quiet. Too quiet. She was up in her own head again, though her worries were always the polar opposite of mine.

She worried about *me*. My stress levels, my lack of sleep, my unmet needs.

It was a difficult thing to grow accustomed to, as I couldn't remember the last time, pre-Bianca, that someone fretted over me.

Not since my mother, I supposed.

She cleared her throat and brought her level stare to meet my troubled one.

"I heard you talking on the phone earlier, to your Detroit manager. It sounded as though the situation would best be handled if you went there in person. I think you should do it. You can't stay home with me forever. I'm perfectly self-sufficient now, and even if I weren't, I have Stephan and Javier next door, not to mention all of the staff."

I didn't even consider it. She may have been ready for that, but I was not.

"Maybe in a week or two," I told her, not meaning it, but using it as a subject ender.

I went back to my food, feeling her presence acutely to my left. I was a focused man, but I could not be in a room with Bianca without at least half of my attention on her at all times.

Her presence was a great gaping void in my concentration— my ultimate distraction.

I caught her sigh out of the corner of my eye and turned my attention on her fully.

She set down her utensils, sitting back in her chair.

"Was it not to your liking?" I asked her, eyeing up her barely touched dinner. She'd finished only about a third of her filet and less than half of her vegetables.

"It was very good. I just wasn't that hungry. I think you actually need to expend energy to work up an appetite."

The words hungry and appetite coming out of her succulent

mouth with that soft voice of hers was enough to make me hard, though it was a fact that it didn't take much these days.

I looked at her, keeping my eyes squarely on her face.

I'd taken one look at the little dress she was wearing earlier and decided wisely not to look at it again.

My control was hanging on by the *thinnest* thread, and that dress, or more specifically, the body it revealed more than clothed, was more provocative than I could stand.

It was overkill, really.

Inflammatory, when I was already on fire.

Still, if I let my mind wander for even a *second*, I could picture it perfectly—her body in that dress.

It was palest peach, a lovely color on her, feminine and loose, with ruffles at the neck and hem, and so minuscule that it could have been a shirt. I had to force my mind away from any thoughts about her long, bare legs in it.

It also exposed nearly her entire back, just one T shaped strap was all that covered her from her shoulder to the little dimples above her ass, which was torment for all kinds of reasons. One being that her back drove me mindless. The other being that it meant she was braless, and *that* drove me from mindless to madness incarnate.

The neckline was decent enough, but the sides of the dress were cut severely, on account of the back, leaving the sides of both breasts exposed, so much so that the wrong movement could slip her clean out of it.

I took a few deep, grounding breaths for control.

I allowed myself one brief glance at her bare neck. Her choker was locked away, since the injury.

The sight of her neck without it always made my fingers twitch restlessly.

This also brought my mind to other things she'd lost during her long hospital stay.

Like both of her nipple piercings, which brought my mind to her breasts, the absolute last place it needed to go.

In spite of myself, I glanced at the white skin of one rounded tit where it nearly spilled out of the side of that damned dress.

And felt myself begin to *shake*.

I looked away, setting down my fork and knife, attempting to hide the fine tremor that ran through the entire length of me and seemed to be most apparent in my hands.

"James," she said, voice quiet and solemn, almost chiding, like she knew what afflicted me.

Like she held the cure if only I'd reach for it.

She did, of course, but I wouldn't let myself reach. Not yet.

It was too soon.

She'd nearly died and needed time to recover, time unsullied by my selfish, unquenchable need.

I didn't look at her directly, but needless to say, I was still hyper aware of it when she stood and moved to stand at my side.

I took in a deep breath, then let it out, calming myself and taking her in all at once.

She touched the top of my head lightly with her elegant fingers. "Oh, James," she sighed, tone gentle enough to make me ache.

She stroked her hand into my hair, gripped it lightly, and started to pull.

She leaned forward, pressing my tense head to her soft bosom, both offering support and taking succor.

I shut my eyes tight.

The image of me putting my ravenous self on her wounded self was a crystal clear picture in my head.

Obsessively, repetitively, day and night, asleep or awake, I pictured this.

It was very nearly too much to bear; this voracious, prodigious need of mine.

I'd not gone through a celibate stage like this since I'd become sexually active, back in my teens. In the beginning of our relationship, when Bianca had left me, I'd come close, but this spell had since outlasted that one.

It was an ordeal.

I jerked off at least five times a day, to cope with the readjustment, but it was about as satisfactory as eating cardboard instead of steak.

My traitorous hands moved to grip the bare backs of her thighs, keeping her leaning against me.

After one inflamed, torturous moment, I tore myself away.

She let me go, moving back to her seat.

I looked at her, making my gaze go to the bandaged side of her face, which I usually avoided, but not now, because I needed that reminder of why I had to put her needs before my own.

Her injury was still dressed from the latest round of reconstructive surgery, covering one side of her face from cheekbone to jaw.

It was a sobering sight, not because it was grisly, in fact, I couldn't even see the actual wound, it was covered so thoroughly, but because it was a stark and clear reminder of what had almost happened.

That reminder was dampening, which was what I needed at the moment.

I finished eating, and Bianca quietly excused herself.

I knew where she was going, and I forced myself to move in the opposite direction.

If I followed her to her painting studio, watched her work on and around a canvas in that fucking dress, I'd surely snap and lose all restraint.

She was not recovered enough for my unrestrained self.

I tried not to follow her, to hover, as that was not what she wanted, but it was a constant struggle against myself not to check in on her.

Instead, I took up residence in my home office and attempted to work.

That lasted all of thirty seconds.

That fast and my mind was wandering back to her and back to the image of my ravenous self on her recovering self, and I recalled rather urgently that I was do for another jerk off session.

I had just pulled my erection from the oppressive confines of my pants when my office door opened with no preamble.

This was unusual. Bianca never came to my office.

She stepped inside, then shut the door behind her, not looking even slightly surprised at what I'd been up to, while I found myself flushing in embarrassment.

Her eyes were unflinching on mine as she approached.

I'd pushed my chair back from the desk in preparation for my after dinner jerk session. There was enough space between for her to fit.

She did, facing me and leaning back until her ass was perched right on the edge.

I raised my desperate eyes to her devastating ones.

Our gazes never wavered as, at the bottom of my vision, she lifted her wispy little dress up to bare herself.

With a sigh of defeat, I let myself look, but only for the briefest moment.

No panties, as I'd suspected.

My eyes, as they returned to hers, were pleading now.

I couldn't fight her *and* myself.

Myself was bad enough, but I'd never been *any* match for *her*.

Not for one lovesick second since the first time I'd set eyes on her.

"You need more recovery time, love," I told her, voice desperate, heart pounding.

"Shh," she soothed, holding her arms out for me, her skirt falling back down to barely cover the essentials.

With a shudder, I moved into her, sliding my chair close between her legs. I rested my cheek on her soft, bare thigh and attempted and *failed* to hold onto any vague shred of my once dependable control.

She stroked her fingers through my hair.

It wasn't long before I raised my head to take her in again. "Grip the edge of the desk with your hands," I told her roughly, unsteady hands lifting her skirt, letting myself look my fill at last.

"I'm off the painkillers," she told me.

My eyes jerked to hers, nostrils flaring as I caught what she meant me to. We both knew I wouldn't touch her impaired.

"Why?" I asked, just to be sure.

"I don't like them, and the pain is manageable."

"You can't do that. You can't make yourself suffer on my account."

"Don't put this on yourself. This is how I've always been. I never could stand to take pain medication, no matter the reason, so as soon as it becomes bearable, I stop."

I shut my eyes tight and took a deep breath, so torn I was doubting myself.

"Please, Mr. Cavendish," she breathed.

She was ruthless.

I was lost.

I turned my head, burrowing my face between her legs, tasting her.

My moan was almost loud enough to drown out hers.

A taste turned into a feast, and I lapped at her, one hand pinching the tip of my cock to hold off on coming as my other hand delved between her thighs to finger her.

She came undone fast, thank God, as I jammed two fingers into her and pushed my tongue repeatedly against the swollen nub of her clit.

I pulled my face away to look at her as my hands went still, stopping her on the brink.

I didn't have to tell her. She knew what to do.

She begged.

With a smile, I pulled my fingers loose.

She cried out a protest that I had expected. Anticipated.

I wanted to be inside of her before she got off. I wasn't stingy with her pleasure, but it'd been too long, and I couldn't wait even a few more minutes to take my own.

My dick was already out and ready, but I shrugged off my shirt as I stood.

I didn't take off her dress, but pulled the front between her breasts, baring them for my eyes. At the sight, I moaned, and shook, and bent to suck the tip of one quivering globe into my mouth with enough pressure to make her cry out hoarsely. I palmed the other one, filling my hand and squeezing her pliant flesh.

With a curse, I found the buttons at the back of her neck, and pulled the top down, baring her torso. I pushed her tits together, then loudly sucked my way from one to the other.

She panted my name, still begging.

I straightened with a curse and obliged.

I met her devastating eyes as I plunged into her, filling her at last. Her tight cunt enfolded me with a welcoming grip. It was pure heaven to feel what I'd only been able to fantasize about so vividly these past torturous weeks.

Neither of us could stay quiet. A few cursing, groaning, moaning thrusts later, and I laid her back, pulling her hips forward.

"Arms above your head," I told her gruffly, watching her tits move while she did it. "Keep them there," I told her, eyes moving back to her face as I leaned forward to press my chest to hers, lining us up until my face was just inches from hers.

I kissed her mouth with the barest touch, more sweet than passionate.

It was all I would get for a great while, as that was one of the injured areas. Her lips looked fine, still lush and whole, but inside I knew that several of her teeth had been reconstructed, along with half of her jaw. It would take quite some time for her to fully heal.

Even the reminder of her grisly wounds didn't slow my ardor that time. I was already moving my hips in earnest, rutting in her with near mindless abandon.

I watched her eyes as I moved, trying my damnedest to wait for her release.

It was a close thing. I could have come the second the tip of my cock made direct contact with her cunt.

I let myself go the instant I felt her tight sheath begin to squeeze me as she orgasmed. I emptied deep inside of her, pumping out every last bit, still going for minutes afterwards, rubbing it all out, every drop.

I kissed her softly on the mouth again, just the briefest touch before I pulled her dress from where it was bunched at her waist, dragged it down her hips and off her, and tossed it over my shoulder.

I took my mouth to her body again, devouring every available inch of her trembling alabaster skin.

I partook of her like a man starved. Not one bit of her was safe from the base of her jaw to the bottom of her feet.

I pulled out of her as I moved lower, and we both moaned at the loss.

Her arms were still drawn obediently above her head as I suckled my way down to her navel, nuzzling, licking, kissing, *inhaling*.

I was panting like I'd sprinted a mile when I came up for air. "Let's go to bed," I told her, voice thick.

The damage was done, the dam broken open, and as I'd known, once I started, I was unable to stop. I'd wear us both out, rub us *raw*, before I had my fill.

I straightened, my heavy-lidded eyes fixed with obsessive attention on her pink sex as she lowered her arms and sat up.

Something caught my attention, out of the corner of my eye.

My brows drew together as I turned my head slightly to look.

My eye caught and fixated on a tiny drop of blood that had fallen from one of her closed fists, and dripped onto the edge of the desk.

My breath caught, and I grabbed one of her hands, prying it open. I found a bloody mess inside, four deep crescent marks cut into her flesh.

With a savage curse, I checked her other hand. It was the same.

I couldn't even look at her face as I darted away, rushing to grab the first aid kit.

I didn't speak as I tended her wounds, my jaw clenched hard to keep any condemning words from lashing out of me.

Finally, when I was finished, and felt I'd adequately calmed myself, I looked up at her and asked, "Did you do that deliberately?"

She just stared at me for the longest time, her face enigmatic.

Licking her lips, she nodded.

It made me feel desperate and a touch enraged.

Had I made her like this? She'd had a clear leaning when she met me, yes, but I was worried that this was new territory, where she *needed* the pain with the pleasure. Required it.

Had this always been the case, or was I just now seeing it?

It *had* always been there, to some degree, I realized, but was it getting worse?

I took a few deep, steadying breaths, to manage my anger. It was a sharp anger that came from a gripping fear.

I *had* to be good for her, needed to be, like nothing I'd ever needed before.

But if ever there was evidence to the contrary, this was it.

My voice, when I spoke, was hard and cold with an authority that I needed her to respond to accordingly. "You do not hurt yourself, do you understand me? And there are things that we *never* do." My tone went from cold to harsh. "We do not draw blood. We do not *puncture*. Those are not healthy outlets for what we feel or need. Do you understand?"

She nodded, her breath catching. "It was just . . . it's been too long. I've become addicted to this feeling. I was trying to draw it out, and I went too far. I should have done what you were doing, weeks ago, and just started getting myself off in the shower."

I didn't know what to make of that. She always knew how to

throw me.

What she couldn't understand was that it made me panicky to think I'd disappoint her in this. She was a natural, a true purist to the lifestyle, and it terrified me.

I knew she enjoyed the sensation of pain far more than I could ever bear to hurt her. She didn't use her safe word, so I had to be the one to judge the limit for both of us.

I was horrified by that.

And more turned on by it than any other thing I'd experienced in my life.

I set my jaw. "Don't do anything like that again. Understand?"

She nodded.

"Say it out loud."

"I won't hurt myself again. I'll show more restraint."

I kept staring at her, my eyes silently chastising her.

"I swear it, Mr. Cavendish."

CHAPTER TWENTY-FIVE

MY ACUTE ITCH

PAST

JAMES

I took in the room, scratching at the scars on my wrists absently. They weren't fresh scars, had been healed over for years now, but they still bothered me.

I made myself stop, as I always did, lest I make the embarrassing marks even more noticeable.

I moved over to a particularly interesting demonstration, one of several placed throughout the room.

A man had a woman bound to a thick wooden post. He was thrashing her enthusiastically.

It made my blood pump hard through my veins. I'd come to the right place, I had no doubt.

I'd been fixated on BDSM for quite a while, and now that I was eighteen, I was allowed into some of the more hardcore clubs.

I hadn't done much. Some spanking, a lot of dirty kinky talk, and a completely excessive amount of bondage. Even the most vanilla of vanilla girls could usually be talked into letting me tie them up.

I'd done all of the usual kinky stuff.

But I didn't want the usual. I wanted the exceptional, a much heavier dose of the thing that I'd come to obsess about—to crave. I needed more.

It was the most acute sort of itch, the kind that made that first scratch feel so good, like nothing else, so good that once you started scratching, you scratched it raw, consequences be damned.

I was a man of extremes, and I scratched it bloody.

Inside of me was an anger, a rage, an inferno of it, one that didn't need fuel. It never had, that I could remember. It seemed to feed on itself.

It would never go away, but every ounce of control I exerted and maintained made it more bearable. So much of this, of all of the things I did with my body, was about control.

There was a hot young thing standing next to me, watching the couple on stage. It took me about half a second to notice her, and when I did, I turned with a smile, sizing her up.

She wore an interesting series of leather straps, nipple clamps, and thigh high boots.

I wasn't completely ignorant about this lifestyle. I knew about subs and Doms, and I knew that this hot young thing was the former, and I was the latter.

It all seemed pretty simple to me.

"I'm James," I told her, leaning close.

She started, gave me wide eyes, and leaned right back, bringing our faces close. "I'm Rose. Do you have a sponsor?"

"Excuse me?"

"Someone to introduce us."

I shook my head, leaning closer. "I don't. It's a pleasure to meet you, Rose," I lowered my voice into a conspiratorial whisper, "See what I did there? We can introduce ourselves."

"Oh," she said, biting her lip. I could tell she wanted me, and I doubted she'd tell me no.

"Are you with anyone?" I asked her, to be polite. I didn't know the rules here, so I just went with the usual.

She shook her head.

"Do you want to fuck?"

She gasped at the crude question.

I smiled, enjoying the shock on her face. "I'd like to do more. I'd like to tie you to one of these displays in here and put on a demonstration of our own, eventually, but right now, I'm horny, and all of that can wait. So what do you say, Rose? You want to fuck?"

With one more trembling gasp, she nodded.

I had her propped up on a table that held an impressive assortment of floggers. I was on the tail end of fucking her silly, in fact had just made her come, when I heard a throat clearing loudly behind me.

With only the vaguest twinge of annoyance at the interruption, I held up a finger, indicating I'd be with them in just a moment, and finished.

I pulled out, removed the condom, threw it away in a wastebasket just under the table, and tucked myself back into my pants before finally looking at the intruder.

It was a small, beautiful woman. She had masses of ink black hair and had collected an impressive amount of ink on her arms.

She did not look pleased.

I gave her a bland smile. "Can I help you?"

"You're new," she observed.

"Yes. I'm James. Nice to meet you."

She shook her head, looking exasperated. She shot Rose a look. "Get cleaned up, sweetie," she told her, tone soft. "This wasn't your fault."

Rose left, shooting me one last longing look over her shoulder. I gave her a smile that let her know I wasn't finished with her.

"You do realize that what you just did could get you kicked you out of this circle indefinitely."

I cocked my head to the side. "Interesting. Which part?"

"Approaching a sub without a sponsor. This is not a pick up joint. This is not a place where you can operate how you normally do."

"She was amenable."

"That is not the point."

I gave her a wicked grin. "You look like you could use a good fuck, too. I've been remiss. You're a beautiful woman. I'm sure we can figure out a solution here."

She was shaking her head before I'd finished. "You really are new at this, huh?"

"Yes. I just saw this club here with a triskele over the door, figured what the hell, I'll give it a shot."

"If you can't take this at all seriously, you might as well go."

I flashed her a conciliatory smile. "I'm only kidding. I meant no harm. What's your name?"

She smiled back warmly. "I'm Frankie. And I'm going to do you a huge favor, James."

It was on the tip of my tongue to suggest a specific sexual favor that I wouldn't mind from her, but I held it in. "What favor would that be?"

"I'm going to take you under my wing, before you get yourself into trouble. You can thank me later."

Turns out, I did.

CHAPTER TWENTY-SIX

MY OWNERSHIP

PRESENT

For a long time, after the shooting, I couldn't sleep through the night.

Bianca slept like a baby most nights, like she never had before, like every worry she'd ever had had disappeared with the death of her father.

But not me. I was more restless than ever. A miracle had saved her, not me, and I felt helpless because of it.

It was not a feeling that fit me well.

In fact, it made my skin crawl in discomfort. In anger.

It had been months since the attack. She and Stephan were healed physically, and, it seemed emotionally, but I felt the wounds as though they were fresh. What had *almost* happened haunted me. I was a man that needed control, and I'd been shown, in the starkest way possible, that I had *none*.

I sat scant feet away from our bed, watching Bianca sleep.

She was nude, with not so much as a sheet covering her. I'd seen to that. I watched her lithe form shift on the bed, one long leg hitching up to give me a glimpse of the pink between her legs.

I felt like a fucking stalker.

In fact, I was one, watching her for hours on end, night after night.

I tensed when I realized she'd roused. It disturbed her that I couldn't sleep, when she deserved peace more than anyone did.

She sat up, and I watched her heavy breasts swaying with the movement. "James." Her voice was the softest utterance.

"Love," I answered, feeling the dark mood that had overtaken me lift in an instant. Just having her eyes on me could do that.

She crawled across the bed toward me. She'd always had an uncanny ability to do exactly the thing that would drive me the most wild, and she'd only gotten better at that over time. She didn't hide her body from me as she moved. In fact, she posed for me, even the exposure of her body an act of submission. As though reading my thoughts, as though even those were a command, she paused on the edge of the bed, parting her legs to let me look my fill before she rose, approaching my chair.

I stood to meet her, my body drawn tight, my cock throbbing as though I hadn't come, buried inside of her, just hours before.

I was a statue as she leaned up to my ear, my brows drawing together in a question. Her lips touched my ear as she spoke.

"Hurt me," she whispered raggedly.

My eyes shut tight, my jaw went slack, and a shudder wracked my entire body.

I'd avoided all of the rough stuff since she'd been injured, but *God* had I missed it.

"We don't have to, Bianca. It's not necess—"

She gripped my hair, pulling my face down to her injured cheek. She dug her jaw into me so hard that I knew it must have hurt her badly. It was nearly healed now, but I knew it was still tender.

"I need it," she rasped into my ear. "I'll never stop needing it. Please."

I pulled back, and my hands trembled as I cupped her face in my hands, my eyes searching hers desperately for what I wanted to see. Need. *Yes.* She needed this as much as I did. More so.

"Get on the bed," I told her thickly.

She obeyed, backing away from me, keeping her eyes on me the entire time.

"On your back. Spread your legs. Wider. Arms above your head."

We were at the Vegas property, no fourth floor in sight, and so I only had to walk to a dresser to find what I needed.

I was uncharacteristically clumsy as I bound her to the bed. I wanted so badly for everything to be perfect, to the point that I was nervous about it.

Her arms went directly above her head, drawn together, and knotted to the headboard.

Her feet I drew wide apart, spreading her legs until I stretched her. I ran a finger across one tautly drawn inner thigh, shuddering in pleasure at the way it made her quake under my hands.

I bent and kissed the spot briefly. "So sensitive here," I murmured into her skin. I knew just where to start.

I stood back and watched her when I'd finished with her restraints, my lids heavy, my blood pounding.

Every ounce of nervousness left me at the sight. The sight of her bound both soothed and enflamed me.

She gazed back at me steadily, her body shifting restlessly, hips tilting, breasts heaving, pink flesh wet and exposed.

I chose a simple leather flogger, a delicate cat o'nine, to break her back in again.

I propped myself on an elbow between her legs, dragging the flogger's thin tails along the sheets, teasing it across her inner thighs.

Abruptly, I snapped it up and back, watching her face as I struck the bed.

She jerked, giving me wild eyes when she realized I hadn't touched her.

I gave her a smile that made her squirm, back to dragging the tails against her sensitive flesh, back and forth, from knee to groin.

The torment of anticipation was every bit as sweet as the bite of the whip.

My cock pulsed, my heart pounded.

With a wicked grin, I snapped the tails against the bed again. Hard.

She gasped, hips circling.

I trailed the flogger up her leg, passed it briefly over her sex, moving it toward her belly.

I met her eyes as I flipped it, suddenly and abruptly, whipping it back to lash her inner thigh with a quick flick of my wrist.

She jerked and moaned.

I swung my wrist again, catching her other thigh, then slowly, almost lazily, I began to whip it back and forth.

I never rose off my elbow, never used my other hand as I slowly tenderized her pale flesh.

It was not a punishment. We had worked beyond that. This

was so much more than the usual game of bondage and submission.

Bianca was a purist of the form, a masochist that enjoyed being dominated sexually.

We needed no artifice, no little lines to justify the things we needed from each other.

I looked down at her thighs, watching the whip as I set to work on her in earnest.

Her inner thighs, from a few inches above her knees to just below her groin, were pink with lash marks by the time I finished.

Even so, she didn't want me to stop. She moaned out a protest when I so much as paused.

I shot her a chastising look as I leaned forward, shifting until my mouth hovered over her slick flesh.

With a soft groan of my own, I bent down and started sucking hard on her clit.

She was primed already and came screaming with a few rough pulls of my mouth.

I'd reached my limit, as well.

I rose from my lazy elbow, climbing up her body. I left her bound while I fucked her rough, sucking her tongue while I drilled my hard length into her soft body repeatedly.

I pulled back to watch her face as her cunt began to clench around me, I shoved harder into her, rocking my hips from side to side to jar along her walls.

I came hard.

I rocked into her roughly and shot deep inside, rubbing out every bit of my seed, letting her milk me to the last drop.

She'd be sore tomorrow; every shift of her body would remind her how I'd taken her repeatedly through the night. Remind her of my total ownership of her body.

It was only fair. After all, she had claimed complete ownership of my soul.

It was minutes later, when I'd caught my breath that I got off her and went to the closet.

When I came back, I paused to take her in for a long time. She was still bound, body limp, eyes sleepy but on me.

I opened the large jewelry box in my hands, watching her face.

She gasped.

I took her delicate collar out, approaching the bed. I climbed between her legs, to hover over her prone form, propping myself on one elbow, setting the collar against her chest with the other.

"Are you ready to wear this again?"

Her eyes were pure liquid on mine. Enough so to drown in. "Always," she said, with relish. "I never wanted to take it off."

I hadn't wanted that either. They'd cut it off, in fact, in the hospital. I'd had to have extensive repairs done to it, but it was as beautiful as ever.

I moved up her body to straddle her, using both hands to fasten it, my fingers smoothing over it.

"Aren't you going to lock it?" she asked.

That warmed my chest. Her willingness. Her enthusiasm for a thing that had once intimidated her.

I smiled into her eyes. "Of course, love."

I had to untie her to get at her nape. She bent forward eagerly, flipping her hair out of my way.

A shiver of delighted relief ran through me as I locked it into place.

CHAPTER TWENTY-SEVEN

MY VERDICT

We were at the New York apartment for the first time since the shooting, and she was at least healed enough for us to make full use of it.

We'd just barely started traveling again, and it was a fact that we'd both been looking forward to this.

I was fairly brimming with anticipation.

Bianca was acting giddy with it. She was never like this. She could barely hold still. It was adorable. And sexy.

I gripped her hair at the nape, hooked a finger in her collar, and watched her face, seeing where in the room her eyes wandered first.

We were poised in the doorway of our neglected playground.

I tensed when she looked longingly at the piercing table.

She'd mentioned a few times, lately, about wanting her nipple piercings back. Everything had been removed when she'd gone into surgery, after the shooting.

I was torn on the issue; it had been on my mind, as well.

I'd finally come to a decision about it.

"You won't like this," I began, "but I've decided not to pierce you there again."

"What? Why?"

"It's a bad memory for me, when I did those piercings. I lost it. Lost my mind. Lost my temper. Lost control. I went too far with you, in a few different ways. I've apologized several times for that, and you seem to be over it . . . but the entire thing is a hard memory for me, so I've decided that's not a marker I want to put on you."

"Don't I have a say?"

"You can always say no, to anything, but you don't get to force a yes. I've made up my mind. Also, I learned from that loss of control. I won't be putting my hands on you, not for pleasure *or* pain, when I'm angry with you again. It's a rule I should have made from the beginning. It just wasn't anything I'd run into before. There was always such an emotional disconnect between me and my subs. It left me ill-equipped to deal with my emotions where you were concerned. The subsequent onslaught of feelings was . . . an adjustment."

She looked surprised. "Whatever you're comfortable with."

"This is what I'm comfortable with. The burden is on me, and this is the solution I came up with."

"So no piercings. That's the final verdict?"

I smiled, watching her face as I said, "I didn't say no piercings."

She looked intrigued. "What did you have in mind?"

"Do you trust me?"

She didn't hesitate. "Of course."

Joy bloomed in my chest. I leaned forward, kissing her

softly.

I didn't deepen it. I was still very careful with her face.

The bandages were off, the surgeries done, the wounds healed. She had a scar along her cheek, but it wasn't disfiguring, which was a miracle, all things considered. I didn't think it marred her beauty at all, but I was still wary of touching it.

It continued to be a raw wound for me, what had happened to her.

As though reading my thoughts, one of her hands covered mine, pulling it up to her face, she cupped it over the side of her face that had been injured.

I pulled back, bringing my other hand and cupping her face in both hands.

"You can touch it. It doesn't bother me. I won't break."

I traced it with loving fingers. "It doesn't hurt to kiss, either? It's not tender."

"No. It's not. You don't have to hold back so much."

I just kissed her for a long time, letting it deepen, until passion ruled, and we were breathing each other's air, my mouth relearning hers after so much time away.

Eventually, I guided her to the piercing table. I fastened her wrists to the table, but left her legs unrestrained. I pushed them wide. "Keep them open," I ordered, going to prep.

She squirmed as I slid on tight latex gloves.

I went through the careful, meticulous steps of piercing her naval.

When I was finished, I straightened, and waited.

"That was it?" she asked, shifting restlessly on her back.

I gave her a smile that was all teeth. "Not quite." I pinched the hood over her clit, rubbing the soft flesh.

"Any objections?" I asked her, as I prepped the area.

"You're going to pierce my *clit*?" she asked, sounding a bit panicked at the notion.

I waited a bit to answer, enjoying her tense impatience as I continued to work on her.

"Not your clit. I don't want to risk you losing any sensation there." I pinched the area I was going to pierce. "I'm going to pierce the hood of your clit. It heightens sensation, if done right."

She swallowed hard, chest heaving. "Have you done that before?"

"No, but I've done my homework. I'm confident I can do it. Any objections?"

She took a deep breath, closed her eyes, and submitted to the point of going limp. "No objections. Please, Mr. Cavendish."

CHAPTER TWENTY-EIGHT

AT PEACE

PRESENT

STEPHAN

In front of our loved ones, on a perfect day in December, at a private resort in Bali, our own little slice of paradise, I took Javier as my husband, joined my life with his.

They were not legal vows, but spiritual ones, which was all that mattered to me.

Without even one *ounce* of shame, in front of all of those people, I said I do and kissed my groom.

We kissed like we were just learning how. Like the sensation of my mouth pressed to his mouth was a new invention. I melded my lips to his and kissed him like there was nothing else, nothing to precede or follow, like this was the final act, the only one. This kiss was a vow. A promise. It was the sacrament and the ceremony that bound us together.

This kiss was all.

And then.

We threw one hell of a party.

It was a celebration of pure joy.

We danced. We drank. We howled at the moon. We reveled. We loved.

The party lasted four crazy, wonderful days.

I'd never been so happy. Never felt so at peace with every part of whom I was, what I'd been through, where I was going. Never been so accepting of all that was me.

Bianca gave the best man toast at the reception. It was short and succinct.

She hated hated public speaking, but didn't hesitate to do it for me.

She held up her champagne glass and turned to me, her eyes bright. She was breathtaking in a clingy light blue dress with a simple cut, her hair loose and tousled with the ocean breeze.

"I think everyone knows that Stephan and I have been attached at the hip for quite a while now. We've had each other's backs since we were teenagers. A decade and counting."

There was cheering, and she smiled at me, love shining in her eyes, so clear and true I could have reached out and touched that love, held it in my hands.

"I've always been proud to call you my best friend," she spoke directly to me. "*Always*. Unspeakably proud. You are the kindest person I have ever met. Your kindness has healed me. No one could ever have a more loving best friend. Your love has quite literally kept me breathing on this earth, more than once."

Of course, I was tearing up. Bianca rarely spoke like this, and never in front of other people. I knew how hard it must have been, and that made it all the more special.

"You've always accepted me," she continued. "Categorically. Unconditionally, you have embraced all that I am, every part of me, the good and the bad, the hard and the soft. That acceptance saved me. We had it rough for quite some time, you and I, but having you with me, having you love me, having you there to take care of me—we both know I would not be here without you.

"But as good as you are," her voice caught, and she took a steadying breath to continue, "as good as you are, as worthy of love, we both know that it was a long journey for you to finally learn to love and accept *yourself*."

She turned to Javier, her crystal clear eyes boring into his bright shining ones, tears running down his face. "I hold you solely responsible for helping him complete that journey. Thank you, Javier. Thank you *so much*. I can't express in words, can't ever properly illustrate the level of gratitude I feel for what you've done, for helping my dearest friend finally learn to accept and love himself. I'm so thankful, so happy to welcome you into our family."

CHAPTER TWENTY-NINE

MY TORN LOYALTIES

PRESENT

JAMES

I wiped my mouth with a napkin, setting it down carefully, looking across the table at my friend.

We often met up for lunch, so I'd had no reason to see this coming.

I stared at Tristan. He was one of my closest friends, and I wondered why he was doing this to me, putting me in this position right before my wedding.

I sighed. "Tristan, this is Bianca's department—"

"Bullshit. She hates organizing this stuff. Either you or the wedding planner are handling these kinds of details."

I grimaced, rubbing at my temple, feeling torn by both a need to protect Danika and respect her wishes, and an acute sympathy for Tristan and the way I knew he felt about her. I was one of the few that knew what had happened between them.

"I don't think this is going to go the way you think it is," I told him, my tone careful. Gentle.

"I'm not asking you to control that part. That part is my burden. I'm just asking you to seat me by her. Just give me something, some contact, an opening to get her to speak to me again." He swallowed, looking away. "Please."

How could I say no to that? There was an entreaty in his voice that I could not deny.

I tried one last time, for Danika. "Tristan, why can't you just let this go?"

But I knew. Even after six long years, years of bitter separation, an endless, silent, hostile standoff all laying heavy across each of those years, Tristan was a man obsessed.

"Listen," he started haltingly. "Even if she never—even if I, ugh, there are some things I need to change. I . . . I'm not who I was. I'm not the junkie that broke her heart and ruined her life. I know I'm not. But I need *her* to know that. Her eyes break my heart every time I look at them. If nothing else, I need to look in those eyes and see that she understands that I've changed."

I nodded. "Closure," I tried.

He sliced an impatient hand through the air. "No, not fucking closure. Closure is bullshit. A fucking myth. What I'm looking for is peace. Anything approaching absolution."

"You only love like this once," Tristan explained to me. "I don't know about women, but I don't think men were made to survive this twice. That's okay, though. It's worth it. Even if it all blows up in your face, it's worth it. Don't take one single *second* of it for granted."

Poor bastard. I felt for him, now more than ever. "I'm so sorry, my friend. So sorry you and Danika had to take different paths."

His eyes went wild. "No." He shook his head. "No. *No.* We're not on different paths. *She's* my path."

How could I tell him no, when I knew exactly how he felt? I just didn't have it in me. I could be a very hard man, but not to those I cared about, not to those I loved.

"Swear you'll never hurt her again. Not in any way. Promise me." I had to say it, even knowing how he'd react. Such was the nature of my torn loyalties.

His eyes went wild, his shoulders bunching up, as though it took every muscle in his body to keep his gut reaction toned down to something appropriate for this quiet restaurant. The room was suddenly too small for him.

"You think you need to tell me that? You think it's *your* place?" An impotent rage dripped from his words. He was angrier at himself than he was with me, because we both knew why I had to ask.

He'd broken her once, and though I had faith in him now, in who he'd become, I had to hear the words.

I didn't flinch from his rage, meeting his wild stare with my calm one. "She's my friend. I care about her, and you're asking me to help you get close to her again. It's not a comfortable position that you're putting me in, and I just need to hear you say the words."

He took a few deep breaths, looking away, his rage deflating out of him, and I could see the reason flowing back in. "I swear. I won't hurt her. I'll spend the rest of my life trying to make up for the times that I have."

I nodded, satisfied with that.

"C'mon, James," he said, smiling now, a broken smile, managing his anger like the grownup he'd become. "I keep hearing all of these matchmaking stories about you. Why are you so hesitant to use that talent for my benefit?"

I grinned. "I'm new at it. Not yet qualified to interfere in your mess of a love life. I need to work up to a task like that."

"That's a terrible attitude. Where's the arrogant prick I've come to know and love, who thinks he can run the world?"

I ignored that, sighing deeply, my mind on my future wife. "Bianca isn't going to like this. She's grown fiercely protective of Danika."

Bianca reacted about how I thought she would, though I did my best to put her in a good frame of mind before I told her.

I came home early from work, wandering through the house until I found her playing in the closet, her back to me.

I stood in the doorway, silently watching her for quite a while.

She had her wedding dress out, a veil on her head, more hair accessories laid out on the closet's large table, as though she was deciding which to wear.

She was dressed in some lacy white underthings that I assumed were meant either for under her wedding dress or after the wedding.

I loved her in lace. Pale lace, a perfect foil to her flawless alabaster skin. Antique lace was my favorite, the stiff kind, that upgraded her skin just a bit, but this was up there, too. Just then she wore soft, stretchy lace, all of it starkly white. Every bit of it screamed *bride.*

My blood coursed through my veins, my cock swelling and throbbing in time to the erratic rhythm of my heart.

My eyes moved over the lace topped stockings that ran up her thighs as she bent down.

I moved a few steps closer to her to see what she was doing. She was fastening some delicate white heels on her feet.

Her long hair cascaded over her shoulder as she played dress up with her wedding finery.

God, had I ever looked upon a more lovely sight?

She looked both pure and sinful all at once. It was the most heady combination.

I wanted to ravish her more than I wanted to breathe, but I held back, savoring the vision of her first. Inhaling the feast before I partook.

My cock pulsed persistently as I started quietly unbuttoning my shirt. I reached for my belt next, and the sound of it dropping to the floor finally penetrated.

She jumped, her hand flying to her chest. When she recovered, she glared. "One of these days, I really am going to put a bell on you."

That surprised a laugh out of me.

She glanced down at the front of my pants, where my erection tented the material out.

Her lips parted as her breath quickened

"Isn't it bad luck for me to see you in the lingerie I'm going to fuck you in at the wedding?"

She gave me a rueful lift of her brow. "You're getting things mixed up. You don't fuck at weddings."

"Make love."

She laughed, the sound music to my ears. "You don't make love at weddings, either."

"Why not?"

"It's . . . inappropriate. And besides, there's no place to do it. It's usually in a place crowded with other people."

"The wedding reception, then."

"*After* the reception, maybe."

I smiled at her fondly. She knew me better than that, but I didn't pursue it. It would come up later. Guaranteed.

"Stand on the table," I ordered her abruptly.

"What?"

I pulled a stepping stool that was used to reach shoes up to the closet's large island dresser.

"Get up there," I told her with a smile. "Heels off," I added, when she started to move.

She bit her lip and did it.

I looked up at her once she was up there, gauging the position.

I moved to stand on the footstool, then motioned her to me, until she was close enough that I could lean forward and kiss her naval, tonguing the piercing there.

"Will your wedding dress be too thin to hide nipple clamps?"

"Yes," she gasped.

"Hmm, okay, I'll work around it," I said, then pulled off her thong with my teeth.

I threw her leg over my shoulder, gripped her ass in both hands, and went to town on her pussy, eating her out, *feasting* on her sweet pink flesh.

I used my tongue to move the little barbell against her clit as I shoved my fingers into her, finger fucking her right to the brink.

When she was close, I took my mouth away, ripped my fingers out, and shrugged her leg off my shoulder.

I held my arms up to her. She leaned unsteadily into them.

I lifted her down.

I took off my slacks. There was a long narrow bench along one of the walls, and I pulled it out. One of its sides was much taller than the other, and I leaned back on it. It was meant for putting on boots, but it had other, better uses as well.

I put my arms behind my head and looked at her. "Straddle me," I ordered.

She straddled me easily with those long legs of hers. The bench made for easy access cowgirl.

I gripped her hips and looked up into her face as she rubbed her pussy over my broad tip.

She still had on the lacy white bra, and I left it on. It was transparent enough that I could see her pebbled nipples pushing tightly against the material.

"Give me your mouth," I commanded.

She leaned forward, brushing her lips over mine softly.

I parted her lips, pushing my tongue inside. My hands moved from her hips to cup her face as I pushed up into her.

She moaned into my mouth. I held still like that, not moving my hips as I held her impaled and kissed her, over and over.

"We need to discuss some wedding details," I told her between kisses.

She groaned, and it wasn't with pleasure.

I pulled away, hands going back to her hips, eyes on her face. I lifted her slowly up and down my thick shaft, setting a pace meant to tease more than satisfy. And her tightness, and my thickness, made it so each drag in and out held a little slice of torture.

I quickened the pace, surging up into her harder, filling and withdrawing, time and again, but never enough.

I stopped abruptly, hands going up into her hair. I dragged

her down for another series of long, drugging kisses.

She groaned loudly as my tongue parted her lips, thrusting inside. I kissed her, not moving inside of her, until she was on the brink.

I tore my mouth away, gripping her ass, and slowly began to move my hips, leisurely thrusts.

I quickened my pace, driving in more forcefully, but only for a short time.

I stopped, grabbed the back of her neck, and dragged her down for another deep, branding kiss.

I repeated the teasing process, time and again.

I was moving her slowly up and down my shaft when she cried out suddenly, "Is this a punishment?"

"No," I said surprising myself. "Just a bit of sweet torture. Savoring the bliss, love. Have I told you how much I love it when I catch you playing wedding dress up, oh bride of mine?"

She almost smiled, but I'd put her in a state of rapturous agony, and it was more of a pained grimace.

I groaned. I could feel my balls tightening up, my body long since wanting to come, but instead I lifted her off me.

She cried out a protest, and I shot her a warning glance as I stood.

Hooking a finger in her collar, I pulled her from the closet to the bedroom.

I told her to stand still by the bedpost and went to the toy dresser.

Her lacy white thigh-highs were driving me wild, and I barely took my eyes off her to reach for restraints.

I cuffed her arms up above her head, attaching them to a hook high up on the bedpost.

I filled one hand with a plump tit, the other with her

straining neck, rubbing my broad tip against her slick entrance. With a groan I surged into her, moving fast and rough this time, fucking her with purpose.

I squeezed her neck when she started to come, exerting just enough pressure to enhance her pleasure as she found her release.

I followed with a groan, leaning down to bite the tendon in her neck.

Later, over dinner, I told her about Tristan's request.

She looked as conflicted as I felt.

"Danika won't like it," she said simply. "We can't do it unless she agrees to it."

"I'll talk to her."

She made a face. "I can . . . if you want me to."

I laughed, couldn't quite hide a smile. We both knew how much she'd hate the task. I didn't like it much either, but of course I'd do it, to spare her having to.

Danika took it much better than I expected, quickly making a point to reassure me that she could play nice and wouldn't cause any drama at the wedding.

"Even if you have to sit next to him?" I asked carefully, feeling like I was walking through a field of land mines.

We were at the casino. I'd called her up to the office during working hours, because it seemed like something I should tell her about in person.

She took a deep breath, but then nodded, not even looking upset about it. "That's fine."

"Even if you have to walk with him in the wedding?"

"It's fine. I'm fine with it, James. If I can't be nice to one person for one day, your wedding day, then what kind of a friend would I be?"

I was hugely relieved. I'd been expecting the worst.

"Thank you," I told her sincerely.

"Don't mention it," she said with a smile, shocking the hell out of me, and went back to work.

CHAPTER THIRTY

MY SIN AND MY TEMPLE

Stephan's speech at our wedding reception seemed tailor made to make me embarrass myself. It was short, but packed a hell of a punch, one aimed right at me.

"I think everyone here knows that I'd do just about anything for Bianca," he began, giving her a soft smile.

"And it's no secret that I can be a little overprotective where she's concerned. I don't think anyone will call bullshit on me when I say she's someone I'd be happy to take a bullet for."

Several laughs for that. Their story was well known among our friends.

"It's also no secret that I think she's the most wonderful woman on earth. Best girl in the world, as far as I'm concerned."

He turned to face me. "I never thought I'd find someone that was worthy of her. I always figured, if she finally found a guy she liked, I'd have to put up with it, but I just assumed I wouldn't like him. Who could ever love her as much as she deserved to be loved, as much as *I* loved her? Who could live up to that? Who on earth could possibly be good enough for my Bianca? And then she met James. A man so perfect for her, so *good* for her."

That got to me, and I found myself blinking rapidly.

"That I never could have seen it coming," he continued. "I'll admit it wasn't all that smooth right from the start. We had some hurdles to overcome." He grinned. "I might have tried to choke him out."

Laughs broke out.

"But it was only the one time."

More laughs. He waited for them to quiet, smiling all the while.

"Bianca and I have a friendship that not everyone can understand, steeped in years of history that make it incapable for us to be apart from each other for any length of time.

"And something that always worried me, even more than worrying I'd hate the guy she ended up with, was the idea, the near certainty that he wouldn't understand or tolerate what Bianca and I mean to each other."

He spoke directly to me, his eyes bright. "But I needn't have worried. You are *just* the person that she needed in her life, for so many reasons. Thank you for seeing the same thing in me. Thank you for never trying to diminish what she and I are to each other. Thank you *so much* for never questioning, never complaining about this package deal you got."

I nodded at him, eyes suspiciously moist.

He raised his glass to me. "Welcome to the family, brother."

I tucked Bianca's body into mine, kissing her temple, then nuzzling my face into her soft, white blonde hair as we danced. I'd intended to behave myself for a few more hours, or a few more songs, at least. Really, I had. But it was useless.

I spoke into her ear, "Are you wet?"

Her step faltered. I'd clearly caught her off guard.

"I'm going to take you into the woods and *ravish* you. I'm going to bind you, claim you, brand every inch of you as mine. *Mine.*"

I heard her breath stutter in and out unsteadily, waited a beat for it to steady, still dancing with her, a slow sway to the music.

"I have the perfect spot," I added. "It's a bit of a walk, but we need some distance."

I let her process that before I added, "This won't be quiet."

I could feel her trembling.

I smiled into her hair.

I didn't make our excuses to anyone. It was our wedding, and we'd be back because one thing was certain, we wouldn't be sleeping tonight.

I simply walked off the dance floor, slipped away from the party, and pulled her into the woods.

I'd set a lantern out for us in a spot on the trail that led from the reception tents to the house. There was enough moonlight for me to see the trail, but not much else. I'd be finding the lantern by memory, since I'd hidden it here unlit.

We were nearly to it when I heard a noise that had me stopping in my tracks.

I pressed Bianca to me, putting my hand over her mouth.

"Shh," I breathed in her ear.

There it was again, a soft voice in the dark, one that I

recognized.

"Tristan," Danika said softly.

A short ways up the path, I could make out the shadow of a couple embracing.

A few beats later, the sounds of lips clashing drifted to us, followed by some unmistakably passionate moans.

"Holy shit," I whispered in Bianca's ear.

She didn't answer. She couldn't. I still had my hand over her mouth.

I started inching toward the spot with my lantern, figuring at this rate, if we didn't leave, we'd soon be hearing them having sex.

Danika started whimpering loudly, and it wasn't from pain.

Tristan moaned almost as loudly.

More, louder whimpers, another deep-throated, desperate moan.

I inched a little closer to the lantern.

One of their shadows seemed to climb the other, and they began to move away.

Tristan had picked her up and carried her off. Like a fucking caveman. I covered my mouth with my free hand to stifle a laugh.

Bianca started struggling against my hold, and I took my hand from her mouth.

"Was that Danika . . . with Tristan? Were they . . . ?" Bianca paused for a long moment, clearly at a loss. "What on earth was that?"

"That was about damn time is what that was."

"You approve of that? Them *hooking up?*"

"Wholeheartedly."

"Well, I don't think I do. He hurt her. Badly. I'm team Danika on this one."

I sighed. "He did. But people change. He won't hurt her

like that again. I'm certain of it."

"So you're team Tristan, then?"

I pulled her against me in the dark, finding and kissing the tip of her nose. And copping a feel. "I'm team happily ever after, love. And as impossible as it seems now, those two won't be happy with anyone but each other."

She made a disbelieving noise. "I think you're wrong."

"Well, only time will tell."

"I think we should stop them. Danika will regret that later."

I started walking, tugging her with me. "I think not. We're not interfering."

"That's not what you said when Tristan rigged the seating in his favor. You were all for interfering then."

I smiled in the dark, and knew she could hear it in my voice when I spoke. "Team happily ever after, love."

I snagged an arm around her waist and started tugging her again.

I found the hidden lantern, lit it, and headed into the woods, away from the house and the reception. There was no trail, but I knew the way.

We walked for about five minutes in silence before we came to a clearing. The sound of a nearby creek and our progress through the brush was the only noise that accompanied us.

"Stay there," I told her, and lit four torches I'd driven into the ground earlier.

The clearing was small, surrounded by a tight circle of trees. I'd chosen the area because it was secluded, and one of the trees had branches that were just the right height and strength for what I planned.

Everything was already laid out: Spreader bar with white leather ankle cuffs, an armbinder that had been designed to match her wedding dress, a white riding crop.

I grabbed the armbinder. It was a conical, single glove sheath that hugged her arms from her fingertips to just above her elbows.

I tugged her to stand under a strong low-hanging branch, pulled her arms behind her back, and began to bind them tightly together.

"You planned this out rather meticulously," she pointed out breathlessly.

I smiled down at her, a wry twist of my mouth. "Are you surprised?"

She laughed, a joyful sound. "I shouldn't be."

"While you were off getting hair and makeup done for the wedding, I was planning bondage and debauchery in the woods."

She let out another happy laugh. It rang out loudly.

I pulled her arms up high behind, and strung her from the tree with a strict strappado—a position that stretched her into helplessness.

I pushed the riding crop into her mouth, making her bite down on it, and left it there. It was not meant for spanking, not tonight. Tonight it had other uses.

A dark, heavy anticipation pumped through my body, making me throb.

I circled her.

I kneeled behind her, getting under her long skirt, spreader bar at the ready. I softly kissed the back of each lithe stocking-covered leg, then swiftly strapped and buckled her ankles into the contraption, spreading her legs far apart to do so.

I dragged the skirt of her dress up and pressed hard against her from behind. I didn't take anything off, just pulled my heavy erection out, pushed her panties to the side, grabbed each end of the crop, pulling it out of her mouth and dragging it down flush against her hips, using it as a handle with both of my hands, taking some of the pressure off her shoulders in this position, and started fucking her hard.

She was already sopping the second I made contact with her, but it wasn't a smooth ride. It was jerky, frenzied, and quick. I jarred into her at a pace meant to take her over the edge, and myself in the process, the tight press inside of her squeezing and sucking at me with each desperate thrust.

I hit the end of her, poured my seed into her womb as she clenched and milked me with her own orgasm, and started again.

I took her arms down, used the armbinder to fasten her arms in front of her now, and rigged them up above her head, pulling them high and securing them there.

I released her from the spreader, straightened, wrapped her legs around my waist, and shoved into her again.

I gripped a hand in her hair, the other cupping her cheek, and stared into her eyes as I took her again.

I went much longer this time, rutting in her for long minutes, lost in her eyes. They were pale windows to her soul, and I saw straight to it, with no impediments. It was the most intimate joining.

She was my sin and my temple. I both worshipped and defiled there. Gloried and desecrated. Revered and debased.

In her, I'd found my own earthly paradise.

"You're mine, Mrs. Cavendish," I told her, voice full of wonder.

"Yes," she breathed, "yes, Mr. Cavendish, and you're mine."

I arched my back and came, eyes never leaving her.

I fucked her, made love to her, again and again, cock marking her as mine, filling her with my semen, greedy in the claiming and the taking.

Eventually, I relented and led her, with mussed hair, a wrinkled gown, and on unsteady legs back to our celebration, hand in hand, sated and content.

I felt so complete, so content in my bones, so lucky.

CHAPTER THIRTY-ONE

MY PARADISE

The honeymoon was tailor fit to my own personal idea paradise.

Five days. No staff. Not a soul but us on an island that belonged to me.

She was not allowed clothes, not even at meals.

I lost myself in her softness. Completely and forever.

We wallowed in each other, for days, the perfect celebration of our union.

The first day was a delight of the senses, and I reveled in her body until she was beyond begging for mercy.

At one point she went limp. I'd gotten carried away, and she'd fainted.

I panicked a bit, but got her to rouse and sat her up, so relieved and remorseful that I shook with it.

"My apologies. I forgot myself. Are you okay?"

She said she was.

I let her rest.

The second day we slept, got up once to eat, I lazily got her off with my tongue, and we slept some more.

Day three we walked along the beach for hours, spilling all of our secrets and dancing naked along the sand. It was a joyful outpouring of our souls, one of the most memorable and profound days of my life.

We made love on the beach and got sand in some interesting places.

We went out into the water, our naked forms joined together as the cool water lapped against us. I held her for hours like that, watching the sea and the sky and marveling at the wonder of life.

The fourth day we walked to a hidden lagoon. We spent the day swimming and lazing away the hours.

The fifth day we barely left the bedroom.

I left her sleeping for but five minutes, to get us cups of water, and came back starved for her, as though we'd been apart for days instead of minutes.

I sat carefully beside her sleeping form.

I bent over her, brushing her lips with mine, then slowly, slipping my tongue in her mouth.

She started when she woke, but quickly settled into the kiss. I moaned when she started sucking on my tongue.

I shifted, holding her face to mine as I swept my tongue across her lips. I pulled back slightly to look into her sleepy eyes.

I slipped my fingers down to her mound, rubbing them lazily through her soft folds.

She shifted, a flush rising to her cheeks.

I found her clit with my index finger and circled it. I felt it swell under my touch.

"Did you miss me?" I asked her, rubbing more firmly.

"Yes, and no."

"Both? Why both?"

"Yes, because of this." She gasped as I pushed a finger into her. "No, because I needed a bit of sleep."

I smiled. She had a good point. I'd been an animal, claiming her body in every conceivable way, day and night, since she'd become legally mine.

Speaking of which.

I stood up beside the bed, looming over her, wearing nothing but white linen trousers and heavy lidded desire.

"Sit up," I told her. "Take it out," I ordered, nodding down at the prominent bulge at the front of my pants.

She obeyed, looking dazed, eyes glazed with passion.

Her fingers fumbled with the ties, the side of her wrist brushing against my erection. I pushed it harder against her, clenching my jaw, holding back a groan when she freed it, and it jutted out at her, inches from her face. A whisper from her mouth.

Bianca took a deep breath, as though inhaling it.

I was fully erect, swelled to my full size, the broad head of my cock stretching toward her parted lips.

She licked those luscious lips and stared like she was starving.

My balls tightened, hard length jerking restlessly, then bobbing with the bounce of its own weight.

She gasped when a drop of pre-cum spilled out the aching head, glancing up at me, as though asking for permission.

I pushed my hips forward that last little bit. "Lick it," I ordered her roughly.

With happy sigh, she lapped at it with her soft pink tongue. The look of bliss on her face was gratifying, to say the least. She continued to lick it clean with slow, concentrated zeal until I told her to stop.

She pulled back, staring at my cock, another spurt of liquid rewarding her attention.

She bit her lips and looked up at my face, as though asking for permission.

I nodded. "Go ahead. Lick it clean again."

She obeyed with long, slow swipes of her tongue. I clenched my jaw, hands made into fists.

She pulled back, and more pre-cum dribbled over to tempt her.

"There's more," I said roughly. "Lick it all up. Every drop."

With a moan, she lapped it up.

"Good, love, now suck on the tip."

We both moaned as she slid her soft lips over my engorged head. Her eyes looked up at me as she sucked, her tongue stroking the underside of my tip with each hungry pull.

"Take me deeper," I gasped, "I want to feel the back of your throat."

Tipping her head forward, she slowly drew me deeper, her tight throat hugging my tip, her tongue moving busily along the underside of my shaft. We'd been working on her deep-throating skills. She'd come far in a short amount of time.

I shoved deeper, and she sucked greedily at every added inch.

I grunted and reached down to grab my base, squeezing hard, trying to hold back my release for a few more torturous, blissful moments in her mouth.

She moaned around my length, taking me still deeper.

With an instinctive jerk, I shoved myself down her throat.

She started to gag, and I pulled back, cursing out an apology.

"You can use your hands now," I told her, and she did, taking me back into her hot little mouth while her hands twisted and squeezed me until I felt my seed rolling up my shaft

I stroked her face and praised her as she milked a quick, powerful orgasm out of me and down her throat.

I pushed her down and knelt between her thighs, lapping at her, sucking at her little piercing, stabbing my tongue against her clit, until she came, screaming.

I climbed on top of her, taking her mouth, sliding my tongue inside with a low moan. We kissed like we needed it to breathe, tasting ourselves on each other's lips.

We were supposed to leave the island that night.

We said fuck it and stayed another five days.

CHAPTER THIRTY-TWO

MY MARRIAGE

Marriage isn't easy. It's not meant to be. It is picking a partnership over a solo venture. It is choosing to consider another person in *every* decision you make for the rest of your life, instead of just doing what feels right for *you*. It is choosing to be selfless over selfish.

And like all marriages, ours had its challenges.

Neither of us had ever even attempted to have a committed romantic relationship with another person before. I'd had copious amounts of sex with too many partners to count, but that in no way equipped me for a lifelong partnership with a woman I adored to the point of insanity.

We needed a learning curve, I figured. We *deserved* one.

And so we learned together.

There was more good than bad, much more, always, even at the hardest times. More things I loved than things that I couldn't bear, so many favorite things about her, about our life together that I couldn't pick even a dozen that were definitively ranked into the top spots of my hit parade.

I loved waking up next to her, pulling her naked body close, feeling it warm in sleep, then thrum awake in awareness as I touched her. And I loved touching her, in any way at all—sexually, chastely.

Possessively.

Covetously, tenderly, wonderingly.

Reverently.

I loved the way she looked at me. She devoured me with those gorgeous eyes, swallowing me whole, eating me alive, her loving soul peeking out at me with no filter.

The way she studied me like she was memorizing my movements. Watching me put on a suit was like Bianca-porn. With each piece I put on, she got more worked up. It was a wonder I ever left the house dressed.

She was completely taken with my looks, and I couldn't help but enjoy that.

"You have a perfectly even skin tone. I've never seen anything like it," she said one day, as I got ready to go in to work for a meeting. Her tone was thick with lust, her eyes on my naked torso just before I shrugged into a shirt. That distracted me. Her preoccupation with my flesh, her lusting for my person, always seemed to have that effect.

I was two hours late for that meeting.

I was late for a lot of meetings.

I loved dominating her sexually, craved it, needed it on a steady daily basis, even while I happily surrendered to her the total ownership of my soul.

I had so many things I loved, things I would not, *could not*, do without.

But of course, there were the things we could not take, could not stand, habits we both possessed that were hard to break.

What she could not take: If I kept anything from her, even something minuscule, just to spare her feelings.

And when I became so enraged that I grew cold towards her, and refused to touch her, it upset her nearly as much as it turned her on.

What I could not take: Her silent withdrawals. Her need for space.

And of course the worst of it, for both of us, was my jealousy.

CHAPTER THIRTY-THREE

MY HATRED

I hated him. *Hated.* He wanted what I had, what I *needed.*

I could see it on him, smell it coming out of his pores, that want.

He couldn't hide it from me. He was taken with her. Smitten. Enamored.

Who but me could better recognize the signs of *that*?

Joseph. Fucking Joseph, the amiable security guy. Such a carefree smile, such soft eyes for my *wife*.

He'd been around too long by the time I realized it, and now I couldn't fire him for no reason without looking like a jealous maniac to Bianca.

Because she *liked* him. I knew she did. She was *attached* to him. He was her favorite bodyguard. She enjoyed his company, thought he was funny and 'a nice guy.'

He and Blake were always the ones she chose to take when she needed security to accompany her somewhere. Always.

But I hated him, and that hate went back a ways.

Two years, to be exact. I remembered the very *moment*. I could watch it in slow motion in my memories:

That night I'd carried her, scantily clad, from Stephan's house back to mine.

"Is she okay, sir?" he'd asked, something soft in his voice telling me even back then, when he'd barely met her.

And I knew he'd seen her like that, her beautiful, lush body barely covered, though he'd averted his eyes when I'd looked directly at him.

He'd fallen for my wounded angel from the first.

Why the fuck didn't I fire him right then and there?

If only I had, it would have spared me all of this impotent rage, this daily struggle to have to tolerate his presence.

Hate.

Raw, oozing hate when I caught him looking at her.

Acute, teeth-clenching hate when I knew he was home with her and I had to leave, or when he was out with her, when I couldn't go.

Bianca, who was normally too perceptive for comfort, seemed utterly oblivious to it.

And then, outrage of all outrages, I caught her painting him.

It was at the Vegas property. I'd come home to find her not in the house, searched and asked until I was directed to the large back patio, a spot where she often went to work.

I froze when I saw them, not quite believing my eyes.

It had been building up for a while, my hate, building up in every tender look he sent her way, every laugh I heard him draw out of her.

Years' worth of the build. Of wondering if I was crazy, debating whether it was my imagination, looking for signs, for evidence of it every time I saw him.

All of that hate came right to the surface, nearly spilling out of me as I observed what I was seeing then.

At least I wasn't crazy. There was some relief in that, though not much.

Here he was, not seeing me, and looking right at her, his heart in his eyes, so much longing there that I had to restrain myself from physically attacking him where he stood.

She, for her part, wasn't looking at him. Her head was down, her full concentration on the canvas.

My chest was moving with my heavy breaths. I loosened my tie, trying to drag more air into my lungs, feeling like I had heavily exerted myself, because in a way I had.

It was quite an effort, this restraint I was holding onto by the thinnest margin.

He just kept doing it, his eyes devouring her downcast head, moving lovingly over each strand of her loose hair, hair that he wasn't allowed to so much as touch.

But those looks were worse than a touch.

She worked standing up, as she usually did, palette in one hand, brush in the other, absolutely absorbed in what she was doing.

She was at her most beautiful like this, with those dreams in her soulful eyes, and I knew I looked just as lovesick as Joseph did every time I glanced at her.

She was barefoot, wearing a thin little white tank top with paint splattered on it and loose beige shorts. Nothing too indecent, but it showed off her legs, and hugged her curves. Her soft round tits looked positively fuckable under that thin material.

I approached behind her, and so he saw me first. Instantly and damningly, his expression became closed off, blank, neutral even, as he tried to hide it from me.

But I couldn't un-see what I'd just seen from him.

I fought not to curl my lip at him and moved my attention to her.

I studied her work in progress over her shoulder for a while before she noticed me.

It was a portrait of him from the shoulders up. He was smiling in it, a glint in his eye, but not the one *I'd* witnessed, which was something, at least.

The painting was good, of course, but very far along, almost finished.

This hadn't been their first session.

I caught his eye, jaw clenched, nostrils flared, just staring him down for a long time, not bothering to hide what was in my eyes, like he was.

Finally, she noticed me. She jumped a little, turning, the hand holding her paintbrush flying to her chest.

"I swear I really am going to get you that bell one of these days," she said, smiling at me, looking so happy to see me, no guilt or artifice in her eyes.

It loosened the awful grip around my heart a bit.

I didn't say a word, just moved close, pressing my body to hers, I gripped her head in both hands and started kissing.

I ran my tongue over her lips, then slid it deep into her mouth, moaning loudly at the taste of her.

She still held her palette and brush, arms out wide to try to keep from getting paint on my suit, body rigid against mine.

That was fine. I took it as a personal challenge.

I drew her tongue into my mouth, stroking it with mine.

My arousal hung heavy and conspicuous between us, even through clothes, and I pushed it against her hip persistently.

I deepened the kiss, thrusting my tongue against hers, coaxing her to suck it.

She shifted and acquiesced tentatively. She hadn't forgotten that we weren't alone. She was still aware of him.

I bit her lip, one hand sliding down her body to cup her ass, gripping a fleshy handful to hold her in place while I ground my hardness into her softness, probing, moving it from her hip to her groin, bending my knees until I was making direct contact with her most sensitive nerves, grinding hard enough that I could feel the little bud of her piercing against my seeking cock.

I pulled her hair, grabbed her ass, sucked her tongue, and circled my hips.

Both palette and brush dropped to the floor, her hands reaching to grip the lapels of my jacket like she was holding on for dear life.

I smiled and pulled back, eyes unerringly seeking out Joseph.

He hadn't left, or turned his back, as he should have.

Instead he was staring right at us with his untarnished eyes.

I took a deep breath and set her away from me.

She was dazed, eyes unfocused, lips parted.

And best of all, she'd forgotten all about *him*.

"Go up to bed," I told her, voice low and rough, but loud enough to carry. "Get yourself ready for me."

She nodded, breathing heavy, and obeyed.

I didn't follow her right away.

I tugged impatiently at my tie, loosening it, and then unfastening the first two buttons at my throat.

I shoved my hands in my pockets, shooting a malevolent glare in *his* direction.

He met my gaze squarely, still just standing there. He

looked like he wanted to say something, but he held his tongue.

I stared him down for a solid five minutes, daring him to say anything at all, neither of us uttering a word for that long, awkward stretch.

Finally, I smirked, running a hand through my hair, still not looking away from him.

I shrugged off my suit jacket, finished taking off my tie. I started to unbutton my shirt, illustrating clearly what I was up to next.

"Don't wait up," I told him, my voice mocking, and turned away.

I stopped in the kitchen briefly with instructions for dinner, then moved upstairs, desire beating heavy through me.

I found her waiting on the bed for me.

She'd obeyed perfectly and wore nothing but her piercings and her collar.

She was sitting on the edge of the bed, hands on her knees, legs parted slightly, back arched, nipples pebbled to hardened peaks.

Even with her legs open, exposing her sex, I couldn't see if she was wet, but I would have bet that she was.

We'd had some work done on the house, as we'd taken to staying here more often than not. The room next to this one had been renovated, and I'd had an adjoining door built in.

I went and opened it. I looked at her and lifted my brows. "The *other* bed," I told her with a wicked grin.

The adjoining room had been outfitted into an extensive playground of *fourth floor* proportions, and the space was dominated by a huge, caged bed.

She stood, and I watched her lush body as she made her way across the room.

I grabbed her wrist as she passed me, stopping her.

I turned her to me, fingers going to her nipples, pinching hard.

She arched her back and pushed into my rough touch.

I pulled her into the playroom, snagging her favorite nipple clamps. They were coral pink, a near perfect match for her nipples.

I latched them in two smooth motions, fishing in the same drawer for a very thin silver chain that had four ends, each with a tiny jewelry fastening on it.

She moaned when she saw it.

I attached it first to her collar, an end to each nipple. The other went to her piercing below. It was the perfect length to pull at each zone just enough to tease.

I stepped back, admiring my handy work.

"Go kneel on the bed, facing me," I told her, and shrugged out of my shirt.

I approached the bed, watching her, balls drawn tight.

As she stared, I pulled my cock out of my slacks, pushing my full length out, tucking the material under my scrotum. I gripped myself, one hand firmly stroking my shaft, the other my sac.

I watched her, debating what I wanted to do, what depraved pleasure would best calm the fiendish need that had its hooks in me.

I kept working my cock, jerking it hard.

Her eyes were glued to it.

"You like watching me jerk myself off," I observed.

She licked her lips and nodded, eyes still glued.

I went to another drawer, grabbing a finger vibrator, shaped specifically to stimulate the clit. I moved close enough to toss it on the bed next to her.

"Use it," I told her succinctly, immediately moving away. "Not to tease. I want you to apply it direct."

I was at the wall where all of the restraints hung, picking out a hogtie harness, when I paused as I heard her breath grow ragged.

She was close.

"Don't come," I told her. "And don't take the pressure off.

She couldn't hold back one delicious little sob, but I knew she obeyed.

I moved back to the bed and dropped the restraints beside her.

Without another word I grabbed the toy out of her hand, tossing it off the bed.

I cupped her shoulders in my hands, breathing her in, throbbing in time to her every breath.

"Struggle," I said the one word with relish, and let her go.

CHAPTER THIRTY-FOUR

MY CHAINS

She obeyed, struggling. She did it just perfectly too, attempting to get around me and off the bed.

I didn't use my hands but my body to keep her corralled at first, only resorting to my hands after I had her trapped beneath me, my chest to her back.

I pinned her roughly to her stomach and hogtied her with soft leather restraints, wrists to ankles behind her back, stomach down on the bed.

She was in a state, thrashing even after I had her confined. It was delicious, and just what I needed.

I picked her up by the ankles, lifting her as I bent my mouth to her sex, and started tongue fucking her pussy from behind.

She was whimpering, trying and soon to be failing to hold back her orgasm.

I still hadn't told her she could come.

I did now, breathing it into her hot wet core.

Her hips jerked as I got her off.

I lifted my head as she finished, lowering her by the ankles back down, pausing about six inches off the mattress. I dropped her the rest of the way.

I grabbed hold of her ankles again and mounted her like that, while she was still winded from the fall and completely helpless.

I took her like an animal, rutting, shoving, thrusting, owning her softness with my hardness, mercilessly, brutally.

I was completely insatiable, marking my territory in the most primal of ways—with my seed deep in her flesh. Repeatedly.

I stayed inside of her long after I came, hands moving to rub her ass as her cunt milked me to the last drop.

When I finally pulled out, I grabbed her ankles, tilting her hips back and up, holding her like that, watching her sex while she squirmed in my hands.

I undid her restraints and laid each of her limbs down softly on the bed. She didn't move, still on her stomach.

I went to the other room, fastening my slacks as I moved. I washed my hands in the bathroom, then moved into our closet.

I grabbed her fresh clothes, myself a new shirt, and returned back to where she lay, still limp where I'd left her.

I started dressing her without a word.

She didn't catch on at first that something was off about me. It wasn't exactly unusual for me to come home from work and want to *ravish* her.

I tugged lightly on the thin body chain still attached to her, sliding my fingers down to where it was fastened at her sex, rubbing it to score against her over-sensitized clit.

"Is it very sensitive right now?"

"*Yes.*" She shivered.

"Does the chain hurt?"

She shot me a look that left me breathless.

God, this woman could undo me. Destroy me. Utterly.

My smile was direct, eyes tender. "Let me rephrase. Does it hurt in a way you don't enjoy?"

Her silence was her answer. The chain stayed on.

I finished dressing her quickly. "Dinner time," I said shortly.

She made noises about it, but I didn't let her shower.

I could hear several of our security personnel in the kitchen as we passed. This wasn't unusual. They worked here twenty-four seven, but only Clark and Blake had a house on the property. The rest worked in shifts, came and went, and ate at the house.

I took her arm, and led her in there, to dine at the less formal breakfast nook, as opposed to one of the formal dining rooms.

The staff, who'd been joking and having a general good time, went silent as we walked in, the three security guys moving to file out of the room.

"No need to leave," I said, eyes on Joseph, who was leaning against the counter and watching me warily. "Join us, why don't you, for dinner?"

This wasn't so unusual. We sometimes dined informally, sometimes invited the staff, who we tended to treat more like friends and family, especially since Bianca had come into my life.

But I could tell as I studied him that Joseph knew why I did this now.

I maneuvered it so that Bianca was at my right, Joseph on the other side of her.

I watched him. Watched him sneak looks at her. They were side by side. So close, with me *right fucking there* and still he couldn't stop himself.

God, he could probably smell it, the sex on her. It probably made him want her more, even knowing it was another man who'd put the sex on her to smell.

I reached under the table with my right hand, sliding it up her leg, into her shorts, teasing my fingers through her wet folds.

She met my cold eyes, and I saw the moment when she realized that I was upset.

I stared into her eyes as I found the chain just above her sex and *tugged*.

Her eyes glazed over, jaw going slack.

I glanced over at Joseph. He was watching us, his face flushed in temper.

He knew I was touching her under the table. I saw it in his tight-lipped anger, saw the disapproval in his eyes, the jealousy.

Good. This lesson was primitive, but it needed to be taught, uncouth as it was.

I was feeling far from civilized.

I had an overwhelming need to stake my claim. Mark my territory.

All of these animalistic impulses overpowered so many of my normal inclinations. Normally I sheltered her. But for him, this fucker that questioned my ownership, I wanted to put my possession of her on stark display.

I drew the meal out. I'd had the cook make burgers and fries, an unusual request for me, but perfectly suited to the occasion.

I pulled my hand away when it was time to eat, catching her eye so she saw me lick my fingers clean.

She shuddered, her breath panting out of her harshly.

I devoured my burger with gusto, slowly savoring each bite, watching them the entire time—her reaction to me, his fixation on her.

One by one, each of the staff finished eating and excused themselves to go back to work.

All but Joseph.

I shot him a cold glare, and reached a hand over, gripping a hand into Bianca's hair. I leaned close and pulled her the rest of the way, and gave her a long, hot, bruising kiss.

I pulled slightly back and brought her ear to my mouth. I took a few deep breaths, inhaling her before I spoke.

"You smell like me. Like you belong to me. Because you're *mine*. Go strip down, get in bed, the *other* bed, and wait for me. I'm going to tie you up and make you suck me off. And that's only the start, love. I'll come inside of every part of you before this night is through."

She pulled back, studied my face for a few pregnant moments, and then left.

I didn't watch her leave. I was too busy watching him watch her leave.

I gave him a cold smile when he finally realized I was staring at him.

I waited until I was sure she was out of earshot to speak. I leaned in. "That's my *wife* you're casting those lovesick stares at," I growled at him.

He glared back, looking outraged. "I'm well aware. I'm also well aware of the way you treat her. Like an object. To abuse. I see the marks you leave on her. I see it *all*."

That had me barking out a laugh, at his expense. "Oh that is rich," I told him, cold disdain in every syllable. "A prude, working for *me*. How about this? You keep your prudish mind out of my bedroom, and off my *wife*, you bastard."

I had to clench my fists to keep from attacking him, because attacking him was not what I needed to do here.

I needed to get him to talk. I'd love nothing so much as for him to give me any excuse to fire him, something I could use that was more substantial, in terms of evidence for Bianca, than the way he looked at her.

I sneered at him. "What did you think, that you would sweep in and save her from me? She's *mine*. You think I abuse her? Then wrap your mind around this: She is in absolute *bondage* to me, chained to me for *life*, and the things I've used to chain her to my side are *beyond your ability to break.*"

He didn't say anything else, though I could tell he badly wanted to.

Instead, he got up and walked away.

It was not what I'd wanted him to do and completely unsatisfying.

"I thought you decided a long time ago not to do any of that in anger," Bianca told me later.

We were soaking in a bath. I snagged one of her feet and started rubbing at her arch.

I was trying to relax, to get over my rage, but even several orgasms and a hot bath didn't seem to be curing me.

I was bad at relaxing, always had been.

"I said I wouldn't do it when I was angry at *you*," I told her finally, kissing the bottom of her foot.

"Are you really going to try to say right now, with the way you've been acting all afternoon, that none of this anger is directed at me?"

I gave her very steady eye contact. "Yes, that is what I'm telling you. Not an ounce of my anger is for you."

She sighed. "It's Joseph, isn't it? You can't fire him over something so *silly*. You know you can't. That's insane. He's worked for us for *years*. You can't fire him just because I painted a picture of him. That's what I do. I paint things. I paint people. It's not even his fault. I asked him to pose."

"That's not why I'd fire him."

She gave me a genuinely confused look that went a long way towards making me feel better. "I don't understand."

I watched her face, wondering if she really didn't know.

If somehow she didn't, I wasn't going to be the one to tell her. I didn't want to see her reaction to his feelings for her.

What if she was tempted? What if she had feelings for *him*?

Without another word, I got out of the bath and went to bed.

I approached Stephan about it, a few days later, wanting his take on the situation, and his opinion on how to handle it.

We met up for lunch at his bar in my casino. I got right to the point.

"Joseph's become a problem," I told him bluntly.

He grimaced. Clearly, he knew just what I was referring to. "Bianca sees him as a friend. A good friend. You can't just fire him."

My jaw clenched. That didn't help.

"Does she know he's in love with her?" I asked quietly.

He didn't look surprised by the information, but he shook his head. "No, no I don't think so. If she had a clue how he felt, she wouldn't be so open and friendly with him. She wouldn't spend so much time with him."

I cringed. "She spends that much time with him?"

"No. Stop. Don't do that to yourself. She doesn't spend an excessive amount of time with him, just, you know, he works at the house, he takes her around. He's her *bodyguard*. That's his job. But you've got nothing to worry about. She would never . . ."

I knew I was in a foul mood when even Stephan was agitating me. I couldn't remember the last time I'd gone to him with something and not had him make me feel better about it.

"You find that situation to be acceptable?" I asked him bitingly. "You think this is going to end well? It's *escalating*, I can tell."

He didn't disagree with me, but he didn't have a solution, either.

I went to Clark about it next.

"Did you know that you hired someone with a very distinct distaste for my lifestyle?" I asked him.

He didn't look surprised. The set of his mouth was annoyed, and a touch resigned. "I do now. I've been catching that vibe for a while, but I didn't know it at the start. Of course, they've all signed NDAs that will protect you."

"Yes I know. This wasn't actually my real issue. Can you guess what is?"

He rubbed at a temple, looking tired. "Yes, I can. I don't know what to do about it. Firing is the easiest solution, with a severance package, but you're going to have to get that past Bianca. They're good friends, you know."

I laughed, and it was a bitter sound. "Yes, so I've noticed."

"I spoke to him about it," Clark added. This was news to me. "I told him that he needs to do a better job of staying part of the background. It's not his job to keep the boss's wife company."

"No, it's not. Did you also tell him it's not his job to *lust* after my wife?"

"I did, yes. In so many words. He said he'll do better. We'll just have to wait and see, unless you wanted to handle it more aggressively. Up to you. Just let me know."

I shook my head. "No, we'll wait and see, like you said."

I confronted Joseph at every opportunity, but he was doing much better at keeping his thoughts and his reactions to himself and under control after that. I didn't know if it was because of Clark, or if his own sense of self-preservation had finally kicked in.

As much as it went against the grain, I did nothing, just watched, and waited, feeling sick to my stomach every time I thought of him spending time with her.

It was agony for me. It made me antsy all the time. *Was he with her right now?* Would he slowly worm his way into her affections?

Had he already?

CHAPTER THIRTY-FIVE

MY PROCLIVITIES

I came home in the early afternoon, some days later, to find her riding.

As soon I found out where she was, I headed straight there, not even bothering to change out of my suit.

Our female horse trainer, Cosette, was with her in the corral, helping her tweak her legwork.

Joseph was there.

He was leaning against the fence post, elbows on the top rail, watching them train.

I approached the corral, but kept walking when I reached it, moving into the tack room. I grabbed the first riding crop I saw, and headed back outside.

I went to lean beside him, eyes on Bianca posting, a fucking *indecent* sight, and began to slap the crop against my palm.

I watched him out of the corner of my eye, saw when he caught what I was doing, was aware of his jaw clenching, fists balling.

I smiled, turning my head to catch his eye.

He looked back at me, clearly agitated.

"Beyond *your ability to break*," I reiterated my words from days earlier softly, succinctly.

Temper flared in his eyes, but he held his tongue, unfortunately.

I moved away from him, entering the corral, striding across the large space to where the women worked.

Cosette stood at the center of the enclosure, calling out instructions to Bianca. You could tell just with a few words between them that the women were close. There was much affection and camaraderie in the way she coached my wife.

Cosette was a diminutive woman, delicately built, somehow able to use that small frame of hers to do some of the most skillful riding I'd ever seen, controlling powerful animals with a flick of her wrists.

I'd hired her two years ago, at Pete's referral, when I'd realized that there was no way in hell I'd allow Pete to teach my wife how to ride.

He'd sworn at the time that Cosette was the best, and he'd been right.

She turned to smile at me as I approached. She was a beautiful woman, with delicately defined features, her streaky hair cut into an edgy bob, short in the back and sides, with long straight bangs that framed her face and emphasized her high cheekbones.

"We're finishing up now," she told me. "She's making great progress."

I just nodded, turning to watch my wife, still slapping the crop against my palm.

Bianca guided her horse my way. "You're going ruin another suit," she said, smiling at me.

I smiled back. "Yes, yes, I am."

She had no idea.

"Come here," I said to her, lowering the crop to my side so it wouldn't spook the horse as she walked it closer.

I grabbed her leg with my left hand, sliding my crop up to tap her shoulder with the other. I used a light pressure on it to guide her down to me.

She leaned down until our mouths were touching. I thrust my tongue into her hot wet mouth, moving the crop down her back to play over her ass teasingly.

Eventually I pulled back, tucked the crop into my belt, and dragged her down from the saddle, pressing her against me.

I looked at Colette. "We'd like to have the stables to ourselves, for a bit."

She was unfazed. She'd been working here a while. She knew how we were. "Of course. I'll leave you to it."

I turned my head, hand rubbing over Bianca's back. Joseph was still at the fence, still watching, the brazen bastard.

My hand moved down to her ass and squeezed hard. *Mine.*

"He should not be watching you do this," I told her quietly, voice hard.

She stiffened, turning her head to look. "Joseph? What are you talking about? He's just doing his job, patrolling the property."

I tried hard to control my breathing and my tone. "So he's just passing by. He wasn't watching your *entire* lesson?"

She paused and I gnashed my teeth.

"I guess he has been. I barely noticed. He's harmless."

Gnash gnash gnash.

"Go wait for me in the tack room," I told her, kissing her on the forehead and thrusting her in that direction.

I headed the opposite way, moving until I was standing a few feet from the bane of my existence.

I pulled the crop out of my belt and started slapping it loudly against my palm. I didn't bother to mask my expression to him, and I knew what it looked like—Savage.

Uncivilized.

Slap, slap, slap.

"*Enjoy the show?*" I asked him, tone pointed and biting.

He didn't answer, just moved his eyes from my face to my hands, up and down.

Slap, slap, slap.

"Did you watch her entire lesson?"

Silence.

Slap, slap, slap.

"Do you always watch her ride when I'm not home?" I asked.

He took a deep breath, but still, silence.

Thwack! The crop struck the fence suddenly, right next to his hand.

"You will answer me. That's an order."

He curled his lip at me. "Not always, but often. And yes, I watched the entire lesson, and I did enjoy the show."

My nostrils flared as I sensed my victory. I was nearly as elated as I was furious.

He looked as close to losing his temper as I felt.

"Well, soak it up," I told him, voice low and mean, "because it is the *last fucking time*. You are *never* to watch her ride! If I hear you've even come within a hundred feet of the stables while she's training, I'll have you thrown off the property. Understood?"

I thought for one happy minute he was going to snap, to say

something I could use in my case against him, but unfortunately he did not.

Instead, he opened his mouth once, snapped it shut, nodded curtly, and strode away.

I joined her in the tack room, still slapping the crop restlessly against my palm.

My voice was thick with lust. "Pull down your pants and lean over, palms on the wall."

My suit *was* ruined by the time we were done. Custom-made suits were not designed with stable fucking in mind. They certainly weren't made for rolling around in the straw, wrestling, getting down on all fours in the dirt, fucking like animals, the list went on and on.

The ruination of this suit had been absolute and absolutely worth it.

She could barely walk from the stable to the house. She had to lean on me heavily the entire time.

She'd be sore tomorrow, as much from the rough, excessive fucking as the spanking.

We had dinner plans with Stephan and Javier. I'd almost forgotten, until I saw them waiting for us on the back porch.

Clark was with them, chatting and laughing. Blake was there too, I saw.

And Joseph.

Stephan started shaking his head as we got closer. "I won't ask," he called out, a laugh in his voice.

"That's for the best," I told him. "We'll be down for dinner in thirty. We need a shower. We're both *filthy*." My eyes went to Joseph for that last bit, and I smiled coldly when I saw him visibly flinch.

That jab must have really gotten to him because the next day he made a point of seeking me out, his intention clearly to give me a piece of his mind.

He found me in my study at the house. He knocked, and I called him in.

"Do you have any idea how selfish you are, to keep her with you?" he asked emotionally.

This had been eating at him, clearly. Thoughts of my wife consumed this man.

Hatred, raw and fresh, rushed through me.

"She could do *better*, and you know it," he continued. "She could find a nice man, a normal guy that loved her and treated her with respect, someone that didn't subject her to that vile stuff you do to her for your own entertainment. She could find someone to help her *heal*, instead of exploiting her issues."

"And I suppose you think you're that guy?" I bit out.

He didn't answer, but he didn't need to.

"You don't get it," I said scathingly. "You don't understand her at all. You are *just* the sort of man that would make her miserable. You'd expect her to hide who she is, make her *hate* it. You would make her feel bad about herself, when there is no fucking thing about her that she should feel bad about."

"*You* should feel bad about it. I saw her wrists yesterday. Saw the marks, yet again. Shame on you."

I stood, smiling nastily. The joke was on him. I was shameless, always had been.

I held out an arm, indicating the door. "If you can't reconcile yourself to working for a man of my particular proclivities, by all means, resign. No one is stopping you."

He shook his head, over and over, glaring at me. "No, no I will not quit. You want me gone, you'll have to fire me, and we both know your wife won't like that."

The way he said *your wife,* that sneer in his voice, it was too much.

Some tight thread inside of me snapped, and I had his shirt in my hands between one breath and the next. I shoved him against the wall, getting in his face.

"That's right," I growled at him. "*My wife*. Mine. Mine in ways you'll never know. You think you've seen the marks? You haven't seen the half of it. I've marred every *inch* of her, staking my claim."

He took a swing at me. I was pretty happy about it, even while he clipped me in the chin.

Happy because, well, game on.

I slugged him back, with relish, catching his jaw. I'd wanted to do that for years, and so I did it again.

I had him on the floor, and we were both a few hits in, panting, when he spoke.

"She's not an object to be owned," he gritted, hands on my hands on his shirt. I'd started slamming his back, is head, into the floor.

"Not an object, no, but mine nonetheless. And that will *never* change." My voice was quiet. The words were each pushed out of me on jagged breaths, but they were full of conviction all the same.

I cocked my fist back to punch him in the face when her voice stopped me.

"James," Bianca gasped, sounding shocked, distraught.

With a curse, I straightened, getting to my feet.

She stood in the doorway, Clark just behind her.

I raised a brow at him. "I'm surprised you didn't interfere." As I spoke, I moved to her, pulling her into my chest.

"It looked like you had it under control," Clark shot back. He sounded smug about it, too.

He *had* been the one to teach me to fight.

Protectively, possessively, I took Bianca from the room.

Her reaction was not what I expected. She could still manage to surprise me.

She wasn't mad at me, not at all. Instead she fretted over my bruises, kissed each one, and demanded gently that I tell her everything.

I was helpless against her tender onslaught. I told it all.

In the end, it was Bianca that fixed things. Quietly and resolutely, she fired him herself.

"I'm so sorry," she said simply, right after she'd done it.

My gut clenched. "Why are you sorry? Did you have feelings for him?'

She sent me a baffled look that mollified me. "Of course not. Not like you're suggesting. He was a *friend*. That was all. I honestly think I just got along so well, so comfortably with him because he's a lot like Stephan, personality wise. To be honest, for the longest time, I thought he was gay. Makes this whole thing extra shocking to me."

That startled a laugh out of me. And the first real smile in days.

All was right again in my world.

CHAPTER THIRTY-SIX

MY FAITHFUL HEART

It wasn't long after the Joseph incident that another outside force attempted to assail our marriage.

I wasn't the only one that struggled with jealousy in our marriage, though she managed hers much differently than I did mine.

We were staying in New York for a spell. Luckily Bianca didn't mind traveling, since it was something we did often. She said the changes of scene were nice, and that she liked to paint in different places.

I was working more hours than usual at the Cavendish

Manhattan property. I'd been gone from the city a long time, and had to play catch up on a few crucial business ventures.

Clark had stayed back in Vegas, unfortunately, to represent me at some meetings for the casino. He was more than my bodyguard. He assisted me in all things, was a partner in several ventures, but still worked as a personal assistant/jack of all trades. I paid him dual salaries for it, because the more he could do for me the better, as I trusted him implicitly. He'd been with me since I was very young, and I knew he was loyal to a fault.

His absence was particularly unfortunate, as I needed extra assistance in the New York hotel, and since I didn't want to shake up the normal of order of things there for a temporary stay, I had to hire a new assistant.

I had the hiring handled for me, my only requirement that the assistant be competent and able to work long hours for the next two weeks.

I'd weaned myself off micromanaging a while back, and I wasn't going to start again now.

The assistant's name was Winona, and her main purpose was paperwork and coffee. Important stuff.

She was eye catching. I wasn't blind, and I noticed right away that she had the kind of looks that could stop a man in his tracks.

Hourglass curves, deep red hair that was tousled like she'd just come out of a man's bed, with a face that was simply stunning to look at, green eyes that were a startling emerald that I personally thought must have been contacts.

If that wasn't enough, she dressed provocatively and carried herself with the kind of sensuality that a man like me could recognize for what it was. She oozed sex. Everything she did spoke of her fixation on it. She was the kind of woman a man saw in the office and figured she'd just finished fucking someone in the elevator on the way up, because she just needed it that bad, that constantly.

She was the kind of woman I'd have taken the bait from a few years ago.

And bait was just what she was throwing out. She wasn't subtle. I caught her vibe right away. I'd been single not so very long ago. I knew the signs, hadn't forgotten a single trick, from her sidelong stares to her flashes of cleavage, I recognized them all.

I wasn't flirtatious with her. I didn't think I'd ever been particularly flirtatious, even before. I'd been polite but to the point. Now there *was* no point. Any woman expressing interest in me who was not my wife was nothing but a nuisance.

She was so obvious, in fact, that I found myself addressing it on the first day.

"You're here to do a job," I told her, voice bland. She was bent over my table, pretending to work on something, her cleavage just about falling out of her top. She'd been posing that way for a good five minutes.

"A simple job, no more, no less," I continued. "If you had some other expectations coming into this, I'm going to disabuse you of the notion right now. Do your work, act and dress appropriately, or leave."

She looked up at me, straightened, smoothing her dress, hands running over her voluptuous body to do so. She blinked her eyes slowly, several times, just staring at me.

I thought she might be going for a seductive stare.

Pointedly, I yawned.

Her mouth tightened, and she nodded, then went back to what she was doing.

I sighed. "You have your own desk, out in reception. I'm not particularly keen on sharing mine."

That at least got her out of my hair for a bit.

On her third day, I went into my office's adjacent bedroom, locking the door behind me, and made a phone call to Bianca that was meant to be a simple checking in to say hi call.

Instead, I ended up with my dick out, jacking off into a napkin as she told me what she was doing to herself on the other end.

It was ridiculous. Just out of hand. I'd made love to her that morning, just before work, and still I couldn't help myself. I only let her hang up after she'd promised to come visit me for lunch.

I'd been in the bedroom about forty-five minutes, and I came back out to find Winona was in my office.

She looked startled. She was by my desk but I couldn't for the life of me figure out what she'd been doing.

"What are you doing?" I asked her.

She licked her lips, smoothing her tight dress over her hips. "I—um came to ask you if you needed anything."

I didn't believe her. My eyes narrowed, I looked around my desk, but could see nothing out of place.

"No," I said curtly. "Go work on the tasks I set you to this morning."

"**W**ho's the new girl?" Bianca asked when she came to visit me a few hours later.

I was behind my desk, signing yet another round of tedious

paperwork.

"New assistant. Winona. I don't think she's going to last long."

She was studying my face, her expression very blank.

"What?" I finally asked her.

"Have you slept with her?" she asked quietly.

I was horrified. "Of course not! What kind of a question is that?"

"Not recently. I don't mean, have you slept with her just now, I mean, in the past, sometime before me?"

"No. I wasn't even the one to hire her, but frankly, I'm questioning the competency of whoever did. I'm about one more annoyance away from firing her."

"She's been hitting on you," she guessed.

I grimaced. "She's definitely letting me know she's interested."

She didn't say anything more about it, just walking from the office to the bedroom. I'd already unlocked it for her.

I was too distracted to work with her in there. I didn't last five minutes before I followed her.

I had only planned to take an hour lunch out of the busy day, but we wound up in there for three.

And we didn't eat, well, not lunch anyway.

I straddled her thigh, her other leg hugged to my chest. I leaned forward, stretching her deliciously wide while I moved in great heavy thrusts inside of her.

I'd been going for a very long time, taking her almost lazily after so many rounds. When I finally felt my balls drawing up, my seed pumping to my tip, then shooting into her, it caught me by surprise. I hadn't even been trying to come. At this point I'd been just enjoying the feel of her, my cock putting in time memorizing her cunt, savoring the fuck.

I let her leg down, moving to lie directly on top of her, putting enough weight on her to make her breathing more labored.

Her eyes were closed, and I thought she might have already drifted off.

"I don't like Winona," she said quietly. "She's trouble, I think."

I processed that, moving both our bodies around until I was spooning her from behind. "Should I just fire her, then?"

She looked tempted by the notion but shook her head. "Just be careful of her. Be cautious, and don't trust her. The way she looked at me . . . I didn't like it."

Winona made me paranoid, especially after Bianca's warning. I always locked everything up, but I took to double checking things like that a lot. The last thing I needed was to have her crawl into my office bed and make a scene.

It was the next day that I just decided to fire her. She wasn't worth the thought it took to wonder if she was going to be a problem.

She was leaning over my desk again, doing the same damn thing she kept doing, working on my desk when I'd expressly told her not to, her breasts spilling out of her shirt.

"Don't use my desk. Use your desk. How many times do I need to tell you that?"

As I spoke, I'd already made up my mind, but I wasn't planning to deal with her myself. I didn't have the time to spare on trivialities like that. Besides, the idiot office manager who'd hired her should have the honor. I'd wait until she left my office to make the call.

Only, she didn't move away, but moved farther forward, her

hands going to the buttons at her neckline, and then beginning to unbutton. Her breasts spilled right out. She wasn't wearing a bra.

What did she think, that I'd be overcome at the sight of some big fake tits?

Needless to say, I was not.

"Okay, that is it. You're done. Collect your things. You are out of here. I'd prefer not to have security escort you, but I won't hesitate."

She did the strangest thing then. One of the most baffling things I'd ever witnessed in my life. So crazy it left me speechless. And slow to react.

First, she took off running. Just sprinted from my office to reception then back again, coming back with a phone in her hand.

Looking deranged, her tits still hanging out of her clothes, she moved to my bookshelf, propping the phone there, camera lens facing the room

She was recording us with her phone.

I got up and moved to the door. I knew it was a fucking setup. I would remove myself and have security take her out.

Her face strangely blank, she shrugged out of her dress. She was naked under, not even wearing panties.

I made it halfway across the room when her rushing naked form made full contact with my retreating clothed one.

She was determined, throwing her arms around me, jumping up to try to straddle me as I attempted to move from the room.

I shouted, loudly, for security. Trying to get away from her, not wanting to put my hands on her, but also wanting her to stop.

Luckily, they responded quickly, pulling her off me, taking her out of there.

"Be sure she is banned from the premises. Revoke any

access."

My office manager, Lenny, a man in his forties who had been given the position just over a year prior, went straight for the phone I mentioned to him that she'd left on the bookshelf.

"Erase that video," I told him. "I've no idea what she wanted with it, but I want it gone. Wipe the entire phone, actually. Who knows what else she was up to.

He nodded and agreed, and left with the phone.

I was frazzled. I wanted, first and foremost, to change out of my clothes, that that strange naked woman had been all over. I went to my attached suite, quickly showering and changing into another suit.

I wanted to forget that the entire incident had ever happened.

By the time I got home to Bianca, I just didn't want to talk about it. The whole thing had been odd and pointless, left a bad taste in my mouth, and I just wanted to put it behind me.

We were back in Vegas when the news hit.

A video had been leaked, a drastically doctored video that made it look very bad, made it look like I'd been embracing a naked woman in my office, instead of warding her off.

My first and biggest question: Who had leaked it?

My office manager had a whole hell of a lot to answer for.

My first and biggest concern: Bianca.

Of course. What else?

I was at the casino when it hit. I left right away, as soon as I saw and heard what had been leaked, in fact.

Bianca was not at home and had not answered her phone. It nearly sent me into a panic.

Stephan had not answered his either. A sick feeling was crawling persistently through my belly, snaking its way up to my chest.

Javier picked up on the first ring. "She's with him," he told me.

"Is she all right? Is she upset?"

"Yes. She's upset. Someone emailed her something, a message about, I don't know, whatever is happening with that video."

"How upset?'

Long pause, then, "Very. She's . . . I heard her say to Stephan that you'd lied to her. I think that's the part she's freaking out about."

"Lied? About what?"

"About sleeping with that girl."

She'd seen the video and believed the worst.

It more than stung. It sliced me right open.

In spite of how it all looked, I'd hoped she just knew me better, knew that my faithful heart was *unassailable*.

"She really thinks I slept with another woman?" I asked, feeling lost.

"No! Not like that. She thinks you lied about sleeping with her before, as in before Bianca."

"I just met that woman a few days ago," I told him.

"I don't know what to tell you. You should just come over, talk to her."

I did. She and Stephan were in their den. He had his arm around her, and she wasn't looking at me.

I watched her face, an all too familiar out of control, helpless feeling overtaking me.

Her face was closed off, expression very blank, and when Bianca didn't want you to read her, she was unreadable.

It was so cold, her anger, her silent condemnation.

I couldn't stand it. I'd rather she raged and caused a scene. Instead, she closed me off, closed herself off, while she processed, sometimes asked a few questions, and then eventually came back around.

It was always on her timeline, though, and often after spending copious amounts of time with Stephan, who could soothe her as no one else could.

I looked at Stephan, knowing this wouldn't go over well, but, "Can we have some privacy please?"

He looked at Bianca. Much to my relief, she nodded for him to go.

I sat beside her, but not close, not touching.

She was so untouchable then, and I couldn't stand to even try to when she was like this. That wasn't what I came to her for. Until it was right again, I didn't want to touch her, not even for comfort.

"It was all staged. Clark is getting the full video now. It will show you very clearly that I was not a willing participant in that.

"I know that. I saw your face in the video. I could just tell. That's not what's bothering me. You *lied* to me."

We hadn't had an interaction like this in a very long time. She was acting like she didn't trust me, and I just couldn't stand it.

She grabbed her phone, scrolled through it briefly, and then handed it to me.

I squinted at the picture on the screen, then cringed. It was a photo of me. My college days, I saw. At a frat party. I had my arm around a girl with dark hair. Her hand was on my crotch.

I remembered the college me, and though I didn't remember her, or that night. I knew the college me had fucked her right after taking that picture, or at least it was more likely than not what had happened.

The hair was different, and she was much younger here, but the picture was clear enough that I could tell it was Winona.

I glanced up at her. "I didn't remember her, I swear. Whoever sent you this did a lot of homework into an obscure and unmemorable night in my past. Why? I couldn't tell you, but I did *not* remember this, did not remember her. I swear it. I never would have lied to you on purpose. I never would have let her work there for even *five minutes*, for that matter, had I known.

Finally she looked at me, studied me for a long time, as though working something out in her head.

"You really slept with that *many* women that you could run into some and not remember?"

I looked down at my hands, wishing my answer were different, for her sake. "*Most* of them, I think. Yes. I'm sorry."

She shifted beside me and suddenly she was burrowing into me, her arms wrapping tight.

Shudders of relief rocked through my body.

There she was, my lover was back, just how I needed her.

Touchable.

I could breathe again, the tight thing gripping my chest finally loosening, my hands running over her.

Time passed. And I held her.

"I owe you an apology," she said eventually. "I'm sorry that for that little blip in time, I felt some doubt in you. It was just, everything was laid out so convincingly, so fitted to my own insecurities. Those pictures were so awful, and then to find out you had slept with her and told me otherwise. The idea that you would hide it from me and be working with her, it really messed with my head."

"I swear, I didn't know, didn't remember her at all.

"I know. I know. I believe you. I just, when you've led a life like mine, with so much heartache, and then become so happy you can hardly stand, I guess I was just waiting for something, something to ruin it all. I'm sorry I was susceptible to that awful stunt. I swear to you that it will not happen again.

It took about three days, but finally the rest of the story came out, or most of it.

The woman was mentally unstable, obviously, but the press found proof of it now, and released it.

And the rest of the video was found (thanks to ninja Clark and Lenny's hard drive) the part that showed the whole interaction, un-doctored. Even without audio, it was pretty obvious I'd been ambushed by a crazy woman, and had not been an active or willing participant.

My phone rang. It was my buddy Parker. "Hey, man," I answered. "How are you? How are Sophia and Elliot?"

"We're fine. Listen, I have something to tell you, something I just found out that I figure you need to know."

"Okay. Go on," I said slowly. His tone spoke of something ominous.

"That scandal. That setup with the naked woman in your office that was plastered all over the press—"

"Yes, I'm well aware of all of that. What about it?" It was

the last thing I wanted to talk about.

"Jules was behind it. She was working with your office manager. She was sleeping with him. She set it up. All of it. She was working with that deranged woman. They were old friends from college."

I was shocked, though maybe I shouldn't have been. "Why? What on earth could she possibly have to gain from it?"

"I think she's come unhinged, to be honest. Either she's deluded herself that if your wife left you, she'd have a shot, or it was just some sick sort of revenge. Whatever her motivation, things are going to change now for her. She's won't bother you anymore, I assure you. I just wanted you to know. You see, my parents are aware of her part in it. With you being married now, with no contact with Jules, even they are seeing just how serious her problems are. They've cut her off, won't support her, won't give her a dime unless she gets herself help."

"God, your sister is a psycho bitch."

He wasn't offended. "Yes, yes she is."

"Thank you letting me know."

"Of course. Hopefully it will bring you some peace of mind to understand what all was behind that."

"It does."

CHAPTER THIRTY-SEVEN

MY JOB

"Bronson Giles," I said as soon as Tristan answered his phone.

There was a pregnant silence and then, "Who?"

I sighed. "I'm not the police. I need to hear the entire story."

"No clue what you're talking about."

"Just tell me this: Why him? What on earth set you off about some washed-up old actor?"

I knew it had something to do with Danika. That was a given. When Tristan started breaking things or hurting people, there was only ever one answer.

"This is feeling an awful lot like that Milton Sagar incident," I prompted him. "Remember that?"

"Nope, doesn't ring a bell," he said, sounding perfectly innocent, which of course he wasn't.

"You're an ass," I told him. "I remember damn well when you rearranged Milton's face, just like we both know that, for some reason that can only involve your temper, you broke Bronson's nose at a gallery showing, and then proceeded to knee him so hard in the groin that he had to ice his balls for a week?"

"A week, huh?" he asked, sounding entirely too cheerful about it.

"Yes, a week, at least, you bloodthirsty bastard. And somehow his son talked him out of pressing any charges, or even talking about it. How the hell did you manage that?"

"None of this has anything to do with me."

"Let's pretend, for just a minute, that it did."

"Hmm."

"How about you just give me a hypothetical reason why a thing like this might happen?"

"Hypothetically, I could see the appeal of beating up some old asshole for 1. Being a lowlife and a deadbeat dad, and 2. Hitting on his own daughter. Hypothetically, if I heard about a thing like that, even if it happened years ago, I could see me doing something about it the first time that bastard was unlucky enough to run into me somewhere, even if that somewhere happened to be one of your galleries."

That certainly shocked me speechless. I pieced it together right away. Tristan was not a subtle man, and he'd given me all the clues. I'd had no idea, no idea at all that Bronson Giles was Danika's biological father.

"I guess that explains why he didn't press charges," I finally got out. "Did he know she was his daughter when he hit on her?"

"No, but you know what? I don't fucking care if he knew. Bastard had this coming. Can you imagine how that would mess with your head, to have your own dad trying to screw you?"

"Point taken. Thanks for clearing that up."

"That's it then?"

"Yes. It was my job to scold you, fine you, or penalize you, per the clause in your contract that forbids you from fighting, and the casino's attorneys were breathing down my neck about it, due to the fact that what you did is lawsuit territory, but I find I have no desire to pursue it. Good job, man. I'd have done the same. Have a nice afternoon."

He was laughing on the other end when I hung up.

CHAPTER THIRTY-EIGHT

MY LIGHT

We were driving home when it slipped out. I'd regret it later, but like any deep cut, I didn't feel, or even recognize the damage I'd done right away.

We'd just had a wonderful visit with Tristan and Danika. I'd spent the afternoon watching Bianca play with Ming and hold Nikolaj, and it had gone to my head.

"We could adopt," I suggested.

She'd been relaxed. Happy. Smiling. It all shut down suddenly. And she was stiff, distant, unreadable.

I tried to backtrack as soon as I saw her face. "I mean, if you didn't want to get pregnant, or . . . I'm just saying there are a lot of options. Tristan and Danika have had a great experience . . . I mean, I—it's just an idea." I felt awkward, my usual ease with words just escaping me.

Not a word, not one iota of an expression change, not so much as one minuscule twitch in her facial expression, but I could feel her hurt, her pain, in the air. It scared me.

I hated when she did this, when she shut me out. It happened less frequently the longer we were together, but that just seemed to make it harder to cope with when it did happen.

"I didn't mean to offend you," I finally tried again. "They just seem so happy. It's clearly worked for them."

"I thought *we* were happy. I thought *we* worked." A hint of the accent that I rarely heard was in the words. That's how upset she was.

My stomach dropped. She said it like the careless thing I'd said somehow undid us being happy, undid us working.

Fuck.

"We are. We do. That came out badly. That's not even remotely close to what I meant."

But the damage was done.

She withdrew.

She left me, for a while. Someone occupied that body, but it was not my wife. It was some stranger that shared nothing with me, none of her thoughts, none of her pain.

For days, she left me.

And then, she said it. It. The thing that broke my heart into a million jagged pieces.

"Maybe we shouldn't have gotten married."

I was having the damnedest time getting air in my lungs. *Was this a dream?* A nightmare? Had she really just said that to me?

Those soul sucking eyes of her hit me like a punch. Not only was she not taking back the awful thing she'd said, but she looked like she was getting angrier by the second, like she'd actually meant it.

"You should have always been honest with me about it," she clipped out. "People should not get married until they have reconciled a thing like this. We should have waited. I . . . still don't know if I want to have children, but you clearly do."

"Yes, yes, I can't deny, I would love to have children. With you. I want that. But not more than I want you. Never. I want you above all, over *anything*. This is me being as honest as I can be."

She deflated a little, softened enough that I was dragging her into me, holding her, touching her, when she hadn't been touchable for days now.

"This is hard for me to say, to vocalize, to even utter out loud," she said softly, despair in her voice. "But I'm not sure I can reconcile who I am, what I've been through, with being a mother. There is a darkness in me, a bloody stain that comes from my father."

She was wrong. She was light. My light. All of that darkness inside of her only made the contrast that much sweeter.

"I just . . . I need more time. Please don't rush me. Be patient with me, and I will work it out someday, I promise."

I held her so hard she couldn't have found it easy to breathe. "Take all the time you need. I swear, I won't mention it again. Ever. We are on your timeline here. You know, I know you know, I can't do without you."

CHAPTER THIRTY-NINE

MY BLISS

Something was up. Bianca had locked herself in the bathroom. She'd been in there for thirty fucking minutes.

I knocked again. "Love, are you okay in there? Is something wrong?"

She mumbled that she was.

I left, did a few things, and came back a good thirty minutes later. She was still fucking in there.

I knocked again. "Are you ill? Did something disagree with your stomach?"

I was a TMI type of guy.

She mumbled a no, but she sounded strange.

I was just getting my phone out to call Stephan when he burst into our bedroom without knocking.

I blinked at him. This had never happened before. He knew very well that our bedroom was not a safe place to enter without knocking. Odds were more likely than not he'd scar his eyeballs for life, doing a thing like that.

What the hell was going on?

His eyes ran over my face, and they were bright with

excitement.

And possibly tears.

What the hell was going on?

He was just striding to me when Javier came up behind him to hover in the door.

Without a word, Stephan dragged me into a rough, back thumping embrace.

I patted him back, cause it seemed the right thing to do.

What the hell was going on?

"She didn't tell me first," he said, sounding excited. "I swear it. I just guessed. She said she wanted us to come over so she could tell us all something, and I just knew."

The confusion, the worry, started to change into something else entirely, something powerful and profound blooming in my chest.

"Tell you what?" I asked softly, right as she opened the bathroom door.

I moved away from Stephan to approach her. She looked pale, something vulnerable her eyes.

Her lower lip was trembling, her eyes pure liquid on me.

And she had something in her hand. She held it up with a trembling hand.

Stephan let out a loud whoop, thumping me on the back again repeatedly.

I approached, looked down at the little white stick in her hand. A pregnancy test. With a clear plus sign on it.

I dropped to my knees, burying my face against her belly, rubbing my face back and forth, taking deep steadying breaths, the strongest joy I'd ever known washing over me, head to toe.

I hadn't even been aware she'd gone off birth control. She hadn't told me she was trying, and I understood. She was already so nervous about it anyway. She hadn't wanted that extra pressure on her.

My excited, adoring eyes would have always been looking for signs of a pregnancy, from the second I knew it was even a possibility.

"How long have you been off the pill?" I asked her, lifting her shirt to kiss her stomach. It wasn't enough of her for me, and I dragged her shorts down, too, giving myself a generous amount of skin to wallow in.

I wallowed.

"About a year," she said quietly.

"How far along are you?"

"Twelve weeks."

My hands went to her ass, gripping as I rubbed my nose against her soft skin. Then my lips, my tongue, moving down, kissing from hipbone to hipbone.

Javier cleared his throat.

Reluctantly, I stopped, letting the other men embrace her. Stephan held her for a long time, so long that I just joined them, hugging her back as he took her front, my hands snaking around and between to rub over her belly, my face buried in her hair. We stayed like that for a very long time.

I was holding the magical stick. I couldn't stop looking at it.

"You know she peed on that, right?" Javier called out.

I shrugged. I could not have cared less, tracing that plus sign with my finger.

"James," Bianca called.

She was lying on the bed, side by side with Stephan and Javier, Stephan in the middle, looking at his phone. Javier's head was on his shoulder. Bianca and Stephan were holding hands.

She extricated her hand from Stephan's nudging him in the side. "Tell him what you were telling me."

"You need to get some coconut oil, to prevent stretch marks," he said, reading from his phone. "She's freaked out about what's going to happen to her body. Like, really freaked out."

She elbowed him for that, and he smiled, leaning over to kiss the side of her head.

I moved to sit at her hip, hand going to her stomach. It wasn't enough, and I turned, lifted her shirt up to her ribs, and rubbed my face into her skin.

She gripped my hair in both hands, stroking through the strands.

I started kissing her skin, and quickly got carried away.

"Seriously, man?" Stephan asked as I used my nose to push her shorts lower, mouth following.

I pulled up gasping.

"Just so you know, these sheets haven't been changed today." I waited a beat. "And we had a *busy* morning."

"Oh God!" Javier said, jumping up.

"That's messed up, man," Stephan said with a laugh, getting up more slowly.

It worked. They gave us a moment of privacy. Well, more like an hour.

I couldn't get enough of my mouth on her body. My face in her belly. Hands cupping soft flesh.

I pulled her shorts and panties off, pushed her shirt up higher to bare her bra, snapped it open, pulled it all off, and took my mouth to her again.

I ate her out *excessively*. Tenderly. I kept my tongue on her and in her until she *begged* for my cock.

We were gaming in the den, Bianca in the next room, sorting through baby things.

"I think you should have five," Stephan said to me right before he shot Javier in the head.

Javier cursed. "I vote two. More than two kids is too many, even with nannies."

"My womb is not a democracy!" Bianca called from the other room.

I couldn't stop laughing for the longest time. None of us could.

She'd taken to using coconut oil as her belly started growing. Just another reason I loved her pregnant.

She smelled like coconuts, vanilla, and Bianca. It was a heady combination.

"How many do you think we'll have after this one?" I asked her.

"How many what?" she asked lazily, half asleep.

"Orgasms." That woke her up a bit. I grinned at her. "I'm kidding. Kind of. But I meant babies. Children."

She looked thoughtful. "I don't know. I say we take it one baby at a time, if you don't mind."

"Just throwing this out there, but I love you pregnant. If that helps."

"Noted."

She was lying on her back in bed, and I had both of her feet in my lap, rubbing them. I'd enthusiastically taken over the task of oiling her up. You might say I went overboard with it at times. There was no such thing as having my hands on her too much or too often, though, as far as I was concerned.

We were staying at the New York apartment for a few weeks. I was getting some work done before we went back to Vegas, before Bianca had to stop flying.

She came out of our closet, holding a silly looking pair of pants in front of her. "No, just no. Normally Jackie is pretty reliable, but she's gone *too far* this time."

I smiled, bemused. Jackie was a strange one, with an off sense of humor that I'd always appreciated. I assumed that this was her version of a joke, but I wasn't actually sure.

"Tell her no more hammer pants."

I laughed. That's what they were! "Hammer pants."

She gave me an exasperated, wide-eyed look. "Is this some sort of maternity wardrobe joke?" she asked.

"We can only hope."

Her already ample breasts had gotten *huge*. It didn't matter what she wore, whether she showed her cleavage or wore a shirt up to her neck, they quite simply tried to escape her clothes, pushing at buttons, swelling into and over any single thing that she tried to wear.

Between that perfectly rounded belly and those mouthwatering tits of hers, I was useless as soon as she entered a room, throbbing in seconds, no matter the company. If she came into arm's reach of me, I was done, my hands filling with her lush curves whether I willed it or fought it.

Even after all the years together, she still blushed for me, but never resisted, never batted me away.

I tried to take her out a few times when she was blooming with her pregnancy, but quickly found that this was impossible for me.

I sat across the table from her in Red, drinking her in, watching her take a sip of water, her lips wet, her throat working. That alone put me in a state. Hardcore BDSM porn could not have done for me what just watching her take one draw of water did.

I was sitting beside her, my chair dragged with me, between one drink and the next, my arm around her, the other rubbing at her belly, then her thigh under the table.

Her mouth parted in a gasp, and I bent to kiss her, my intent innocent enough, if anything could be innocent when I had been obsessed with fucking her senseless since the moment I'd set eyes on her.

The years had not softened that need one bit.

One soft wet touch of her lips made me snap, and I groaned

as I nuzzled into her parted lips, sliding my tongue into her mouth, then out to lick her lips. I took them hard, sucking, licking, biting as I wrapped her close with one arm, the other snaking up to fondle her glorious tits.

She murmured something unintelligible, her tone surprised, but I couldn't stop rubbing, fondling, eating at her lush pink mouth. She wore a loose maternity style sundress with a rounded neckline. It showed enough of her cleavage that I almost hadn't let her leave the house in it. My first instinct was quickly proving to be wise, as I barely stopped my hand from plunging in to touch skin.

Attempting to restrain myself, I moved my lips to her brow, and my roaming hand back to her belly.

A soft gasp out of her mouth had me losing it again, bending to nuzzle into her exposed cleavage, my hands cupping her breasts together to better feast.

I tore myself away when one errant hand decided on its own to grab her hand and drag it to my pulsing cock.

I was panting as I said, "I think we need to go."

She swallowed, hand still on the throbbing bulge of my erection. "Yes."

I bent and started kissing her, then tore myself away again.

We didn't even try to make it to the apartment. I dragged her up to my office suite.

The first mating was frenzied and fast. I laid her on the edge of the bed, grabbed her hips, and plunged in, fucking as hard and fast as I dared.

I was obsessed with her tits, and I carefully climbed over her body, pushing them together. I shoved my cock in between, fixated on titty fucking her, but it wouldn't work. I'd have had to put pressure on her belly that way.

I finally settled for sitting her up in a chair, gripping her breasts and fucking them like that, upright, grabbing great handfuls of her flesh and rubbing into her.

Her devouring eyes kept me hypnotized all the while.

I came on her chest and still coming, kneeled down and got under her belly to suck on her clit, fingers driving into her, making her come hard and fast.

EPILOGUE

MY FAMILY

I've been remade five times in my life.

You know about the first four.

And I'm sure you can guess the fifth.

Fatherhood suited me. I'd always suspected it would, but the reality, the day to day of it, blew me away.

And Bianca as a mother was all that I had ever wanted. Watching her grow into the role, growing together, it was the very meaning of my life. The purpose of my existence.

We had three beautiful children, one boy and two girls, each of them roughly one year apart. They were our pride and joy.

Duncan was a brilliant boy. I knew he had a mind for business early on. He was enterprising, born with the shoulders to carry heavy responsibilities. He looked like me and had many of my traits, with little sprinkles of his mother apparent in the little subtle movements of his face. The twist of his smile. The wrinkling of his nose.

He was a charmer, that one. But also sweet and loving.

Duncan worshipped his mother, thought the sun rose and set in her smile, would move mountains to win her approval. He got that from me.

Imogen was passionate and resilient, and terrifying in her stubborn pride. She was a fighter.

She and Duncan could have been twins, they looked so much alike.

She had a strong sense of justice and a compassionate soul. She was versatile in that she could have done anything, been anything, because she always excelled.

We never tried to predict where her life would take her. We were just excited to watch her path.

Isabella was an artist. We knew early on. She was a daydreamer. A stargazer. Our little angel was born with the ability to see and create beauty.

Obviously she got that joyous talent from her mother.

And at last we had a child that favored Bianca in looks. Except for her eyes. Those were mine.

She was sweet to a fault, a lover to Imogen's fighter.

Of course, I was her favorite.

She was a daddy's girl. Absolutely. I would move heaven and earth to keep it that way.

The real romance in life didn't come in that first sweet taste of love, as profound and life changing as it was. There was love then, yes. Obsession, passion, infatuation. All of that and more.

But the true romance came from the slow lapse of time, the inexorable passing of days, weeks, months, years, decades.

I'd hold onto her with the last breath in my body. My final thought would be that I hadn't gotten enough, I just knew it.

Because I would never have enough.

Never enough sweet moments. Never enough shared smiles.

Never enough of touching her.

Never enough grabbing her face in both of my hands and marveling at the miracle of love.

Never enough of watching her grow as a person. Growing with her. Watching her journey as the mother of my children. Taking that journey with her.

Never enough of sharing every single burden, big and small, that she would let me, and sometimes not giving her a choice, taking those burdens from her, prying them from her elegant hands and carrying them myself.

And the fights, yes, even the most horrible ones we ever had, because they taught me something about her, and more about myself.

The inside jokes, the shared humor may have just been the best part about sharing my life with my soul mate.

Nothing on this earth was more romantic than a private inside joke still going, still bringing us joy, still making us laugh as we added layers to it, after twenty years together. Then thirty. Forty.

True love was a language, so many looks, touches and one word references that told the other more than full sentences or paragraphs, more than full outpourings of speech.

Our language was extensive and beautiful, and over a joyful lifetime together, we stayed fluent in it.

Our wives were having a mommy pamper day at the spa with the girls while we had a BBQ with the kids at Tristan and Danika's house.

It was a disaster, because that was the day we realized something very troubling, something that would haunt us for many years.

We were on the patio, Tristan grilling us burgers, as we watched the kids playing in their park of a backyard.

We were both dads that prided ourselves on being our kids'

favorites, but when this group got together, they forgot we even existed.

I pointed at Nikaloj, huddled together with Imogen. "No *fucking* way," I told Tristan. "That right there is *not* happening."

He curled his lip at me, waving a hand at Cleo and Duncan. They were *holding hands.* They were only six, but that wasn't the point. "What about that right there? What the ever-loving fuck is up with that? I'll tell you right now I won't stand for it."

"Oh you think you have it rough?" I stabbed a finger towards Isabella and Jared. They were *wrestling.* Oh, the *outrage.* "By my math I have it at least twice as bad as you."

The bastard laughed, threw back his head and laughed like crazy. "Oh man, you are right. That's so true. You do have it worse. When these kids are teenagers you are going to *hate* your life."

"Ming will be a teenager first," I pointed out, as it was only fair. She was the only child deemed mature enough to embrace a day at the spa with the mommies, so she wasn't there, but I felt she should be included here.

"Fuck," he said, low and succinct.

This time it was me that couldn't stop laughing. The idea of Tristan as the father of a teenage girl as she started to date was just priceless.

"All of the kids are closely paired up in ages, every one but Ming. Our *daughters,* Bianca, Tristan's rowdy boys are going to try to take our daughters!" I had to get it off my chest. It was too much for any father to have to bear alone.

She laughed, not looking at all worried, not understanding how serious and terrible this was. "Yeah, we figured that out already. And they all like each other, too. Imogen told me the other day that she was in love with Nikolaj and wants to marry him."

I shook my head. "No, no, no. Just no. I forbid it. Categorically, no."

"And Duncan, too. Him and Cleo. They're inseparable."

"That's not as bad, since he's a boy."

"That's sexist," she pointed out.

I supposed it was, but something about boys getting near my little girls was just much more disturbing to me, more inherently unacceptable. It went beyond logic and into gut reaction territory.

"Jared and Isabella are sweet to each other, too," she added, rubbing salt in my wound.

I thought of something that cheered me up. "Can you imagine Tristan, when Ming or Cleo start dating?"

She got a real kick out of it, too.

We were still laughing when Imogen busted in on us.

We were in Bianca's painting studio, at the Vegas house. She was painting, and I was sitting in my favorite spot, a sofa angled just perfectly to watch her work. As always, it was a joy to watch her, one of life's greatest pleasures. Sitting right here, in this exact spot, brought me peace, more peace than I thought I'd ever have, ever deserve.

Imogen took in the room, zeroed in on me, a brilliant smile breaking out across her face.

I smiled back. She was drop dead gorgeous and a shameless heart breaker to boot.

She'd recently had her dark blonde hair cut into a bob with

short bangs that made her eyes positively glow in her face, their brightness contrasting in a startling way with her dusky skin.

She was bouncing on her feet, her bob bouncing with her. It was about the cutest thing I'd ever seen.

"What's going on, princess?" I asked her, knowing there was something.

She kept smiling, batting her lashes as she came and climbed on my lap.

I tousled her hair and kissed her temple.

Bianca and I shared a smile. She was up to something, for sure.

Isabella came skipping into the room, her tangle of blonde hair flying wildly. She scrunched her face up and blew me a kiss before heading to her own workstation beside her mother, setting up her small easel and canvas all by herself and without a word, absorbed in her task. Bianca incarnate.

Duncan came in next, holding a phone and looking at Imogen, his expression stern.

"What's with the phone, bud?" I asked him. He was six. He was not old enough to need a phone. "And whose phone is that?"

"Clark's," he said, pointing at the little angel in my lap. "Ask her what she did."

I scooped her up and cradled her, smiling down into her guilty face. "What did you do?"

She scrunched up her nose, craning her head to glare at her brother. "Tattletale. I'm going to tell Nikolaj and Jared that you're a tattletale."

"Wouldn't that just be you tattling on my tattle? What's *that* going to solve?"

I tried and failed to hide my laughter.

"And I guess you get to ask them soon," Duncan added,

246

"since you invited them over."

"How long have you had Clark's phone?" I asked.

Duncan pointed at Imogen. "She had it. I just now got it from her. She's been using it to call the Vega kids. She invited Nikolaj over for tea. And now they're *all* on their way over."

I bent down and kissed the tip of her nose. "You been talking to boys? No more of that, princess. Not until you're thirty."

She giggled.

I set her on her feet. "I want you to return Clark's phone to him. You need to say sorry, since you were the one to take it." My tone was gentle but chiding.

As she left the room, Duncan on her heels again, I called Tristan.

"My daughter stole a phone to make a call to your son," I told him.

He laughed and laughed. "Oh man, that is the best. What will they do next? My money is on them knocking off a bank. We'll have a little Bonnie and Clyde on our hands. Better start setting aside the bail money now."

"I heard a rumor that you're on your way over here."

"Not me, no. Didn't you hear?"

"Hmm?"

"We're not bringing the kids over. They left without us."

"What? How?"

He was laughing hard. "Imogen sent them a car and driver."

BOOKS BY R.K. LILLEY

THE WILD SIDE SERIES

THE WILD SIDE

IRIS

DAIR

TYRANT - COMING SOON

THE OTHER MAN - COMING SOON

THE UP IN THE AIR SERIES

IN FLIGHT

MILE HIGH

GROUNDED

MR. BEAUTIFUL

LANA (AN UP IN THE AIR COMPANION NOVELLA)

AUTHORITY - COMING SOON

THE TRISTAN & DANIKA SERIES

BAD THINGS

ROCK BOTTOM

LOVELY TRIGGER

THE HERETIC DAUGHTERS SERIES

BREATHING FIRE

CROSSING FIRE - COMING SOON

TEXT LILLEY + YOUR EMAIL ADDRESS TO 16782493375 TO JOIN MY EMAIL NEWSLETTER.

Visit my website for news and new releases here.

HERE'S AN EXCERPT FROM MY UPCOMING NOVEL,

THE OTHER MAN

THIS IS LOURDES AND HEATH'S STORY

LOURDES

I felt eyes on me all through the grocery store. I had good instincts, and so when I turned and saw no one, I was surprised.

It was a quick run, mainly for fresh produce and meat, so I was in and out quickly, my mind on Dair.

He was hot. Tall, with a body to die for. Huge arms, a rock hard chest. And the rest was just as nice, with messy brown hair and kind eyes that always made me feel like I was with an old friend.

Hot, successful, and almost too easy to talk to. I found myself spilling my guts to him practically every time we spent any time together.

Still, we seemed destined to stay in the friend zone, and even I couldn't have said why.

I collected my organic Swiss chard, spinach, kale, tomatoes, zucchini, onions, leeks, just grabbing the usual, no specific meal in mind. I was a vegetable junky, so I'd find something to do with it all, and force as much of it on my boys as I could. Cooking healthy and feeding it to them was a compulsion for me at this point.

They were great sports about it and rarely complained. They were good boys.

My pride and joy.

My divorce had been ugly, but so had my marriage, and over a year later I found myself in a strange place. I loved my work, my children were grown and thriving, and I was enjoying life more than I could ever remember. There wasn't much romance in my life, but there hadn't been much even when I'd been married, so it still felt like a clear turn for the better.

Perhaps I was one of those women that were just better off alone.

Certainly, I was happier.

I collected some fresh organic chicken, and some grass fed beef, enough for one small woman and two large men. I still cooked family sized portions, as my boys often showed up for dinner. I hoped that would never change.

They were so good to me. They were as busy as I was, but always made time to check in with their mother. I couldn't have asked for more.

I was in the checkout line and had just finished piling my items onto the belt when I felt eyes so intently on me that I had to check again.

I glanced behind me and found my eyes meeting icy blue ones.

I quickly looked away. The eye contact had been uncomfortably intense.

I waited a beat, then looked again, assuming the large blond man would have had his fill staring at me by then.

He didn't, meeting my eyes even more brazenly the second

time.

My eyes darted away again, but I'd had enough of a look, with my photographer's eye, to take inventory.

Tall, blond, tan, big, and muscular. Gray T-shirt, dark gray jeans.

Hard jaw, harder eyes.

Smoking hot.

He could have been any age from twenty to thirty, going by his mean, unlined face. The scruff on his hard jaw and his aged blue eyes made it impossible to say.

I instantly wanted to photograph him. If he wasn't a model, he should have been. There was just so much character in his face. And so much to read in his hard expression.

Aggressive and a touch of something else. Something akin to hostile, though I couldn't imagine it was directed at me. Just a restless man that hated standing in line for even five minutes, I figured.

I glanced furtively at his single item on the belt, my eyes snapping away, face flushing when I saw that it was a twelve pack of magnum condoms.

Well, shit. Why did that turn me on? It shouldn't have. The guy was probably a jerk, and off to have sex with what I assumed would be a random woman. Men that good-looking buying condoms generally were.

Tell that to my libido.

We were waiting forever for an old, white hippie lady to count out exact change, and I didn't last long before checking him out again, this time my eyes below his belt, the magnum thing making it impossible not to be curious.

I flushed as I looked away again. His jeans weren't tight, but I'd made out enough of a bulge to embarrass myself.

What was wrong with me? I was not turned on by strangers. Even the idea was ludicrous. I needed more than looks to even consider getting physical with a man.

Finally I paid for my things and carried them out toward my car.

I was nearly there when the sound of something hitting with a splat onto the pavement had me whipping around.

I blinked up at the big blond stranger, who had apparently been following close behind me, then glanced down at the single tomato that had managed to fall from one of my bags and onto the ground.

I lifted the paper bag, brows drawing together at the very neat hole in the corner. It looked like it had been cut, but that was impossible.

"Let me carry that for you, before anything else manages to fall out," a deep, gravelly voice said to me.

I looked at the stranger.

He was offering to do something nice and polite, but his tone wasn't even remotely friendly.

It was odd.

"No, that's all right," I told him with a shake of my head, balancing both of my bags into one arm, and bending down to collect the ruined tomato, then straightening when I saw that was clearly pointless. It was a goner.

My hair had fallen over an eye when I'd bent down, and without missing a beat, brazen as you please, the stranger reached a hand over and stroked it away from my face, then let it linger there, in my hair, bold as you please.

I just stared at him, a bit shocked. I couldn't remember a time in my life running into such an aggressive stranger.

His mouth shaped into the barest shadow of a smile as he

gripped a light handful of hair at my nape, his big body shifting closer.

He didn't say a word, but as his eyes moved over the masses of my hair, I felt and knew that he was clearly admiring it.

He didn't *have* to say a word. His eyes were the compliment.

"I insist," he finally said, taking both bags out of my arms before I could protest. His packet of condoms (not in a bag) was held, shameless as you please, in the hand of the arm he shifted my bags to.

My slack jaw snapped shut and I turned on my heel, heading to my car. I'd thought I knew how to handle every kind of man, but this one left me baffled.

I would let him load my bags into my trunk and politely send him on his way. As far as I was concerned, that was the easiest and best thing to do.

I opened my trunk for him, then watched him, and his Mack truck arms, as he shifted both bags into my car.

He straightened and stepped close to me.

He let his eyes run over me, top to bottom, and I just stared up, struck dumb by his unapologetic boldness.

This man had a strange effect on me. I really needed to get a handle on it.

Finally, the once-over stopped, lingering on my cleavage. I was dressed up a bit in a sexy white dress that had been meant for another man, one who was not a bold stranger, but this one seemed to appreciate it more than I'd ever intended. Certainly Dair never would have admired my breasts so openly.

My chest swelled out in a shocked breath as he brought a big hand up to lightly finger my collar. It was wide, and cut down from my neck down to the lowest point of the opening, right between my pushed together cleavage.

"You're a very beautiful woman," his gravelly voice mused idly, as though he was talking to himself more than me.

His eyes returned to mine as he addressed me directly, "But then, you know that, don't you?"

I shook my head, at a loss.

"I'm Heath," he told me, like this was all perfectly normal. "And you?"

"Lourdes," I told him breathlessly.

His touch was light but very deliberate as he let his knuckles brush directly over my nipple. It swelled and hardened instantly, as though it was trying to return his touch, with or without my consent.

With a ghost of a smile, he pulled his hand away and stepped back.

"I'll see you around," he said, tipping an imaginary cap at me.

Without another word, he turned on his heel, and strode away.

I watched him walk away, fascinated with the way he moved, fast and purposeful, with complete confidence.

And that was that.

Or it should have been. If things were normal, and life was still sane, it would have been.

But something had shifted, and it wasn't a subtle shift.

I'd come to the attention of a man who didn't play by any normal rules, and my life was about to get very interesting.

I was at the dog park the next morning. It was a brisk fifteen-minute walk from my house. I was letting my blue Great Dane, 'Tato, run in the park. This was a daily ritual, even in the worst of the Vegas heat. My great beast of a dog needed the exercise.

I threw 'Tato's slobbery tennis ball as far as I could, for the umpteenth time, and he took off after it with great bounding strides.

"Morning, Lourdes," a gravelly voice said just behind me.

I jumped about a foot.

I knew that voice, but what the hell?

I turned, letting my face show how perturbed I was by his unexpected presence.

I wasn't wearing a scrap of makeup, and my heavy hair was in a heavy, messy braid that I was sure couldn't have been my best look, not to mention that I was wearing baggy sweats.

Yes, my first thought was vanity. Of course it was. This guy was sex on a stick.

"What are you doing here?" I asked him, my tone bordering on hostile.

He smiled; the first full smile I'd ever seen on him.

He liked me hostile. It was twisted.

He indicated the sweats and running shoes he was wearing. "I was jogging. Imagine my surprise when I spotted you. Nice dog."

I supposed it kind of added up. The store where I'd met him was pretty close by.

He must live nearby, I decided.

But to be sure . . . "Do you live around here?"

"Not too far," he said, and didn't elaborate.

'Tato returned with his slobbery tennis ball, and I threw it again.

"What's your dog's name?"

"'Tato." I caught his look. "Short for couch potato. My kids named him."

"How many kids do you have?"

"Two. Well, they aren't kids anymore. Now they're grown men, but my youngest was twelve when I first got 'Tato, and he named him."

"Both boys?"

"Yes."

"How old are they now?"

"Twenty and eighteen."

Even his stoic face couldn't hide his surprise. "Did you have them when you were *twelve*?"

I laughed, flattered and a touch chagrined, though I got this a lot. "No. I had my oldest at twenty. I'm forty-one."

I laughed again when I saw his eyes widen. "What, did you think you were hitting on someone closer to your own age?"

Something in his expression changed, something worrisome that made his nostrils flare. "I never thought about it."

I let him off the hook. "Don't worry. I'm not a cougar."

"Oh, trust me, I'm not worried. Let me walk you home."

What did that mean? And how insane would it be if I let this strange man walk me home?

"I don't know you that well," I told him warily.

"So get to know me. Let me walk you home, make me a cup of coffee, and we'll talk. I'm harmless." He smiled a sharp smile that illustrated clearly that he just might be the least harmless person I'd ever met.

Why did that harmful smile make me wet?

"You're not harmless," I pointed out wryly.

"To you, I am. And look, 'Tato thinks I'm all right."

As he spoke, my traitorous dog was nudging Heath's hand with his nose.

I watched for a minute as he crouched down, petting my dog until he had him on his back, completely submissive.

That was when I decided to let him walk me home. Why not?

Was it dangerous? Yes. But going by my suddenly throbbing body, my tingling thighs, my aching breasts, perhaps I needed a touch of danger in my life.

It had been so long since I'd felt desire like this.

It wasn't something I wanted to disregard.

It was something I wanted to explore. Thoroughly.

I put 'Tato on his leash and started to leave the park.

Heath took my arm like it was the most natural thing in the world.

It didn't feel natural. It did, however, feel good.

I found myself leaning into him. Even with that small contact, of the back of my arm against his chest, I noticed that he felt amazing, so hard and big.

I'd been married young, and never in my life so much as considered having a one-night stand. That seemed suddenly like an oversight. Perhaps I needed to do it once, just to try it out. And Heath was a man who seemed more than capable of making it worth my while.

Rough, dirty, sheet-clawing sex fairly radiated off him.

And I wasn't forgetting for even one millisecond about those magnum condoms.

"Don't make me regret this," I told him quietly, stealing a glance at his face.

His mouth quirked up. I was already learning things about him, and one was that he *never* smiled with his eyes.

They stayed cold, always.

I should have been more worried about that.

"You won't," he assured me, voice quiet and steady. "And you won't forget it, either."

I took a deep breath, looking ahead, blinking rapidly. He was arrogant. Why did that turn me on so much?

"What do you do for a living?" I asked him, figuring I should know *something* about him.

"I work in security."

That could have meant anything, really. "Care to be more specific?" I prodded.

"Not particularly."

Well, that was to the point.

"What do you do for a living?" he shot back.

"I'm a photographer."

"Care to be more specific?"

I almost smiled. "Specifically, I photograph *everything*. People, places, things. I'm freelance, and I basically work at whatever catches my eye."

"You could say I'm freelance, as well. See how much we have in common?"

Not one thing. Still, it didn't make me want to turn around.

Or if it did, the slow burn that had started up low in my belly overshadowed it too completely for me to linger on it.

Hopefully this sudden desire I had for a bit of strange wouldn't blow up in my face.

Something occurred to me. "Maybe we should go to your place, instead."

It seemed wiser not to let him know where I lived.

Another humorless smile. "It's not big enough for that dog of yours. Let's drop him off at your house, first."

I chewed on that for a bit, but I decided that it didn't really matter.

More than anything, he seemed like the kind of guy that you had to worry about never seeing again, the opposite of the kind you couldn't keep from staying away.

"How long have you lived in Vegas?" I asked him, still grasping for a bit of common ground.

"Not long at all. What about you?"

"I've always traveled a lot for work, but I've had a house here for over a decade. I only started staying here full time in the last year or so, though. Been taking a break from traveling, but it won't last forever."

I was babbling. Why was I telling him so much? He clearly wasn't going to reciprocate, and he likely didn't care about anything I was saying.

"Why were you taking a break?" he asked, as though he *was* interested.

I'd have figured he was just being polite, but I already knew him well enough to understand that he was *never* polite.

"I . . . went through an ugly divorce, over a year ago, and I decided to stay in one place for a bit, get my head on straight."

"Vegas is an interesting place to stay to try to get your head on straight."

That made me laugh, because it was very true. Still, somehow it worked for me. "My boys enjoy it, and they enjoy staying in one place. I took them everywhere with me when they were kids."

"Do they live with you?"

"No, but they live close and visit often."

"So now they hate to travel?"

"No, I think they still love it, I just think they're more well-rounded than I am. What about you?"

"I enjoy traveling, and I've done my fair share of it."

That was it, nothing else. He wasn't a sharer.

"Where did you live before Vegas?"

"Here and there."

"Which was your favorite? Here or there?"

I got a slightly bigger smile for that one. "Here. Right here. Do you have any other pets?"

Hello, random. "No. Just 'Tator here. How about you?"

"No pets. No kids."

I'd figured. He didn't seem the type to have any attachments at all, let alone *dependents*.

I turned my head slightly and found his eyes on me, full of a disconcerting razor-sharp focus.

It was so disconcerting, in fact, that I began to question what I was doing. This wasn't me. I'd felt a surprising surge of lust and let it temporarily cloud my judgement.

"Knock it off," he said lightly, or as lightly as he could with that gravelly, bar brawler voice of his. "Quit thinking so hard. I told you, you won't regret this. You might be too sore to walk without a limp tomorrow, but you'll be happy about it."

Something heady and electrifying shot through me.

My nostrils flared, and my breath grew short.

He'd guessed what I was thinking. That, and all of the sexy, arrogant things he'd just spouted, had me back to being too turned on to think properly.

A man that knew how to read a woman. That combined with his knockout body, and those magnums, well, I couldn't help it, expectations were getting very unrealistic.

This was not good. It'd been too long for me, and it had just occurred to me that I was a bit desperate.

I missed penis. I liked penis, and this sexy creature apparently had an impressive one. The inner hussy that I never knew I had wanted badly to see it. See it, and a lot of other things that flashed through my head quite vividly.

Beyond my impeccable instincts, and against my better judgement, I kept right on walking with him, all the way to my front door.

I let him into my house, and he prowled inside.

I followed him, letting 'Tato off his leash.

'Tato bolted straight for the kitchen, then out his oversized doggy door, into the backyard.

Acutely aware of the eyes burning holes into my back, I went into the kitchen and got a pot of coffee brewing.

When I turned to look at him, Heath was leaning against my counter, bulging arms crossed over his chest. It didn't even feel like my kitchen anymore, with him in it.

The man staked his claim on everything. He owned whatever space he occupied.

That sparked a visual that made me shiver, head to toe.

He just watched me, eyes way too intense, not even a hint of a smile on his mouth.

"Come here," he said, voice low and guttural.

The most unnerving shock went through me, but I went.

I was standing almost close enough for our chests to touch when he reached up with one hand, gripped my thick braid, and began to wrap it around his heavy fist. He did this until his knuckles were digging into my scalp and then he pulled a little harder.

It stung, but it wasn't the sort of pain you wanted to shy away from. Not at all. It was the kind you wanted to lean into, to explore to its fullest, because you knew that just on the other side of that pain was intense pleasure.

"How rough can you take it, Lourdes?" he asked, bringing his mouth very close to mine.

I was trying not to pant. "I don't know," I replied honestly. "Why don't you show me what you got?"

He smiled, and this time, it very nearly reached his eyes. "You asked for it."

For my *Breathing Fire* fans.

Thank you for being so patient with me.

The second book in this series has long been in the works. It is close to my heart, and I'm hoping to have it finished very soon.

So here is a bit of never before released info about *Crossing Fire.* These books were meticulously plotted out when I first started this story, over seven years ago. The love story in the book was always so screwed up that it was nearly hopeless, and the history between Jillian and Dom was always a story in itself, though it wasn't one I was necessarily going to give to the readers in its entirety. The mystery of it sort of tickled me. The torture of what you do and don't know. This still holds true, but as I've worked on book two, it's changed shape with the evolving plot of the story, and I'm excited to tell you that this book has turned into a journey of past and present, of before and after, where you will get to see Dom's POV over the years in a very unique and twisted way.

Translation: You will get some of the dirty details of Jillian and Dom's past, and many scenes in Dom's point of view.

Here's a little teaser for you:)

CROSSING FIRE (HERETIC DAUGHTERS #2)

JILLIAN

I was a fool. A masochist. A glutton for punishment. I was the type that kept picking at a scab, keeping the wound open until it scarred, then scratching at the scar until I created another deep, jagged cut.

Knowing all of this, I still found myself seeking out the grove, yet again.

"More," I spoke, my voice throaty with need.

I said it to the blood red water, and that evil water answered.

I knew it would, even before I saw the creature emerge.

It didn't take long to present itself. A white body, that odd, wrong, creepy as hell presence, was out of the water and nearly to me in the strangest motion. It never looked like it was moving fast, but it covered ground between one blink and the next.

It paused when it reached me, and I clenched me teeth.

I felt like a junkie looking for a fix, and perhaps I *was*. My fix just happened to be pieces of my past, *our* past.

And I just kept coming back. I wanted to eat every scrap of meat off this dysfunctional bone, then split it open, and suck out the marrow.

"Don't draw it out," I told it, my voice harsh. "I don't have much time."

"You know how it works here, first-born," it breathed on me. "Time stands still."

Wasn't that just the brutal fucking truth of it?

Without another word, it struck my neck and took me under.

Some part of me remained while I was in his head, in his

past now, and the more I did it, the stronger it was. I could form thoughts as a watcher now, cohesive ones.

And as I came into his body for this memory, I thought: *Oh no, not this one. My heart can't take this memory. It's too much.*

Not only did I see what he saw when I came into his memories like this. I also felt what he felt. And the instant I got there, I felt the pain.

It was fathomless. Infinite. *Never ending.* So flooring I wanted to sink to the ground and never rise again.

Raw, oozing agony.

Pulsing, bleeding anguish.

Thrumming, gushing torment.

Mental, physical, spiritual, I was tormented on all fronts.

I was looking at a very somber Sloan. She had a manila envelope in her hand, but she was shaking her head, over and over.

"You don't need to see this, Dom," she told me, a weak thread to her voice I'd never heard before.

I held out my hand. I *had* to see. I already knew it would be bad. My lover had left me, breaking all ties, leaving chaos in her wake, and the harder I looked for her, the more damage I found.

That was Jillian for you. She never did anything half-assed. Never pulled any punches when she was being self-destructive.

She should have known me better. I'd never stop looking for her, no matter what she'd done.

No matter what things she'd destroyed, what laws she'd broken, what beliefs she'd set asunder.

I would save her from herself. That was my job. She needed me as much as I needed her.

She'd already broken our blood bond, parts of me breaking with it. What could be worse than that? What could a manila envelope hold that was more profoundly detrimental to me than the loss of her, the only woman I had ever loved?

Sloan handed me the evidence, and I asked her for a moment alone.

"Please, Dom. Don't look."

I shook my head, and she left. She knew me better. I was resolute.

I stood there for a long time before I opened the envelope, time bracing myself, staring at the thing like it held horrors I could not bear to stomach.

It did, of course. I'd known it as soon as I heard there were pictures, had it reinforced when I saw the defeated look on Sloan's undefeat-able face.

My hands shook as I pulled out the stack of photos and began to flip through them.

I was three pictures in when I began to shake so badly that I fell to my knees.

Six pictures in when I began to wretch.

Ten pictures in when I began to weep.

Not only had she left me, broken oaths, severed bonds.

She'd been *unfaithful*, done the thing she knew would break me the most, and with a man I despised. She'd shared her body, all of that beautiful flesh that belonged to *me*, with my enemy.

I was blind in my agony, lost in my pain, but even crippled and broken, I knew there was calculation behind this thing she'd done.

Why? And . . .

How could she?

It didn't matter what she'd done. And it didn't matter why she'd done it. I'd still never stop looking for her. What I'd do with her when I found her, well, that wasn't a productive line of thought.

Turns out, hate didn't kill love. In some extremely fucked up cases, the two things could coexist together.

But him. *Him.* I knew what to do with him. To him I'd show no mercy. Not an ounce of it. I had a target now, a focus for the unadulterated fury that had gripped me from the moment she'd broken our bond.

Heads would roll.

.

Here's an extra little treat for fans of Tristan & Danika. I couldn't help myself. I love them so much.

LOVELY TRIGGER BONUS EPILOGUE FROM TRISTAN'S POV

TRISTAN

That morning I'd learned everything. Every awful thing that I'd put Danika through revealed to me at last.

I'd been nothing so much as a mess on the floor after that, after she'd left me with a few last debilitating shots.

I'd managed to make it off the floor, eventually.

Baby steps.

And eventually, hopefully within a few days, I'd be able to function again, able to think up a proper plan, and work up the nerve to go and get her back.

Frankie came to see me that night.

Her jaw was set, her eyes animated. She looked ready to raise hell.

I loved hell-raising Frankie best, even on my worst day.

I let her in.

She didn't waste any time. "So that's it then? You're just going to give up now? You're gonna lie down and die, let the love of your life walk away?"

I held up my hand. As much as I hated to interrupt an impassioned speech . . .

"Of course I'm not giving up," I reassured her. "Thought never even crossed my mind. I'm just . . . building up my artillery for the next battle. She pulled out some heavy guns in our last round. I need a few days to recoup, let some of these fresher wounds heal.

"Oh Tristan," she said sadly.

"The person you love the most on this earth is the one most able to *hurt* you," I said softly. "And Danika does nothing in half measures. I'm not gonna lie, she did some damage back there."

Her cute little hell-raising face scrunched up like she just might cry.

I reached for her hand. "I'm okay. I'm fine. I know what I need to do. I have so much clarity now, and most of the things she said, well, as much as they broke my heart, I needed to hear them."

One week later, reinforcements in hand, I knocked on Danika's door.

She opened it, eyes wary, sad, six long years of heartbreak pouring out of them.

I'd be fixing that. I'd be fixing everything.

If it took the rest of my life, I'd fix it all.

We had a surprisingly peaceful marriage, for the most part. No one was more surprised by that than I was.

We'd been at war for so many years that we were *good* at it. In general, I found that people tended to keep doing the things they were good at, even if those things were destructive.

And oh boy were we good at waging that futile war on each other, at fighting a battle where both of us did nothing but lose.

But when that awful war was finally over, we stopped fighting, for the most part.

I decided that we must have just gotten it all out of our system. Both of us had suffered a lifetime's worth of pain early on.

And now, *at last*, our golden age of peace.

Ming had just turned fifteen. We were celebrating, a small party with just the family.

She beamed at me, words coming out of her mouth that I did not understand.

She was petite and slender, and just a beautiful girl, inside and out. And she was *brilliant*, top of her class.

And coincidentally, at that moment, she was attempting to give me, her father, a heart attack.

"You *what*?" I asked her. I'd heard her wrong, obviously. There was *no way* she'd just said that to me.

"I'm going to senior prom with Alex Bancroft, a *senior*."

I started shaking my head. She'd said it again, repeated the same crazy words.

"The *hell* you are," I finally got out.

She didn't seem to hear. "It's the best thing ever," she explained to me. "He's *really* cute."

"He won't be cute when I destroy his face," I told her. I held up an open hand and smashed my fist into it, grinding it hard against my palm. The palm represented this bastard Alex's face.

She blinked at me, cocking her head. "Dad, you are *so weird*."

Danika intervened, and I was grateful. She spoke teenage girl much better than I did.

She put an arm around Ming, patting her back, and guiding her from the room. "Let's go talk about this away from the boys, sweetie," she told her.

"**I**'ll kick his ass for you, Dad. Don't you worry about it," Nikolaj said behind me, sounding gleeful and bloodthirsty about it. "And then I'll kick him in the balls so hard that he'll have to stay home from prom to ice his *nuts*."

I turned and glanced at him, lifting a brow, trying not to smile. He lifted a brow back at me and started popping his knuckles. Our oldest son cracked me the hell up. He'd been born with a sense of comedic timing, and a fun-loving spirit.

He was tall, his hair darkening since childhood into a dirty blond that he kept long enough to fall into his startling blue eyes. He was slender to the point of thin, but you can bet your ass that my boys knew how to fight.

My girls, too. I taught them all well.

The girls especially fought dirty as hell. It tickled me to no end. I was just waiting for someone to mess with them and get the surprise of their lives.

"Language!" Danika called from a few rooms over.

"She has supernatural hearing," Jared said, drawing my attention. He was sitting at the table, eating his second piece of cake. "It's scary. We should all be afraid." He pointed at Nikolaj. "Especially him. You don't even want to know the things he does in the bathroom."

Jared was a riot, too. I covered my mouth to muffle the sound of my laughter. If Danika heard me, I'd be getting another lecture on not encouraging the boys to misbehave.

It wasn't my fault, they were both incorrigible.

"Jared, knock it off!" Danika called.

"See," Jared whispered, grinning at me. I grinned back. He looked like me, was built like me, but sometimes I swear I saw my brother peeking out of his playful silver eyes.

"Heard that!" she yelled.

He bit his lips to try to hold the laughter in.

Cleo came charging into the kitchen, iPad in hand. "Hey

Dad, you want to take a look at this face you guys are planning to destroy?" she asked archly, her curly hair wild, her eyes mischievous.

We'd adopted her a year after Jared as born, domestically this time. Her parentage had been a mystery. She'd been abandoned. All we'd been told was that she was a mix, and all we knew for sure was that the mix was *beautiful*.

Her beauty was wild. It was huge. The room could barely contain it.

She was the baby of the family, and we all doted on her, even Jared, though he was only a few months older.

"Yes," I said with no hesitation.

"Hell yeah," Nikolaj chimed in.

"Um, duh, yeah," Jared added.

The boys swarmed me, huddling in close so we could all see, my hands automatically going to the top of each boy's head and ruffling.

She showed us the screen of her iPad.

I glared at the picture of Alex Bancroft. I hated his face.

"I hate his face," Jared said.

I started laughing and couldn't stop.

"Asshole," Nikolaj added.

"Nikolaj, language!" Danika called.

"*Bastard*," Cleo said, glaring at the picture. "I hate him, even if he *is* cute."

"Cleo, language!" their mother barked out again. She could barely be heard over my laughter.

"Tristan, stop encouraging them!" She raised her voice louder.

"Duncan is coming over, hope you don't mind. I just texted him," Jared informed me. "I know we're having a family day, but isn't he basically family?"

"Why didn't you tell me?!" Cleo screeched, moving out of the room. "Now I need to do my hair!"

I lifted my brows. "Yes, he's family, but how is he getting here?"

"He has a chauffeur, remember?"

I went to check around the corner, making sure Cleo was out of earshot. I moved back to Jared, voice pitched low. "Listen, I want you to do something for me."

He nodded, eyes wide with excitement. "Sure, Dad, what's up? We doing another prank on Mom?"

"Maybe later," I said.

I waited a beat.

"I heard that!" Danika yelled. I grinned. Tormenting my beautiful wife was one of life's greatest joys.

"Listen," I told him again. "I know Duncan is your best friend. And he's a great kid. Seriously, I *love* that kid. But you need to do something for me. A brotherly duty. I want you to be sure to let him know that he's *never* to go near your sister. You have my full approval to kick his ass if he even looks like he's going to."

He smiled and rolled his eyes. It reminded me so much of my brother that it made my breath catch.

You'll never be gone, I thought, *not for one day.* He'd passed over twenty years ago, and I still felt *so* close to him. He was a part of me, and the passage of time couldn't change that.

"You do realize they are only eleven, Dad, right?" Nikolaj called out sassily.

I shot him a look, a dad look that said, 'Watch it, son.' I pointed down the hallway, where Cleo had run off. "She's already doing her hair for him. It's never too early to start keeping an eye on your sisters, boys. And Duncan is a Cavendish, so you should both know that, though he's family, that means he's extra trouble. As your mother would say, he's trouble with a capital T."

"**Y**ou do realize what you're doing to our sons, don't you?" Danika asked me later, when we were alone in our room, getting ready for bed.

I grinned. "Those two, Lord." I shook my head. "They crack me up."

"Yes, I know. They have well developed senses of humors, there is no doubt. But they're little hell raisers. Seriously. They're little mini yous. Did you know that Jared can already pick me up? He lifted me clean off the ground and carried me from the living room to the kitchen yesterday, just because I told him he couldn't. He took that as a *dare*. Sound like anyone? It's insane."

I couldn't hide my huge grin with any success.

"And Nikolaj. Don't even get me started. He was trying to skateboard off the roof of a house the other day, because someone *dared him to*. What am I going to do with those boys?"

"And what about our girls?" I asked her. "Our little sarcasm generators? You gonna pretend they didn't get all that sass from you? And if you didn't notice, they also never turn down a dare, and *neither do you*."

"I'm perfectly capable of turning down a dare," she said firmly. She'd never admit it. I hadn't gotten her to cop to it even once, but we both knew she was as bad as I was when it came to being challenged.

"I gave the boys an okay to go open season on Duncan if he looks even remotely like he's making a move on Cleo."

She laughed at me. *At* me. Loud and mockingly. "They are eleven, you caveman. Slow your roll. And what about the boys, with Imogen and Isabella? How come you aren't worried about that?"

I went and grabbed her, throwing her over my shoulder, tickling her in revenge to the mocking.

"It's not the same," I told her. She thought it was sexist, but it just *was*. Our baby girls were to be protected from boys for as long as we could manage. That was the order of the universe.

I tossed her onto her back on our bed, getting on top of her, wedging my hips between her legs, cupping her beautiful, smiling face in one hand, the other tracing softly over every beloved feature. Time had done nothing to diminish her beauty. I personally thought time had enhanced it, added to it with still more depth in those eyes of hers that enslaved me at a glance.

She was as beautiful, as sexy, and had me wrapped as tightly around her little finger as she ever had.

"I love you, sweetheart." I didn't so much say it as breathe it against her. It was a quiet utterance, not meant to be heard so much as *felt*. From the outer edges of her skin to the marrow of her bones. *Felt*.

She blinked up at me, her heart in her eyes. She didn't even have to say it. I felt it back.

She sucked in a gasp as I moved against her.

"Did you lock the door?" she asked, as I started to inch her shirt up.

"I did," I assured her. "But they're all old enough to know better than to bother Mom and Dad after nine p.m. unless something's on fire."

She hummed out a low noise of pleasure as I took my mouth to her stomach.

I stripped her down, then myself, moving on top of her, hands everywhere, mouth everywhere.

I took my time with her.

I drew hard on her nipple, two fingers plunging smooth into her core.

"I love your hands," she said softly, wonder in her voice. Even after all these years.

Wonder.

She was not alone.

Not alone in her wonder. Not alone in her joy or her love. Not alone in her powerful, grasping, weak-kneed gratefulness of all we'd been given, all the ways we'd been blessed.

She was not alone in *anything*. Not the burdens or the blessings.

For the rest of our lives, we shared it all.

2D

JAMES

I caught a glimpse of her back as I walked to my seat. Good, I thought, relieved. At least I'd actually gotten the flight right. Getting her schedule had turned out to be a challenge. It had taken over a week of calling in favors, in fact, and that was with me knowing the CEO of her airline personally. The comings and goings of airline employees were well guarded, I had learned.

She was in the front galley, bent down to dig through one of the drink carts. She turned her head slightly, and I was almost relieved to feel that foreign punch in the gut from the first time I'd met her. I hadn't just imagined it, as I'd tried to convince myself that I had.

I watched her straighten, pulling a bottle of champagne out of the cart, before she moved out of my sight.

Reluctantly, I took my seat.

Scant seconds later, the big blond man who had greeted me at the aircraft door swept by. He was a flight attendant, but he didn't look like any flight attendant *I'd* ever seen. He was good-looking and big, and you could tell he was muscular at a glance. I didn't like that—didn't like such an attractive man working in close quarters with her. *How could I feel so covetous of a woman that I'd met only once, and briefly?*

I didn't know, but I couldn't deny the feeling, or name it anything but what it was.

He swept past me again, heading back to the door, a pleasant smile on his face.

My entire body was drawn tight as a bow, but I tried my best to hide it, pushing my back into the seat—relaxing my body, when she swept from the galley. I didn't think I hid a bit of my intense reaction to her as she approached. I came to the quick and brutal conclusion that I would never be able to fake a second of indifference with this woman.

She was carrying a round silver tray, laden with champagne flutes. She was every bit as lovely as I remembered, with soft, beautiful features, and sad eyes. *Those eyes* . . . They got to me, on a number of levels.

Her pale hair was pulled back as severely as it had been the first time I'd met her, but the severe hairstyle didn't detract from her beauty. I didn't think anything could. She had clean, even features. Her eyes were captivating, her nose straight and perfect, and her mouth was sexy but serious.

She was no flirt, and I knew that I would have to work to get so much as a smile from her, but I had no doubts that it would be worth the work.

She walked down the aisle like someone who'd done it a thousand times, her step brisk and steady, right up until she raised those ageless eyes to look at me.

She was composed to a fault, but *I* got to her, and I loved that. She froze at the sight of me, her expression arrested. I smiled, pleased down to my soul at her reaction.

Finally, after a long and telling pause, she swallowed hard and said, "Hello again, Mr. Cavendish." She nodded, her heavy drink tray wobbling.

I stood, reaching to steady her tray, never taking my eyes off her.

"I'm so sorry, Mr. Cavendish," she said breathlessly.

I ran a hand through my hair, trying to figure out why she was apologizing. I couldn't have cared less about the champagne on my sleeve. "Don't be sorry, Bianca," I told her, loving her name on my lips, though I loved my name on hers more.

I steadied her, letting go of her reluctantly when she had the tray again.

"Champagne?" she asked.

I shook my head. "Just some water, when you get a chance." I gave her a warm smile.

My phone beeped a message at me after she'd left to serve the other passengers.

Tristan: You have any luck finding that flight attendant you were stalking?

My lip curled in a smile. I couldn't blame him for giving me shit. I'd been the one who had told him about my sudden infatuation when we'd had lunch at my casino the day before. Still, my response was quick and succinct.

James: Go find some rabbits to pull out of a hat and oh yeah go fuck yourself.

His reply was just as prompt.

Tristan: Hope that's not all you end up doing tonight. Good luck with the stalking;)

I looked up from my phone as Bianca approached me again with a bottle of water.

"Can I take your jacket, Mr. Cavendish?" she asked softly, handing me the bottle. "I could try to get the champagne out or just hang it up, if you like."

I rose, stepping into the aisle, deliberately crowding her as I did so. I could see how it unnerved her when I stood close. I shrugged out of my suit jacket, nearly brushing against her with the movement.

She paused for a long moment, staring at my chest, before she took the jacket from me. She was very careful not to let her hand touch mine. It made me smile.

"Just hang it, please, Bianca," I told her softly, enjoying that I could shatter her composure.

"Yes, sir," she murmured hoarsely.

I watched her every move with fascination, knowing that she was aware of my intense regard, though she tried hard not to so much as glance at me. I was fine with that, content to study her as she worked, and to affect her just with my presence.

I was just enjoying the view right up to the moment that I saw the male flight attendant, Stephan, grip her hand as the plane took off. It wasn't a tentative touch, but a very familiar one. My fists clenched. I couldn't say why, but the thought that she might have a boyfriend had never even occurred to me. I chose not to examine how much it bothered me that she apparently *did* have one, instead focusing my efforts on how I would deal with that.

She flashed a warm smile at the other man—a look that made my heart seize up in my chest. I wanted that smile. It should have been for me. It infuriated me that she could react the way she did to me, when she obviously loved another man. I knew it wasn't logical; the one had little to do with the other, but I was still *incensed* at the sight of that affectionate smile, and if looks could kill, Stephan (I'd caught his name during his announcements) would have fallen dead on the spot.

I couldn't seem to take my eyes off those joined hands, my mood growing dark. I felt like I'd been played, as though our off-the-charts chemistry was somehow something she could have controlled, since she was apparently attached. I could barely stand to look at her as she served me, pulling out my laptop for distraction.

She approached me after she'd finished her service. Her face was earnest, her brow furrowed, as she spoke to me quietly. "Can I get you anything else, sir?"

My mind went a little crazy at the question, several things, most of them X-rated, coming vividly to mind. I decided on the spot on a direct approach, knowing that I didn't have the patience for anything else with her. I kept my face and voice as civilized as I could manage. "May I ask you something, Bianca?"

She raised her brows in a question. "Yes, Sir. What can I help you with?" Her tone was the epitome of professional.

I sighed, waving at the seat beside mine. "Can you sit for a minute to talk?"

She glanced around, as though sitting beside me was somehow out of line.

"Sit, Bianca," I coaxed. "Everyone else is beyond caring."

She perched on the seat nervously, her every movement careful.

She smoothed her skirt down as she sat, drawing my attention to her legs. They were long, slender, and shapely. You usually only saw legs like that on models with boyish figures, but she didn't have *that* problem. Her chest was ample, her hips shapely. That killer body, mixed with her cool reserve, was a heady combination that I simply couldn't resist shaking up.

"Are you and Stephan together?" I asked her, watching her carefully.

She blinked at me, obviously caught off-guard. "No, sir," she answered quickly. "We're friends, but it's platonic."

I studied her carefully. I thought that she was telling the truth. To say I was relieved was a vast understatement. In fact, I suddenly found it impossible not to touch her.

I caught her wrist, smiling warmly as I studied her downturned face. She was taking deep breaths as she looked up into my face, as affected as I; I watched her large breasts rising and falling with her breaths. Her hard nipples were clearly outlined through her sexy-as-hell uniform, and if she'd bothered to look down at my lap, she would've seen that I was having the same reaction to her.

I reached a hand to the thin tie she wore, running a finger down it, my touch light. I hummed deep in my throat with pleasure as her breasts quivered for me.

I cleared my throat, looking back into her eyes. "Are you seeing anyone?"

She bit her bottom lip and shook her head. I watched the motion with fascination, wondering how I was going to keep my hands off her for another second. "Good," I told her. "I assume you're taking a nap when you get to your hotel. What time will you be waking up?" I knew I couldn't wait even another day to have her.

"I usually sleep for about four hours, so I can still get to sleep at night. We have an early flight to Las Vegas on Saturday morning. If I slept any longer than that, I'd be up all night."

I processed that briefly. "So noon?" I asked, planning to take the afternoon off work and in bed with her.

She nodded, looking a little stunned.

"I'll send a car to pick you up for lunch," I told her firmly. This thing we had between us needed to be addressed in a hurry. "You and I need to talk," I continued. "I have a proposition for you."

She stiffened, shaking her head, her eyes suddenly cold. "No, Mr. Cavendish." Even in that icy tone, her calling me that made my cock twitch with need. "I'm flattered that you're . . . interested in me in some way. But I'll have to politely decline. I don't date."

I blinked at her, surprised that she could turn me down when she so obviously felt this crazy attraction just like I did. I didn't even have to think about it to know that I didn't have the self-control to stay away from *her*. I tried another tactIC. "I don't date, either, actually." Which was true, and frankly, I'd go along with any arrangement she was amenable to just to get inside of her. I could always change her mind later, though as I thought about it, keeping her away from the media circus aspect of my life was a sound idea all around. "That was not exactly what I had in mind."

Her eyes had gone cold before, but they went glacial as I spoke. "Then what did you have in mind?" she asked, her tone hard.

My brain, or other things, completely ignored her tone, focusing only on her question. I wanted badly to show her just what I had in mind, though I knew that I wasn't treating the situation with the finesse it required.

I ran my finger along her tie again, watching her quivering breasts with hungry eyes. I thought I would do anything to have that lush body under me, and under my control. "I think you and I are very compatible," I told her thickly, thoughts of her tied to my bed naked, writhing at my touch, running rampant through my mind. "In fact, I'm sure of it. Come to lunch with me today and I'll show you. If you still aren't interested, I will, of course, leave you alone. But I promise I can make you interested. I'll treat you very well, Bianca. I'm a very generous man—" It was the wrong approach, I saw immediately. Everything was coming out all wrong with the way she was affecting me.

She held up her free hand. "Please, no more," she told me stiffly. "I'm not interested in any of that, believe me. I don't know what impression you think I've given you, but I'm not some kind of fortune hunter. I don't want your generosity. I don't want anything at all from you." *Fuck.* Her tone sounded final. I'd already royally fucked things up, but even her flat-out refusal did nothing but turn me on.

"We have a girl that works in back who seems more your style," she continued, making me want to put her over my knee right there. "I'll send her your way if you're so hard up that you're offering random women money." *Fuck,* I had sort of implied that in so many words, though I'd been thinking farther ahead than that. That was the problem. I'd been so obsessed with her since our first short meeting that we'd progressed much further in my head, and my fantasies, than where we actually were. It was a problem. "Or whatever the hell it is you were suggesting," she was still ranting. "But I can tell you for sure that I am not the kind of girl that you're looking for." She tried to rise, but I tightened my hand on her delicate wrist. It was a perfect wrist, just begging to be bound.

She sat, glaring at my hand.

"That's not what I meant at all, Bianca" I said in my most conciliatory tone. "I didn't mean to sound so . . . indelicate. But I am very, very attracted to you, and I would very much like to do something about it." I smiled at her, catching her eye. As our gazes met and another sizzling burst of heat passed between us, I couldn't even comprehend how she could turn *this* down. I would do anything to see where *this* went. "Have lunch with me," I continued reasonably, "where we can discuss this at length, and with some privacy." I let her go reluctantly as I finished speaking.

She didn't even hesitate, standing and rejecting me within quick moments. "No, thank you, Mr. Cavendish." She strode away.

I processed that for less than thirty seconds before I was standing, striding to follow her, not even approaching deterred.

I swept the galley curtain aside with one impatient movement, moving straight to her.

She was leaning heavily against the galley's metal counter, her breathing unsteady. She opened her mouth to tell me no again, and I crushed mine over hers, effectively shutting her up. It was a desperate, ravenous kiss, having none of the finesse that I wanted to show her. It was an honest kiss, though, showing her that I wanted to own her—to possess every inch of her. And by God, I would have her submission.

Despite her rejection, her kiss was just as honest. Like me, I didn't think she could help it. Her mouth softened under mine, obeying my order to submit as though I'd spoken it out loud. It was just what I'd pictured for all the days I'd been fantasizing about it. It was perfection.

I stroked my tongue into her mouth and she moaned, which

made me shake.

"Suck on my tongue," I told her roughly, when I came up for air.

She obeyed, tentatively, and then harder. I groaned, losing my mind for a minute. Blind with need, I pressed slowly into her, grinding my erection against her. In my blind need, I'd fucked up again, too much too fast, and she pulled back, giving me wide eyes.

"Touch me," just slipped out.

I was shocked and delighted when that didn't make her recoil. She swallowed hard, watching me with raw need written in every line of her face. *Good*, I thought. *At least she feels this, too.*

"Where?" she asked unsteadily.

My cock twitched, but I did show an ounce of restraint. "My chest and stomach. Touch all the places there that you want to be touched on your own body."

She did, kneading at my chest with an absolutely riveting look of want on her face. I thought about the tiny commercial airplane bathroom, just a few feet away. It wasn't the easiest place to fuck, but I knew all the tricks to fucking in hard places. *No*, I told myself. *I have at least that much control.* The first time had to be in my bed, under my absolute control. I'd fantasized too much about that to allow anything else. All I could allow myself here and now was the groundwork for the seduction.

She moved her hands tentatively lower, and I licked my lips, nodding at her to go on. She ran her hands along my abs, and I thought I was going to lose it again. I had to make myself count for control as she stroked my stomach and then my arms.

I couldn't seem to resist further torment, unbuttoning my shirt from chest to navel. I had to feel her, skin on skin, even if it was only the briefest contact. I *needed* it. Touching *her* was out of the question. I *would* lose it then. "Touch my skin," I ordered her roughly.

She didn't even hesitate, obeying me automatically. *So fucking perfect, as though I've dreamed her up.*

She tried to fit both hands into my shirt, and I tugged one out, bringing it to my mouth for a soft kiss. I put that hand on my shoulder while she tortured me with the hand in my shirt, stroking my stomach with a firm touch. I wanted that touch on my cock so badly that my eyes clenched shut with the need.

As though she'd read my mind, her hand wandered down, gripping my erection with a firm hand. *So fucking perfect for me that she can read my mind*, I thought, even as I groaned, wrenching her hand away.

I grinned at her, thinking that I was already far too fond of her. *I'm keeping this one*, I thought, even knowing how insane that was.

"Not here. Not yet," I told her. "The first time I want you in my bed." *Need you in my bed.*

Taking a step back took every ounce of control that I possessed. I buttoned and straightened my clothing, watching her beautiful face watching my hands.

Determined as ever, I pulled my phone out. "Give me your number." It was a command.

She shook her head, infuriating me. "No," she said firmly.

I couldn't believe her gall. How could she deny me, even as every inch of her body submitted? My mouth twisted in amusement. I rejected her denial completely. This was happening. Her submission had revealed so much more to me than her words ever could. She had more self-control than I did, but it couldn't be limitless. I would break her down.

She studied my crooked smile, glaring. She backed away until she hit the counter. "Not interested," she stated.

I will count down the hours until I can put her over my knee, I thought with relish. A corner of my mouth kicked up involuntarily. Torturous as it was, I was going to enjoy every *second* of this pursuit.

I put my hands in my pockets, mostly to keep from touching her. I leaned against the counter beside her.

"How about coffee?" I asked, suddenly amused at the entire situation. Images of her sipping a cup of coffee while I licked her pussy flashed through my mind. "Is that neutral enough? Give me your number, and we'll go for some coffee."

She shook her head, not even hesitating. "No, thank you." She waved a hand. "I don't do this sort of thing. I'm just not interested."

I had to smile at her blatant lie. You didn't melt under a man's touch when you weren't interested. I didn't entertain the idea for even a second. I watched her ample chest rise and fall, her nipples visibly hard. She glanced down as though her own chest was disappointing her.

"I will put you over my knee every time you lie to me, Bianca," I told her quietly, determined to be very clear about my intentions.

Her face went a little slack, and I almost lost it. I had to wage another short inner battle for control. It didn't help that she trembled where she stood, visibly affected. "See. I'm not into any of that stuff, so we are clearly not compatible."

Even as her obvious lie infuriated me, her self-control impressed me.

I ran a finger down my tie, my eyes on her own indecent one. That little fucking tie was sinful, sitting right between her perfectly rounded tits.

"I'm not sure if that one was a lie, or if you just don't know how pleasurable 'that stuff' can be. Or how well suited you are to it. I can show you. I would love to show you." My thoughts went to dark, uncivilized places. "When I'm done with you, I'll know your body better than you do, and you will be begging me for it. Every inch of your body is submitting to me even as you're turning me down. Can you honestly tell me that the thought of submitting to me in bed doesn't make you wet?"

She shifted on her feet, unable to hide her reaction to my words. *Good*, I thought. This needs to affect her like it does me.

She studied my face, as though deciding if I was serious. I grinned. "I meant what I said about the spanking, Bianca. And the submission. You're going to learn very quickly that I always mean what I say."

"Please leave my galley, Mr. Cavendish. I won't change my mind," she had the gall to say.

She'll pay for that, I thought. She would soon learn not to give me orders, especially while calling me *that*.

I pulled out my wallet, taking out a business card. I touched it to her lovely cheek, running it lightly down to her chin, and then her neck. She shivered as I reached her collarbone, and my cock ached. I was going to spend *days* buried in her cunt. *She'll be too sore to even leave my bed after I break her in.* And that will just be the start of it . . .

I dragged the card over her breast, slipping it into the pocket right over her nipple. Just touching the card to that hardened crest had my body thrumming with a nearly uncontrollable need.

"The number on the back is my cell," I told her, trying my hardest to sound civilized. "I would love to hear from you. Anytime, night or day."

I tore myself away with reluctance, returning to my seat.

I don't know how long I sat in my seat, tense with desire and fighting not to go back into that galley to change her mind. I only stirred as Stephan appeared, walking slowly towards the front of the plane, solicitously meeting my eyes to see if I needed anything.

I promptly waved him over, sitting up from my slouch.

He had no qualms about occupying the seat next to me. He gave me a friendly grin, brows raised.

"Bianca told me that you were best friends. Purely platonic," I told him bluntly, studying him.

He blinked, looking surprised. He studied me right back. "You're interested in her," he said in such a way that made me think he had this conversation often.

I nodded, deciding to go for broke. "*Very* interested. You're close?"

He looked around, as though he were about to make a confession. "She told you we were platonic?" he asked carefully.

I tensed, but nodded.

He sighed. "That's unusual for her." He chewed his lip. "I'm gay, and she and I are closer than family, but I'm surprised she told you that we were platonic."

I arched a brow at him, waiting for him to explain the meaning of that riddle.

He shrugged. "Normally, she puts guys off by telling them I'm her boyfriend. She must be at least a little bit interested in you."

I gave him a wry smile, relieved at what he'd revealed. "Well, I'm more than a *little* interested in her. Do you guys have plans while you're in the city tomorrow?" I wasn't going to admit that she'd shot me down—hadn't even given me her number.

He glanced around again, chewing his lip, as though afraid we'd be overheard. "We'll likely be going out to a bar tomorrow night. Just hanging out."

I smiled my most charming smile for him. "I think your best friend is lovely, and I would really enjoy seeing her again. Would you mind giving me the name of the bar?"

He stared at me for a long time, looking torn. "We're just hanging out, so I'm sure it would be fine if you wanted to stop by to say hi."

I nodded, schooling my face into a bland smile. "Sounds great."

"We'll be hanging out at O'Malley's Irish Pub, on the corner by our hotel."

"I know where that is," I assured him. I'd gotten the location of the crew hotel when I'd gotten Bianca's schedule.

"It's karaoke night, so it might be kind of loud."

"That's fine," I assured him, already making plans to remedy the problem of the too-public venue. "Thanks for letting me know. I owe you."

He shrugged. "It'll be fun. The more the merrier."

"I look forward to it," I told him. It was a vast understatement.

R.K. LILLEY

KARAOKE

JAMES

My heart started pumping hard as I spotted the back of her head. I'd pulled a ridiculous amount of strings just to get a chance to talk to her, and I knew she wouldn't even be happy to see me. Still, I didn't think for a second that it wouldn't be worth it. I hadn't felt so alive since I could remember. I also couldn't remember a time when I'd felt this level of anticipation. I couldn't think about anything but her. *What was it about her?* She was beautiful, sure, and her body was fucking hot, but it wasn't as though I hadn't had my share of that.

Her reaction to me, I thought. She'd said that she wasn't into the lifestyle, but I knew beyond a shadow of a doubt that she was wrong about that. She might not have tried it, but I'd never seen a more perfect sub in my life.

The chemistry . . . We would be perfect together, I was certain. *That must be it.* And it was that. But still . . .it was more.

Her eyes, I thought. There's something in those eyes, something that called to me, some kindred spirit that I needed to explore.

I had no doubts that I could seduce her—her reaction was just too volatile to give me any doubts. She worried me though, and my entire body felt drawn tight with tension. She was skittish. If I didn't pursue her relentlessly, she would walk away from me and not regret it. I *hated* that. I wanted to affect more than her body, and that was the strangest thing. I'd never had that urge before, and I barely knew the woman. Still, I *felt* like I knew her. She was reserved, but I felt like I could read some things about her like a book. Like her eyes. She was young, possibly a little younger than I'd like, but those pale blue eyes of hers were ageless.

I shot a glance at Clark, who was at the door, helping to execute the slow evacuation of the club. He nodded at me, not quite hiding a tiny smirk. I wouldn't have caught it if I didn't know him so well. He thought that these were ridiculous lengths to go through for a woman. I mentally shrugged. The sad part was, I would have done more. Already, my obsession with this woman didn't seem to have a limit. I should have been more troubled by that.

I began to approach her. I had to stop, my fists clenched hard, when I saw a pilot touching her hair. I counted to ten, my vision growing cloudy with a fine red film. *Beating a man to a bloody pulp for laying a finger on her would surely scare her off.*

I saw her reaction to the man, the slight recoil, but he didn't seem to notice, leaning close to her. I had to take another long pause, repeat another long count, before I resumed my stride towards her.

I rudely moved the pilot out of my way, shouldering in with no apology. I didn't even look at him. I didn't want to see the way he looked at her. I might lose it, then.

I was directly behind her chair as she shook her head, talking to Stephan. "Not like that," she was telling him in an infuriatingly drunken voice. "A different kind of scary. I haven't figured it out. All I know for sure is, I need to stay the hell away from Mr. Beautiful."

Perversely, her words made me hard. I was glad her chair obstructed the room's view of my growing erection.

Stephan spotted me, his eyes widening in recognition. I nodded at him. I liked him, and there was no doubt in my mind that I had to stay on his good side. That would be essential if I wanted to get close to her.

Bianca had been slouching against the bar, but with the look on Stephan's face, she straightened suddenly. "What?" she asked loudly, drunkenly. I hated how drunk she was with a singular passion. "What? Is Mr. Beautiful standing behind me or something?"

Stephan pursed his lips, and she spun to look at me. She gazed at me, looking drunk, and dazed, and too beautiful to keep my hands off of. *Fuck.* I was in trouble. I hated alcohol, and drunk women were not something that had ever tempted me, but I still wanted her as badly as ever.

"Hello, Mr. Beautiful," she said softly in that slurred voice. The dazed look on her lovely face quickly turned to an accusing one. She spun on Stephan. "Traitor!" she slurred.

Stephan threw his hands up, giving her a completely innocent look. I'd need to watch out for that one, I thought. He was a bit of a hustler. "I didn't give out your number or anything. He asked if we were going out tonight. I just told him where. No harm done."

I looked down at her head, at that smooth, pale golden hair. I had to touch her. I couldn't stop myself for even another second.

I pressed my cheek to her hair, my mouth close to her ear. It was an effort not to shudder at the brief contact. "Mr. Beautiful, huh?" I whispered in her ear. She'd gone stiff. "I'm going to take that as a compliment, though I have to say, it's a new one."

"Hello, Mr. Cavendish," she said stiffly. She didn't turn.

I smiled, loving the sound of that on her lips. Too much for public, in fact. "I told you, call me James," I said quietly into her ear. "Or Mr. Beautiful, if you prefer. You can save Mr. Cavendish for when we're in private."

I felt a fine tremor move through her before she pulled away. I relished her reaction.

I straightened and grinned at Stephan, and he smiled tentatively back. "How's it going?" I asked him.

His smile widened. "Good. I've had a few more than I meant to, but I can't say I care at the moment."

I sighed, looking at Bianca. It was the first time I'd seen her hair down. I found it nearly impossible to keep from touching the soft fall of it. "You aren't the only one," I said wryly.

He grinned. "We've got a great bartender tonight. What can I say?"

We chatted companionably for a few minutes while Bianca ignored us both. He was easy to talk to. I was glad we'd have no trouble getting along, since he and Bianca seemed to be a package deal.

Bianca lurched to her feet suddenly and drunkenly.

"Whoa, careful there, Buttercup," Stephan told her.

I moved closer, wrapping my arm around her waist. "Buttercup?" I asked him, distracted for a moment from the dark mood her condition had put me in.

He gave me a sheepish look. "It's an old nickname, from when we were kids. Bee will have to tell you the story sometime."

"I look forward to it," I said. She swayed a little, and I had to grit my teeth to remain calm. "Does she drink like this often?" I asked him, my tone deliberately bland.

"All the time," she said loudly. I wanted to spank her right there.

"This is the first time she's had a drink since the month she turned twenty-one," Stephan corrected. "At least two years ago."

I felt a wave of relief at his words. This wasn't a pattern for her. Good.

I put my mouth to her ear again. "You remember what I told you about lying to me," I warned quietly. "That's two."

"He's a kinky bastard," she said in a whisper, looking at me with very wide eyes.

I bent to make sure she was looking into my eyes and nodded. It was best that she understood that right away.

"I need to go to the bathroom," she announced to the room.

"I'll help you get there, Buttercup," I told her. Strangely, I loved the ridiculous nickname.

Stephan rose as though to help. I waved him off. "I've got her," I told him.

She'd left her phone on top of the bar. She didn't notice as I grabbed it, shoving it in my pocket.

I led her through the room, taking the brunt of her weight as she stumbled along.

"Why are you here?" she asked me.

I gave her the short version. "Well, I came here because I very much want to fuck you until neither of us can walk." It was the most polite way I could word it. "I want you so bad I can't see straight." It was an understatement. "But since that won't be happening now, I'm staying to make sure you make it back to your room in one piece."

"Why won't that be happening now?" she asked me, sounding putout about it.

I had to work to keep a straight face, loving what her statement told me about her willingness.

I raised a brow at her. "I won't touch you while you're impaired. Never. I just don't do that." I wanted to be very clear.

"So you give up?" she challenged.

I kissed the top of her head to hide my grin. "Far from it. I still intend to fuck you senseless. Just not tonight, Buttercup. And I'd appreciate it if you could refrain from ever getting yourself into this condition again." I couldn't keep the irritation out of my voice as I thought about her getting this drunk.

She stopped suddenly, turning into my arms, pressing into me. I sucked in a breath at the feel of her against me. Some graphic pictures of me buried inside of her flashed through my mind. *God, I wanted her.*

She made a point of meeting my eyes, her lush breasts plastered to my chest. If she weren't so drunk, I'd have given serious thought to nailing her against the nearest wall. She was just the perfect height for a good wall fuck . . .

"Yes?" I asked her, my tone as hard as my cock.

"My condition isn't your business, James."

I didn't even entertain that idea. It was *all* my business. "I intend for it to be my business," I said diplomatically.

"You don't want to date me, you said," she told me. She sounded a little wounded over it, which made me mentally flinch. I hadn't handled that delicately enough, hadn't explained that my need to keep my personal life very private was for her benefit. Of course, to tell her that, I would have to explain how infamous I was, which would inevitably lead to her discovery of how promiscuous I'd been. My reputation was beyond tarnished, and I knew instinctively that it wouldn't go over well with her. She would never trust me if she had an inkling of my past. I thought that one was better put off as long as possible. I didn't think it would take much to scare her off at this stage in the game.

I sighed, debating with myself on how to handle her. "It's true," I said. "But I want other things. I at least want the chance to talk to you about what I do want."

"So talk," she told me. I had a very brief but vivid fantasy about spanking her bare ass right there.

"We will talk. When you're sober. And when we have some actual privacy."

She wagged a finger at me, then stood on her tiptoes, speaking directly into my face. "That doesn't sound like talking," she slurred.

I flinched, hating how intoxicated she was.

It was an effort not to follow her into the restroom, her steps were so unsteady.

A cheap looking redhead passed me, giving me a lascivious once over. I ignored her, used to the type.

I made good use of the five minutes she was in there, programming my number into her phone, and then calling myself so I had hers.

I took Bianca's arm the second she staggered out of the restroom.

"Have you ever been so drunk that you can't look yourself in the eyes when you see a mirror? she asked.

I watched her, keeping my face blank. I thought that she was *trying* to piss me off.

"Answer me, James," she said.

"No," I told her.

"Dance with me," she told me.

"No."

"Fine. Somebody'll dance with me. Just you watch."

I gripped her arm when she tried to move away. "No, they won't. If you have to dance, it'll be by yourself tonight," I told her, leading her by the arm back into the main room of the bar.

"Whats 'appened to all the people?" she asked, looking at me.

I shrugged.

"Is it that late?" she asked, rifling through her handbag. "Where's ma phone?"

"You left it at the bar," I told her.

She started to move in that direction.

I held her back, holding her phone in front of her face. "I grabbed it for you."

She snatched it from me, giving me a glare that I found way too adorable. She glanced at it, checking the time. "'S only eight clock. Why d'ya spose everyone is leaving? Is something happening? Are they closing?"

I shrugged, saw that it infuriated her, then shrugged again, keeping my face carefully blank.

Her eyes narrowed on me. "You don't have to stay here," she told me. "I'm just fine."

I pulled her against me, pushing her cheek into my chest. The urge to touch her was overwhelming me. I couldn't remember a time when I'd fought so hard for control, both of my anger, and of my physical response. I buried my face in her soft hair. It felt like silk and smelled like heaven. "You're an infuriating woman," I murmured. She struggled a little at that, but I just held her tighter. "I would be happy to walk you back to your room, but I'm not leaving you here when you're acting like this."

"You don't know anything about me. I may act this way all

the time," she said into my shirt.

She started nuzzling into my shirt, and I clenched my jaw hard to keep from touching her. I wouldn't so much as kiss her when she was this plastered, and I was shocked at myself for wanting to.

She pulled back to study me, focusing on my chest. She started running her hands over my chest, kneading at my skin. I had some vivid images flash through my mind of tying her to my bed and fucking her senseless.

"Someday soon I'm going to tie you up and tease you just the way you're teasing me right now," I told her, my voice pitched low, "with no hope for release for at least a night."

Her hands stilled, and she pulled back to give me wide eyes. Her expression changed in an instant into one of determination. She snapped her fingers at me. "I have a surprise for you," she told me darkly, swiveling around to stalk towards the karaoke stage.

The DJ sent me a questioning look as she spoke to him, and I nodded slightly, folding my arms across my chest and schooling my features into passivity.

When the first notes of S&M started to play, I just stared at her, a little shocked. *I'm in trouble with this one*, I thought. For the first time in my life, I had the thought that I was in over my head with a woman.

She started giggling and singing in her soft voice and my brain did a little short-circuiting. *Fuck. I'm in trouble.*

She was doing a distracting little wiggling dance when she stumbled, and I moved closer to catch her. I swore to myself that if she fell off the stage I was going to carry her straight out of there.

The trashy redhead approached me, getting way too close. I didn't want anything to do with this one, I thought.

She flashed a sultry smile at me. "Hi, I'm Melissa. Are you friends with Bianca?"

I nodded slightly, just wanting her to go away so I could focus on Bianca's performance. I had a feeling she wouldn't be doing this for me often, going by her usual reserve.

"I work with Bianca. She and I are real close," she said, showing a lot of teeth in a strangely feral grin that struck me as a little crazy. I ran into fortunehunters like her all the time. *Fuck*, I thought. I didn't want to have to hang out with this one all the time. Stephan I could take.

She leaned into me, pushing her silicone breasts into my arm as she craned up to speak into my ear. "Just so you know, if you want a wild time in bed, you should always go with a redhead. Blondes are on the cold side, if you know what I mean."

I looked at her. "Are you referring to Bianca?" I asked. If she was doling out information, I wanted all I could get.

She shrugged, still standing way too close. "Maybe. I can't say for sure about her, but you can find out for yourself about me."

I gave her very solid eye contact, trying my hardest not to be openly rude to one of Bianca's friends, though she seemed like a pretty shitty friend from where I was standing. "No, thank you," I said slowly and clearly. "I prefer blondes."

The music stopped, and I smiled at Bianca as she strode towards me with a purpose.

"Thank you for the surprise, Bianca," I told her, meaning it. "I won't forget that for as long as I live."

"Do you two know each other?" she asked, looking between Melissa and I suspiciously.

That baffled me. "We just met. She works with you, right?"

"So what were you talking about?" she asked.

"She said she was a good friend of yours," I said, beginning to suspect that Melissa had been lying when she'd said they were close. "I was asking her about you."

Bianca gave Melissa an inscrutable look.

Melissa did a quick one-eighty, grabbing Bianca's hand. "Come on, chicky," she said, leading Bianca back to the stage. I'd been right, I decided. *The redhead is mental.*

I folded my arms across my chest, just raising a brow as they started rapping a duet of a crude rap song. I didn't even spare Melissa a glance, just watching Bianca rapping with a silly smile on her face. *Ah, now, there it is.* I needed more of that smile. It affected me. *She* affected me.

Stephan was moving towards me, giving Bianca some intense best friend looks. I imagined they had their own language just with those looks they shared.

He approached me, his mouth tight. He spoke quietly, his tone serious. "This isn't her," he told me flatly. "She's drunk, and she never drinks. I don't want you to get the wrong impression of her."

I nodded, meeting his eyes. I'd known as much. The only impression I'd gotten that evening was that she was way too fucking drunk.

"I hope you aren't thinking she's someone that you can just play around with. She doesn't sleep around, not ever. If you aren't seriou—"

I interrupted. This part would be easy to put to rest, if he didn't object to me seeing her altogether. "I'm very serious, Stephan. Earnestly so. I want to take care of her. I'm *not* playing around. Not at all."

His brow furrowed. "If you don't treat her well, I will hurt you. I don't care how rich you are, I will kick your ass." He said it as though he honestly couldn't help it.

I nodded at him to show I understood. "I want you to trust me, Stephan. As I said, I want to take care of her. I swear to you that I'll treat her like a princess. I'm not in the habit of stalking women. This is all new to me, but I . . . just want to care for her."

Stephan cleared his throat, suddenly looking down at his feet. Even in the dim bar lighting, it looked like he was blushing. "She's a virgin," he said quietly.

My eyes went wide and shot to Bianca on the stage. My brain did another little short circuit. I was a little shocked at myself. My first response was one of overwhelming pleasure at the revelation. *Mine*, I thought. She was all mine. I couldn't help but relish the thought. I'd never felt so possessive of anyone or anything in my life.

"I'll see her home tonight," I told him quietly. "But I want you to know that I would never touch her in this condition. She's too drunk to make a decision like that, and I would never take advantage."

He studied me closely, then nodded.

Bianca stormed from the stage as the music ended, walking right into Stephan. She was clearly irate. It was a sight. They huddled together for a solid five minutes, obviously hashing something out. I shamelessly tried to eavesdrop on them, but I couldn't hear a thing.

Bianca pushed back from Stephan suddenly, pointing at the bar. "Go. Back. To. Your. Seat."

He went, looking dejected.

Bianca turned her wrath on me. "So, are you done yet?" she demanded. "You can see now that this is not going to happen. My V-card should be more than enough of a reason to make someone like you run screaming in the other direction."

I schooled my features into passivity. I wasn't feeling

civilized. The things I wanted to do to her *weren't* civilized, and I didn't want to shock the poor girl any more than I had to.

"Come here," I ordered, watching her. *Mine.*

I gripped a hand into her hair very carefully. I pulled her head back slightly, leaning down to her. "I'm going to ruin you," I breathed into her ear. "I'll be your first, and I'll fuck you so thoroughly that I'll be your last, too. You won't want any other man after I've gotten my hands on you. Every last inch of you."

She shuddered deliciously against me, and I had to struggle for control. *Mine.*

She pulled back a little to look at me, her brow furrowed. "So you prefer virgins?" she whispered.

My brows shot up. She had the strangest notions. "I've never been with one, so no. But I can't say I'm displeased with the notion. In fact, I love it that I'll be your first."

R.K. LILLEY

SLEEPOVER

JAMES

"I'm ready to go," Bianca said.

About fucking time, I thought. "Good. Let's go tell Stephan."

We approached the slumped form of Stephan. Whatever Bianca had said to him had him in a state. "Bianca is calling it a night," I told him. "I'll see her to her room. What time should I set the alarm for?"

"Five," Bianca and Stephan said.

I nodded goodnight to Stephan, and he nodded back.

Bianca moved to Stephan, kissing him on the forehead. They had another quiet but intense exchange before we took our leave.

I gripped her arm as we left. "Stephan and I spoke at length. He knows I would never take advantage of you when you're impaired. If I didn't know otherwise, I would think he was your older brother. How long have you two been close?"

She gave me a sideways glance, her expression unreadable. "A long time," she said.

I changed the subject, since it was obvious she wasn't in a sharing mood. "You need to get on the pill," I told her. It was a polite order.

She sent me a cute little glare. "My body, my business," she said stiffly.

I felt a little thrill move through me when she said that, because I was going to show her beyond a shadow of a doubt that her body was *mine*. I would own every inch of it.

"When we're having sex, it will be my business, as well," I told her, trying to sound reasonable. "And you need to get started. It can take weeks to months before it becomes effective."

She glared. "For your information, I'm already on the pill. I have bad periods, and it helps make them milder. I've actually been on them since I was a teenager . . . for personal reasons. But you are outrageous, you know that? I've never agreed to have sex with you."

"What personal reasons?" I asked.

"I prefer to keep those reasons personal." She had the nerve to stick her tongue out at me.

I squeezed her arm, some very vivid images of what I wanted her to do with that tongue flashing through my mind. "You are exasperating."

"Let me bombard you with a bunch of personal questions and see how you like it."

The idea of that strangely wasn't troubling to me. "Give it a try. I think the tradeoff might just be worthwhile for me."

She got very quiet for the rest of the walk. She greeted the girl at the front desk as we walked by. That was it. No doorman.

No security to speak of. We just walked right onto the elevator.

I shook my head, appalled.

"The security here is deplorable," I told her.

She giggled. "What did you expect? It's a crew hotel in downtown Manhattan. The security isn't deplorable. It's non-existent."

I stared at her. "It's terrifying. Anyone could come in here."

She just kept giggling. "That's what locks and police are for. If you think this is bad, you should see some of the places Stephan and I have stayed."

I searched her face, a strange feeling of alarm gripping my chest. "Where? What do you mean? Do you still stay in those places?"

She shrugged. "Um, not really. I guess this is our least secure crew hotel at the moment." She burst into another giggling fit. I held out my hand for her key, and she handed it to me.

"I would prefer if you stay at a more secure place when you visit the city. I'll arrange it," I told her.

She shook her head, her smile fading. "No. No. No. I don't know what you think is going on here, but you are not going to take control of my life. You can just rule out that scenario right now."

"We'll talk about it when you're sober."

"You can talk all you want. That is not happening." She sounded so sure of that. I could admit to myself that she scared me. She was about to make my life very difficult.

We stepped into the room, and I couldn't help but notice the open door of an adjoining room. I strode inside. A men's flight attendant uniform hung in the visible closet.

"Stephan's room?" I asked loudly.

"Yes."

I went back into her room, shutting and locking the door behind me.

I watched her flop onto her bed, still fully clothed. "I need to set my alarm," she said.

"I've got it," I told her, moving to her purse.

I plugged her phone in to charge and set her alarm.

"Thank you," she murmured. "You can go now. I'll wake up on time. I've never been late to work. I'm not gonna start the habit tomorrow. As soon as my head stops this spinning, I'll be falling asleep."

I moved to her suitcase, checking for something for her to sleep in. I wasn't sure if I wanted to curse or cheer when I found a tiny, sheer slip of a nightgown. A fucking virgin that looked like a playboy model and wore sexy lingerie to bed. *Fuck.*

I set it on top of her bag, going into the bathroom. I saw the package marked 'makeup remover wipes' and grabbed one.

I moved back to the bed, perching beside her. I gently wiped her face. Her skin was perfect, and as I wiped it clean, I realized that she barely wore any makeup. She was so lovely. I wanted so badly to kiss her that my hand shook with a fine tremor as I cleaned her eyelashes carefully.

"You hardly wear any makeup. You have a lovely complexion." It was an understatement. She was perfection.

She snorted. "Look who's talking, Mr. Beautiful."

I smiled. "Perhaps I'll just call you Mrs. Beautiful." I kissed just the tip of her nose.

I got up and turned out the lights, then moved to undress her. That was for my benefit as much as hers. I didn't completely trust myself. My reaction to this woman had become too volatile.

She moved her hands to block me as I began to unbutton her shorts. "What are you doing?" she asked. She didn't sound alarmed, which did nothing good for my self-control.

How wrong would be if I just used my mouth on her? I had become obsessed with making her come.

Not tonight, I told myself firmly. She was beyond my reach tonight.

I brushed her hands away, removing her shorts quickly. "Taking care of you," I told her, trying to shake off the images flashing through my mind of me really *taking care of her*. "I told you and Stephan that I would. I'm getting you ready for bed right now. And if you start throwing up all of that poison you drank tonight, I'll take you to the bathroom and hold your hair out of your face for you. Hold still. I'll have you changed faster if you don't fidget so much."

She submitted, which made my hands shake a little as I quickly stripped her and slipped her into that obscene slip that no virgin should have been wearing to bed.

I put her clothes away carefully, fighting hard for control. I tucked her in carefully.

I looked down at her when I'd finished, at a loss. I couldn't leave her, but I also didn't see how I could stay.

"You can sleep here," she told me in a drowsy voice. "If you can handle the lack of security."

I sucked in a breath. *Fuck.* I was lost. There was no way I could say no to that.

"Do you mind if I just sleep in my boxers? It's much more comfortable, and I swear I won't try a thing. Tonight."

"Okay," she said softly.

I stripped down to my boxers, wondering if she could see my obvious erection in the shadows. I got on the bed, staying as far from her as I could get. I stared at the ceiling, knowing that I wasn't going to get any rest that night, but I still didn't even consider leaving. She'd told me I could stay, and I couldn't resist, even if it *was* pure torment.

I could feel her watching me. "Go to sleep," I ordered.

"Are you tan like that everywhere?" she asked sleepily.

I smiled. Her breathing changed almost instantly, becoming deep and even with sleep.

I gave some serious thought to going into the bathroom and jacking myself off. There was no way I was going to rest with my cock so hard that it had taken on a life of its own.

I was a second away from doing just that when she rolled into me. I stiffened, but I could tell from her breathing that she was still sound asleep. I mentally cursed as she nuzzled her face into the side of my chest, her hand moving to rest on my sternum.

Fucking hell. She cuddled in her sleep. I didn't know how I was going to manage, but I didn't think I could bear to leave her touch.

"Stephan," she murmured contentedly.

I processed that. Stephan was gay. He had told me as much. And she had told me that they were purely platonic. I believed them both. *Why does she seek him out in her sleep? Were they really so close?* A part of me was insanely jealous at the thought that he was that important to her, but I knew instinctively that I couldn't indulge that jealousy. The two of them were too close to tolerate anyone coming between them, and I wouldn't be making that mistake.

She nuzzled against me, throwing a leg over mine. I could feel her sex moving flush with my thigh. I couldn't quite stifle a moan.

"James," she said softly in her sleep. *That's more like it*, I thought. That one little telling admission made the entire night worth it. I was getting under her skin, as well. It was only fair.

"*Mine*," I whispered back, closing my eyes. Her hand was on my stomach, and I wondered if I'd be breaking all of my own rules if she just happened to give me a hand-job in her sleep. In my current condition, a few strokes would do it.

I mentally berated myself for even having the thought.

I moved my thigh against her sex, telling myself that I was just getting comfortable.

She gasped softly and pressed harder against me. In my mind, I was burying my face between her legs and lapping at her core like my life depended on it, but I only allowed myself the fantasy. This was a test of my self-control that I was determined to pass.

She stiffened suddenly rolling away to huddle in on herself. Her breathing became ragged, and not with passion.

She's having a nightmare, I thought.

I wrapped myself around her back as she began to shudder. "Shh, love," I told her soothingly.

What I'd called her shocked me enough that I lay thinking about it for a long time. *I'd named her love.* I'd never said anything like that to a woman before, but I couldn't make myself regret it. It just felt right to call her that.

She relaxed eventually, her breathing evening out into a more peaceful sleep.

"Yes, love," I told her softly. "Rest."

She'll be the only one resting tonight, I thought wryly.

We suffered a few more close calls that night, as she shifted restlessly in her sleep, sometimes plastering her body to mine, other times facing away, curled in a ball.

She pressed herself to me, hand resting on my stomach again, making me hold my breath. Her breath grew ragged, though sleep still held her, and her hand wandered lower.

I put my hand over hers, gently stilling it.

But then she grunted my name in her sleep, and I let her do as she liked.

At the first touch of her fingers to my hard length, I twitched, a spurt of pre-cum spilling from my tip.

I was panting, but she'd said my name, and I needed to hear it again, so I let her sleeping hand explore me, moving until I'd maneuvered a sneaky thigh between hers, letting her ground against me while she tortured me with her touch.

Wake Up Call: Part One

JAMES

I slid my arm out from under her head, very carefully replacing it with a pillow. I pulled the thin blanket up to her shoulders and got dressed swiftly. It had been a long night, and I hadn't slept, but I wouldn't have done anything differently.

It was four a.m. I had just enough time to get home and get dressed before she woke up.

I sent Clark a text as I slipped out of her room, snagging her key card.

He was waiting at the curb, on top of things as always.

"The apartment," I told him as I slid into the backseat. "And wait at the curb. I'll be in and out."

I saw his brow rise in the rearview as he pulled the car away from the curb. "Going into work this early?" he asked.

"No. Coming back here. I may be flying to Vegas today."

"May be?" he asked. I could hear the smirk in his voice.

"I'm going to get dressed and go back to the hotel. I'll let you know the plan after that."

"You want me to get you a commercial airline ticket?" he asked.

"That sounds like a good idea."

"Do I even need to ask what airline?"

"You do not. Make sure it's the very first flight."

"Am *I* taking this flight, as well?"

"No. You can fly out this afternoon. Paterson will pick me up. Get some sleep. I know you've been up all night waiting for me."

"Yes, sir. How long will we be in Vegas?"

"I'll let you know when I figure it out."

"I take it you're pretty serious about this girl."

"You could say that, Clark."

"Should I expect a lot of unexpected trips like this for the foreseeable future?"

"That wouldn't be a bad idea. My schedule is going to be very . . . flexible, while I figure this thing out."

"Good to know."

There was virtually no traffic that early in the morning, so Clark was pulling up outside of my building within five minutes. I moved briskly through the lobby and to the elevator. I felt a strange sense of urgency to get back to her, as though she might disappear if I wasn't fast enough. I felt anxious and almost panicked, though I knew it was unreasonable. I'd given myself plenty of time.

I showered and got dressed, grabbing the first suit I saw. I was ready and striding back out of my apartment within thirty minutes.

I stopped at the closest coffee shop, my mind on hangover remedies. I wasn't used to waiting in line, and I found myself tapping a foot impatiently and checking the time. She'd be awake any minute, and I didn't want to miss her.

I made a last minute stop at a drugstore to grab aspirin, feeling silly but unable to stop myself.

I felt a very unfamiliar nervousness course through me as I arrived back at the hotel, unsure of my reception.

I opened her door quietly, but I saw right away that she was already awake.

The bathroom door was slightly ajar, the light on. As I closed the door behind, she peeked her head out. I didn't hesitate to join her inside. She had to be sober by now.

All bets were off.

I handed her the coffee and aspirin, setting two bottles of water on the counter for her. "The pills are for the hangover," I told her. "And the water will help. You're dehydrated." I kept my voice carefully blank, my eyes running over her body.

Fuck, I thought, growing hard in an instant. She may as well have been naked in that damp, clingy slip. She was sober and practically naked. *How the fuck was I supposed to keep my hands off her?*

She took the pills, drinking most of one of the bottles of water. She took a long drink of her coffee. I watched her throat work, my eyes moving irresistibly to her chest. That obscene slip pulled tight across her breasts. She had a phenomenal rack, her breasts heavy and round, with small, pale pink nipples.

"You went back to your place?" she asked.

I didn't answer, my eyes glued to her body. I could make out just about every delectable inch of her in that joke of a nightgown. She was surprisingly curvy, even her hips rounded just perfectly. In clothes, she looked slender with large breasts. I knew that she was twenty-three, and I couldn't wrap my mind around the idea that a woman who looked like her had made it that long without having sex. Every inch of her was made for sin. I wondered if she was just a technical virgin or a literal one. *Had a man ever gotten her off? What had she done? Was she completely inexperienced?* I wanted to know everything. But more than anything, I wanted to make her come.

I moved close against her back, my eyes on her chest. With the slightest move, she arched her back, her nipples rubbing against the fabric of that fucking awesome little slip, growing into tight little buds. I was lost.

"I don't want to make you late for work," I murmured to her. "But I need to do something."

I pressed against her back, wanting to moan as my cock rubbed hard into her. I palmed her breasts, kneading firmly, and she moaned, arching into my touch. Her response was perfect, as though her body knew instinctively what I needed from her.

Her eyes fell closed. *No,* I thought. I need those eyes the most. It was a shocking realization. My subs, as a rule, kept their eyes lowered. It was one of my staunchest rules.

Not anymore, I realized.

All of my fucking rules were about to be broken, and I couldn't bring myself to give a damn.

"Look at me," I snapped.

She obeyed, meeting my eyes. I felt such a sense of relief at her compliance that it made me a little weak. No sub rules for my Bianca. Oh no. She would get her own set of rules. First of all, she would give me those glorious eyes every fucking time she came for me.

"I like this nightgown," I told her idly, still kneading her perfect breasts. "Spread your legs more," I ordered.

She obeyed with no hesitation, and I almost came right then.

I wouldn't be training this one, I thought. She may be inexperienced, but I thought she just might be training me. I could only hope to be a good enough Dom for such a perfect sub.

I plucked at a tight little nipple with one hand while the other ran along her ribs, stroking along her flat belly and between her legs. She began to squeeze her legs together.

"Open wider," I told her, and she obeyed me again with no hesitation. "I want to pleasure every inch of you," I told her, my voice a little hoarse with need, "but for the moment, I'm just going to make you come. I just need to touch you. Lay your head back against my shoulder."

I moved my hand over her sex, my thumb going directly to her clit, my other fingers brushing over her entrance. My vision blurred a little, and I sucked in a harsh breath as I found her already wet.

"God," I rasped, "a fucking wet virgin. You are too much, Bianca."

I pushed a finger into her and groaned. She was so unbelievably tight that I could hardly stand it. I imagined pushing my cock into that tiny entrance, breaking her hymen, and I came so close to losing it that I forgot where I was for a moment. *Control yourself*, I told myself firmly, working my finger in very slowly. I stroked her walls, watching her, my thumb still busy on her clit. Her eyes were still glued to mine, glassed over with her passion. I stroked her slowly and thoroughly, grinding my arousal against her back. I slipped a second finger inside of her, and she cried out, arching against me.

Her automatic surrender snapped my mind back to my purpose. "Ask me for it," I ordered, lost in her eyes.

Perfect fucking Bianca didn't hesitate. "Please."

"Say, please, Mr. Cavendish, make me come."

"Please, Mr. Cavendish, make me come."

I pinched her nipple hard, stroking harder. I knew that she would always need at least a touch of pain to attain her pleasure. *So fucking perfect.*

She came, and I thought that it was the hardest thing I'd ever done to resist taking her right then. I could have bent her over the counter and pounded into her, but I needed the first time to be in my bed. I had such a perfect picture in my head of how her first time needed to be that I would have gone through hell to make it happen. *Was going through hell,* I thought.

Her eyes glazed over, and she shook with her climax. I was panting with need when her vision finally cleared, and she blinked at me, looking startled. She watched me steadily as I dragged my fingers out of her. Her jaw went a little slack as I raised those fingers to my mouth and licked them clean, loving the taste of her. *Mine,* I thought, a little savagely.

I grabbed her chin roughly, craning my neck and hers for a deep kiss.

Wake Up Call: Part Two

JAMES

"**Y**ou are the most perfect fucking thing I've ever seen in my life," I murmured into her mouth.

I'm keeping you, I thought.

Her hand moved suddenly, touching my thigh, obviously on its way to my cock. *Fuck*, I thought.

I caught her hand, fighting for control. "There's no time. Get dressed," I told her, feeling violent. If I distracted her with pleasure, and made her late for work, I knew she'd avoid me for it. When we weren't caught up in our passion, she was all too willing reject this thing between us. It infuriated me on every level, but there was nothing to be done but work around it. *For now . . .*

She seemed to come back to herself, moving away from me.

I followed her out of the bathroom, watching her get ready with hungry eyes. She put on her little dress suit of a uniform, with that little tease of a tie.

I was shocked at how quickly she got ready. She was low-maintenance, I was surprised to realize, but she certainly didn't look it. She wasn't wearing a scrap of makeup, and I knew I'd never seen a more beautiful woman.

"That is the hottest fucking flight attendant uniform I've ever seen," I told her as she tucked in her shirt. "That thing should be illegal. I'm going to do some illegal things to you with that little tease of a tie."

Perfect fucking Bianca laughed. My jaw went a little slack at the sight. She was glorious.

"I can do my hair and makeup in the van," she told me with a lovely smile. "Stephan will help me."

She licked her lower lip, waving a hand at me, her eyes going to my crotch. "I still have ten minutes to spare. There has to be something I can do for you. I don't like feeling like I've left you unsatisfied." I didn't think I'd ever been more shocked and pleased by any words in my entire life.

I tried to smile at her, but it was an effort. "You are too perfect," I told her, meaning it to the depths of my soul. "But it's not happening this morning. I'm not coming again until I can be buried inside of you. Preferably for days."

My perfect Bianca only took a step closer, licking her lips.

I sucked in a breath as she suddenly knelt in front of me.

"You could bury yourself somewhere else," she said breathlessly.

She gazed up at me with those breathtaking eyes of hers, her face inches from my cock, but not touching.

I grabbed a handful of her silky hair, feeling covetous and violent and absolutely desperate with need. "Have you done that before?" I asked her. I would punish her if the answer were yes. It was insane, but in my mind every inch of her had always been mine. If she'd given any of it to anyone else, I was determined to show her just how big of a mistake that had been.

She shook her head, licking her lips. I could read in her face that she was sincere. "Like I've told you," she said steadily, "I don't date. I don't do any of this stuff. I don't know what's gotten into me, but you should take me up on the offer before I change my mind."

I couldn't have turned her down to save my life. I ripped my slacks open, and had my cock in her face before she could take another breath.

She blinked at me, her perfect mouth opening wide to latch onto my tip. She sucked at me, her mouth wet and hot. I wanted to ram deep into her throat, but controlled myself.

"Use your hands at the base," I ordered, seeing that she couldn't fit much more than my tip into her mouth.

She obeyed, her delicate hands gripping me. I put my hands over hers, using the moisture from her mouth to lubricate. I showed her how to stroke me at the base.

"Harder," I ordered. "Pull your lips over your teeth and suck harder." She obeyed instantly and perfectly, and I gasped. "Yes, that's perfect, Bianca."

She kept it up, doing exactly as I'd ordered. She was a perfect study. *Absolutely perfect*, I thought.

"I'm coming," I warned her roughly as my vision went a little hazy, still glued to that rosy mouth on my cock. "If you don't want me to come in your mouth, you should pull back now." I didn't want her to. I wanted so badly for her to keep sucking, but I didn't want to push her too hard.

As though she'd read my mind, she just sucked harder. I was lost, coming in her mouth, losing myself harder than I could ever remember.

I'm keeping you, I thought possessively, pulling her up and hard against me.

I kissed her, my hands pulling roughly at her hair.

After long, drugging moments, I pulled back, glancing at the clock.

"You're late," I told her unsteadily. "We'll talk later. I don't want you to get into trouble. I've seen how important your work ethic is to you."

She just nodded, looking suddenly distant, as though she'd just forgotten everything we'd done together. That look, that distance in her eyes, drove me fucking up the wall crazy.

She was ready to go in swift instants, not looking at me.

I almost lost it on her, the knowledge that she wouldn't hesitate to drop me for good all that kept me from shaking up her composure.

She walked out of that room without looking back. I'd never felt so desperately covetous of anyone or anything in my life.

I straightened my clothing and took a few necessary minutes to compose myself before I followed her.

Her back was to me as I approached her and Stephan in the lobby.

Stephan glanced up as I neared, giving me a tentative smile. Bianca turned, looking comically shocked at my presence. She recovered quickly, though, running her eyes over my body, and when they reached my cock, she licked her lips. It was too much.

I waited for her eyes to meet mine before looking at Stephan and nodding. "Good morning," I told him, keeping my voice as polite as I could manage.

"Morning," he said with a pleasant smile.

I laid my hand at the nape of her neck. Her eyes moved to my cock and my grip tightened. Her gaze shot back up to mine.

"Our Buttercup is a handful, Stephan," I said idly. I was trying out the word 'our.' It went against every instinct I had to share her with another man, but from what I had observed of their relationship, I knew that I would have to share or get *nothing* at all. At least he was only a friend, and a protective one at that.

Stephan surprised me by laughing. "She is that."

"A fucking perfect handful," I murmured to Bianca.

Stephan laughed harder, not taking offense. "Well, I wouldn't exactly know about that, but I'll take your word for it."

"Walk me to the door, please?" I asked Bianca.

She didn't hesitate, moving with me.

I lowered my hand from her nape as we reached the door.

"I'm going to tie you to my bed and take your hymen," I told her quietly, unable to keep the words to myself, even knowing they would shock her. In fact, saying them because they would. "I can't seem to think about anything else. Tell me when I can see you again."

She swallowed visibly. I watched her lovely throat work. "I'm not sure," she said unsteadily. "I have a twelve hour day tomorrow. We're doing a turn to DC."

"What about today?" I asked, watching her face closely.

She blinked at me. "I'm flying back to Las Vegas."

I nodded and strode away.

BREAKFAST SERVICE

JAMES

I'd barely taken my seat on the plane when she was sweeping out of the galley, drink-laden tray in hand. She didn't even glance at me as she passed. I watched her every move unabashedly, turning to watch her serve the other passengers.

She served a group of loud New Yorkers first. They were loud and boisterous, but fell silent as she moved through the cabin.

"Hey, sugar. You're a sight for sore eyes," one of them said in a loud New York accent. The words, and the greasy tone of his voice, made me tense.

"Good morning," she murmured back in a quiet, neutral voice. She handed them their drinks swiftly. She didn't linger, heading back into the galley for the next round within seconds.

"Look at the fucking rack on that one," one of the men said loudly.

"Great tits," another agreed.

My vision quite simply went red with temper. I couldn't decide which inflamed me more; that they were thinking about her like that, or that they were saying it out loud. I knew one thing for certain, it was unacceptable. I would need to find her another job immediately. Something that didn't put her within contact with men like that.

She came and went from the cabin, again not seeing me, which drove me crazy, but not as crazy as the loud comments from the men sitting two rows behind me.

"The flight attendant is a fucking ten," one said when she went back into the galley again.

"Between her eyes, the tits, and the legs, she's at the top of my Vegas fuck list."

"She ain't interested."

"There're plenty of ways to get her interested. Don't you worry 'bout it."

"As long as I get my turn."

My jaw clenched so hard that it ached. I wondered if I would be finding new and interesting ways to despise commercial air travel on *every* flight I took during this unorthodox courtship. And I also wondered if I was going to get myself added to the commercial no-fly list before *this* flight was over.

Finally, she noticed me, and her immediate, drastic response was gratifying. Her composed, professional mask slipped for a moment, and the smile froze on her face as her gaze met mine, and she just stared at me as though she couldn't believe that I was there.

She recovered quickly enough. "May I get you anything else, Mr. Cavendish?" she asked. "May I hang your jacket?"

I stood, moving into the aisle to remove my jacket, crowding her as I did so.

She sucked in a breath. "Why didn't you tell me you were taking this flight?" she asked quietly, her lovely brow furrowed.

"It was a last minute decision. I didn't know until this morning that I had urgent business in Las Vegas that needed attention today." I tried to make my tone quiet and neutral. It would do me no favors to reveal to her that I was very close to getting myself arrested because of the crass men behind me.

She studied my face briefly before moving away, working busily to prepare for departure.

I continued to watch her as she worked, studying her as she moved through her safety demonstration. She carefully avoided so much as glancing at me, even skipping over me as she did her obligatory seatbelt check for takeoff.

"You can check my lap a little closer, doll," I heard one of the obnoxious men say as she passed over him.

"Pull tight on my strap, sweetheart," another muttered.

My hands tightened into fists. *The fucking nerve of them.*

Bianca stopped by my seat, looking completely unfazed by the things that I knew she must have heard. *Was this a common occurrence? Was she subject to treatment like this often?* The very idea made me feel murderous.

"Can I help you with anything, Mr. Cavendish?" she asked softly, her tone concerned. She was already too good at reading me. I shook my head slightly.

"Tell Stephan I want to speak to him as soon as he's available," I told her, unable to help myself. Perhaps he could handle the men without resorting to violence, because I was beginning to seriously doubt that I could.

"Okaaay," she said, sounding perplexed. She moved away.

Stephan was approaching me within moments, bending

R.K. LILLEY

down to speak quietly. "Is everything okay? Bianca told me that you were upset about something."

I grimaced, and told him everything I'd heard. "The men behind me are out of hand with the comments about Bianca," I concluded. "If they make one more comment about her tits, her legs, or fucking her, I'm going to lose it. Does this sort of thing happen often? Men talking about her like this? Are you okay with it?"

He gave me a level stare, and I could see the rage just under the surface that he hid so well. "Of course not. Do I look like I'm fucking okay with it? If anyone so much as hints at crossing a line with her, I kick them off the fucking plane. She gets hit on, but what you heard is definitely crossing a line. I'll take care of them after we reach altitude. It's too late now. We're next in line for takeoff. I'll handle them. Don't do anything crazy, okay?"

I looked away. "I'll try my best, but I can't make any promises if they keep it up."

We were taking off when the bastards started up again, talking so loudly that I could hear them even over the plane's engines.

"I get first dibs on blondie's pussy," the main offender said loudly.

"That's fine. You know I'm an ass man," another one said with a laugh. All of the bastards laughed.

My eyes widened, my hands going to my seat belt. I saw the alarmed looks on Stephan and Bianca's faces as they watched me.

"You two are so full of shit. She hasn't even looked at either of you twice," another loud voice told the other two.

I carefully let go of my seatbelt and unclenched my hands. I shut my eyes, counting to ten, trying hard not to lose it.

"I don't give a fuck where she's looking. She can point her

334

eyes at the ground, as long as her ass goes in the fucking air."

"Well, she ain't interested, no matter where she's looking, and I don't see how you're gonna change that."

"One pill in a drink, and she'll be our party girl for as long as we want."

"You're so full of shit, Donny. You talk out of your ass more than you talk out of your mouth."

"How's this for talking out of my ass? We follow her through the airport," I was out of my seat, rage in every step, as he continued, "talk her into one drink, and I'll handle the rest. Who's full of shit now, huh?" He looked a little surprised as I reached his seat on his last sentence, but not at all alarmed. The man had terrible instincts. I was a word away from beating him to a bloody pulp.

I pointed at him. "Don't say another word. I'm having you arrested on the other side of this flight, but one more fucking word and you're going to lose some teeth first."

I felt Stephan moving in behind me as the man raised his hands in an innocent pose that I didn't believe for a second. "We meant no harm, man. Just talking. Talking ain't against the law."

I leaned very close to the scumbag. "It is when the talk involves drugging and gang-raping a woman."

I heard Stephan suck in a breath just behind me.

"*What did you say*?" Stephan said loudly, sounding as angry as I felt. "This ends now," he addressed the group at large. "One more of you say another crude word and we will divert this plane and have you arrested at the nearest airport. Do you understand? It's going to be perfect silence or police."

"What hotel are you booked at?" I asked the one I had singled out as the worst offender, while Stephan continued his tirade

His eyes were wide, and he looked genuinely surprised that there had been a negative reaction to his outlandish statements. *Who the hell was he used to dealing with, that he thought it was okay to talk like that where anyone could hear?* Or at all, for that matter . . .

"The Middleton Hotel," he said, sounding meek as a lamb now.

"No, you're not," I told him. These sick bastards were about to find themselves blacklisted from every decent property in Vegas. No hotel wanted a gang of roving sexual predators on the premises, and I would make all the calls to assure that everyone had their names.

"Chill out. I was joking about drugging her. You can check my bag, if you don't believe me."

"I mean it," Stephan said, his voice raised to a near shout. "One more word out of any of you, we are diverting this plane, and there will be law enforcement waiting for you at the gate." Stephan turned and strode back to his seat, but I wasn't done.

I made very solid eye contact with the man. I knew he was lying. Every instinct I had was telling me so. "If you so much as look at that flight attendant funny, I swear to you that I will make you regret it. This won't be a short-term regret. It will be a, holy fuck what happened to my life, kind of regret. I won't tell you again."

I returned to my seat. I sat down, closing my eyes, making an attempt to retain some semblance of calm and composure.

I didn't stir until Stephan approached me while he was handing out hot towels. I took one, waving him closer. Like me, he still looked tense, but he leaned forward.

"Even if they don't make another sound back there, they need to be arrested and searched when we get to Las Vegas," I told him quietly.

He nodded. "I know. Even if it was all talk, they need to be questioned and searched. I'll arrange to have law enforcement meet us at the gate."

I nodded, leaning back and closing my eyes.

I didn't see Bianca again for the entire first half of the flight, but all things considered, I was actually relieved that she wasn't out in the cabin, going near those men.

I was too distracted and agitated to work or sleep, so I just sat and thought, which was troublesome, because all I could think about was Bianca, and the things we'd done, and of course, the things we *hadn't* done. I was particularly obsessed with the fact that she had gone down on me, and I hadn't reciprocated, hadn't had the chance. I needed that first, needed to taste her and feel her shake with need under my tongue.

Bianca and Stephan both had their backs to me as I went into the bathroom, but I could hear their muffled voices through the door as I washed my hands.

"I'll be back in a few minutes," Stephan was telling her. "Brenda is baking the cookies back there right now. I'll bring some back to add to the cheese service."

I smiled. At last, a bit of luck. I was moving quietly into the galley to join her scant seconds later.

Bianca gave me a small, rather shy smile when she saw me.

"Hey," she said, watching me.

I smiled back, moving the cart she was handling into position to give us a few moments of much needed privacy behind the curtain.

"Oh," she said softly, her eyes glued to me.

I loved having her focused on me like that.

I set the brake on the cart with my toe, taking a deep breath, fighting for control.

I turned, striding to her. I grabbed her braid, pulling her head back roughly, and kissing her without holding back.

She submitted instantly and perfectly, and I pushed her by the hips to the tiny galley counter, lifting her to perch there, my lips still crushed to hers.

She made a startled sound of protest as I began working her pencil skirt up her legs. "What are you doing?" she asked when I had her thighs bared.

"Shh," I told her, kissing her while I shoved her skirt higher. "I need to do this."

I just stopped and stared when I saw her garters and the tops of her stockings. I recovered quickly, shoving her skirt up roughly.

I cursed when I saw the tiny scrap of lace she was wearing underneath. "This is the type of panty you were wearing last night, too, wasn't it? But that one was blue."

She nodded, looking dazed. "They're the most comfortable underwear I've ever worn. I can't wear anything else, since I discovered them."

"I fucking love them," I told her, meaning it.

She smiled at me.

I knelt in front of her, handing her a handkerchief. "Put that in your mouth and bite down. Try not to make too much noise."

She obeyed with no hesitation, her body trembling, and I felt my cock twitch. This would be torture, since I couldn't be inside of her for hours yet, but it would be worth it.

"Grip my hair," I told her. She stroked her hands into my hair, turning it into a caress.

I shoved her thong to the side and buried my face between her legs. Her entire body was shaking under my hands as I nuzzled and licked at her core.

Knowing that I was the first one to do this to her, the first to taste her like this, gave me the most primitive and overpowering sense of satisfaction. It was an anomaly for me. I could be possessive, and had been in the past, it was a Dom's prerogative to own his sub, but it had been such a fleeting sort of possession, belonging solely in the short-term. What I felt just then was so different that what the word possessive meant to me was irrevocably changed. *This* was mine. *Her* I possessed. Not just today, or tomorrow, but for all of the befores and all of the afters.

I pushed two fingers inside of her, stroking along her tight walls. If I let myself, I thought that I could come just from feeling her clench against my fingers. I moved my mouth up to suck mercilessly at her clit, and she came, violently, her entire body rocking with her pleasure. I felt that strong sense of satisfying possessiveness so strongly then that I shuddered, nuzzling into her as she calmed.

I lifted my head to look at her as she stilled, propping my face on her skirt to study her. She had the most adorable, dazed look on her lovely face.

"One more," I told her, relishing the way my words made her jaw go slack with need.

I licked at her, going straight for her clit with time in short supply. She came easily, letting out a muffled scream around the cloth in her mouth; our chemistry and my experienced tongue making it seem effortless.

I licked her once, twice more as she recovered.

"I could eat you all day," I told her, standing. I decided it was better to keep it to myself that eating her pussy had been close to a religious experience for me.

I pulled the handkerchief from her mouth, and used it

between her legs. "I love how wet you are," I said softly, bending down to kiss her deeply. Perfect fucking Bianca sucked on my tongue. I groaned, and she sucked harder.

I pulled back, knowing that things would get out of hand if I didn't. I pulled her off the counter, shoving the handkerchief into my pocket and straightening her clothes as quickly as I could.

Stephan burst through the curtain just as I was pulling her skirt down. He looked shocked, and then scandalized, blushing scarlet. "Was that noise you? That muffled scream?" he asked her.

She blushed, but she nodded.

Stephan turned a stern look my way. "Really, James? On a morning flight? With a group of perverts just a few feet away?"

I flushed, agreeing with his censure wholeheartedly. I had lost my mind for a few minutes, and as her protector, I couldn't be upset with him for calling me out for it.

Stephan pointed towards the first class cabin. "I think you should go sit down now."

I went back to my seat without comment.

The rest of the flight was basically an exercise in torture, while I just sat in my seat and tried not to think about Bianca every single second. Even with the most optimistic estimate, it would be hours before I could bury myself inside of her, and I'd never been so impatient for anything in my life. Hours seemed like years from where I was sitting just then.

The only highlight of the flight from that point was when she served me.

I was trying to relax in my seat, but I had the handkerchief I'd used on her clutched in my hand, and that wasn't helping a bit. Still, I couldn't bring myself to put it away. I wanted her to see it, and to know just what I was thinking about. And I loved to shake up that perfect composure of hers.

I could tell that she was trying not to look at me as she served me, and that made me smile. I made a point of folding out my tray table and perching my arm there, the handkerchief blatantly on display in my hand.

I clenched and unclenched my fist, watching her closely. The moment when she saw what was in my hand was as gratifying as I could have hoped. She went white, then pink, then looked away, a scandalized look on her face. I grinned, admitting to myself right then that I was infatuated. As if I'd had any lingering doubts about that fact . . .

I watched her as she finally took her seat, just as I heard the wheels coming down for landing. I waited patiently until she finally glanced at me. I smiled at her. It was a fond smile, I couldn't help that.

She just stared back at me, blushing. She gasped loudly as I brought the handkerchief to my face and inhaled deeply, my eyes closing.

"What the hell?" Stephan said loudly.

I was grinning like a fool when I opened my eyes again, watching her stare at anything but me, completely scandalized.

R.K. LILLEY

BIRTHDAY

JAMES - BETWEEN BOOKS 1&2

I checked my phone again, feeling pathetic. It was my birthday today, and all I was hoping for was a text, and even that wasn't likely. My mouth twisted bitterly when I saw that she hadn't responded to my latest inquiry about her welfare. She usually didn't.

I checked my computer. I had an entire network keeping tabs on her—sending me every photo and scrap of information that they found. I was basically torturing myself, because most of it was taking the form of petty tabloid gossip. Still, I looked.

The first picture I saw made my jaw clench. I gritted my teeth hard enough that the sound of it filled my office. I had the childish urge to throw my computer across the room in a fit, but I tamped it down. It wouldn't make me feel better to break something. *Nothing* would make me feel better, aside from hearing from her.

In the picture, Bianca was lying on a pool lounger, wearing a see-through black cover-up with a little bikini under it. Her face was peaceful. She could have been sleeping, in fact. It was *his* face that bothered me. Damien was sitting on a lounger beside her, and he was staring at her breasts. Even in a picture, I could read his filthy thoughts.

Mine, I thought savagely.

I clicked to the next picture rather violently. It was no better. Worse, in fact.

I studied the picture for a long time. I rubbed at my chest. It hurt. The picture troubled me on a number of levels. She was with Damien again in the picture. They were walking on the beach. Even the lighting was romantic.

They walked side by side, barefoot in the sand. They looked like a fucking Hallmark card, and he was *touching* her.

Mine, I thought again.

Her expression was hard to read. She was wearing dark shades, but I could tell that she was blushing. I didn't know what to think of the look on her face. Again, it was *his* face that made me want to break things. Namely, his *face*.

I was well aware that the man was infatuated with her. I'd known it from the first time I'd met him. It actually pissed me off even more that he'd been nothing but polite to me, as though *I* was her passing fancy, and he was content to wait me out.

And that was my fear.

When I looked at her, some part of me thought I'd walked into the most beautiful love story. Looking into her eyes, I imagined that there was someone for everyone, and that I had finally found *my* someone. It made me feel optimistic—and I began to dream that even the severely damaged could have happy endings.

But when I looked at him, or them together, I felt my gut churn and doubt fill me. Perhaps this was *their* love story, and I *was* just the passing fancy. I could see Bianca thinking of our tempestuous affair as a brief passionate interlude before she set her feet firmly back on the ground again and found a normal guy. *Would that be her happy ending? Is that what would be best for her, in the end?* I didn't know the answer. All I knew was that I wasn't unselfish enough to let it happen without a fight.

I spent too long looking at that damned picture—that hand touching her. Abruptly, I picked the computer up and threw it as hard as I could across the room. It hit the wall with a satisfying crash.

I'd been wrong. I did feel a little better after breaking something.

Clark burst in the door, looking a little ruffled, though he quickly shook it off when he saw the mess that used to be my computer. He looked between me and the iMac, raising his brows. "Time for another workout?" he asked mildly. He was always happy to hit the gym.

I nodded.

"I'll have that taken care of," he added, nodding towards the mess that used to be my computer.

I just nodded again.

We were nearly to the elevator when my phone beeped at me. I checked it way too eagerly.

Bianca: I'm doing fine. Please stop worrying about me.

It had taken her over six hours to text me back, but I was messaging within five seconds of reading hers.

James: Thank you. I miss you desperately, Love.

As sad as it was, it made my day when she responded right away.

Bianca: I miss u 2.

I was smiling as we boarded the elevator.

POST AND TROT

JAMES

The horses were saddled and ready when we got to the stables. Good.

I outfitted Bianca myself, head to toe, even fitting on her gloves.

I was working on my own gloves, pushing my fingers in, smiling as I caught her eyes, which were glued to my hands.

"I love your hands," she uttered softly. "So much."

I threw my head back and laughed, a feeling of purest joy blooming in my chest.

I put her on her horse myself, and she shifted until her seat was just right, a natural at it.

"Perfect," I told her, meaning it, for so many reasons.

I vaulted onto my own horse, well aware that her devouring eyes were eating up my every movement like it was foreplay.

I took the lead, fingering her collar as I rode past her. I touched the hoop as I murmured, "I should get a lead rope for this, as well."

That stopped her in her tracks, which made me smile. "Follow me," I ordered.

I led her through the woods, anticipation strumming through me in delicious waves. My heart was pounding, breath heavy, though I'd barely exerted myself.

I knew what was coming, had planned it down to precise detail, but she was oblivious. That only served to heighten my own excitement.

I stopped when we reached a smooth dirt road that ran the length of the property. I sent her a sidelong, wicked glance. "How do you feel? Are you sore?"

She shook her head, looking bemused. She knew I was up to something.

I laid my reins across Devil's neck, stilling my mount with a word.

Watching her face, I undid the buttons at the top of my riding breaches, folding them down as I tugged out my thick, throbbing cock, tucking the material below my scrotum.

I shrugged off my shirt, tucking it into one of my chaps.

Her eyes one me were like hungry hands, stroking every bared inch of me.

I smiled at her. "Come here."

Her horse sidled toward me until she was close enough for me to pluck from her saddle to mine. I swung her to straddle me, perching her just in front of me.

"Don't move," I ordered, pulling a large pocketknife from my boot. I worked her higher on my thighs.

I took the knife to the waistband of her thin leggings, cutting towards myself, just a few inches before I put the knife away.

With relish, I used the cut in the material and ripped her pants clean off.

Devil sidestepped at the loud noise, but I calmed him, and focused back on the delicious task at hand.

It was an incongruous and arousing sight, to see her bare from thigh to stomach, the rest of her still covered.

I reached behind her, untying the reins, making them longer, arranging them so Devil could move with just my legs controlling him.

I gripped her hips and lifted her until her wet entrance hugged just the tip of my cock, moving my hips in small circles to tease her.

She moaned, moving her hips, trying to take me deeper.

I couldn't resist for another second. I clenched my jaw and thrust straight in, burying myself to the hilt.

"Oh, James," she cried out, her hips jerking against me.

I moved Devil into a walk, moving my hips with him, thrusting inside of her just enough to tease, watching her beautiful eyes all the while.

"Do you want a posting trot, Bianca?" I asked her roughly.

"Yes," she moaned.

"Beg me for it," I said archly.

"Please, Mr. Cavendish, bring us to a posting trot."

I tsk'd at her impatiently. "That was a sad excuse for begging, Bianca. Now you only get the sitting trot."

I clicked Devil into a trot, keeping my seat smoothly, thrusts barely deepened from the walk.

She made a noise of frustration, gripping my shoulders. "I beg you, Mr. Cavendish," she said. "Please, fuck me at a posting trot. Please, please, please."

I instantly moved the horse into a faster trot. "*That* is the tone I was looking for. Hold on, love."

I began to move up and down on the saddle, thrusts going

349

longer, harder, deeper with the exaggerated movements.

She fell apart in seconds with the new rhythm. "Come," I growled, pushing her over the edge.

I kept going, driving into her, over and over, relentlessly. I pleasured her again, then again, before I found my own toe curling release.

I kissed her, still buried deep, as Devil slowed to an aimless walk.

This horse was getting a full bag of carrots when we got back.

"Have you ever done that before?" she asked, sometime later, when she'd pulled back from our deep kiss.

I stiffened, anxiety churning in my gut.

"Made love on horseback?" I asked.

Her eyes narrowed. "Fucked someone on horseback," she amended.

I felt myself flush. "I've fucked a woman on horseback before, but it wasn't like that. It was far more technical, almost clinical. It was more about seeing if it could be done, for me, than the actual doing. And I was barely an adult at the time." I hated how her eyes had turned cold, her face shutting against me. I knew what she was going to do. "Please don't try to demean what we just shared."

"Was it *her*?" she asked, tone horrified.

Fuck.

I squeezed her more tightly against me, burying my face in her neck.

If I could have erased my entire past, I would have, for her. It all seemed so pointless now. Acting out with sex, being with too many women to count.

"Who are you referring to?" I finally asked.

"Jules," she said, stiffening, tone gone glacial.

I sighed. Of all the damned lucky guesses in the world. She must have heard something.

Jules' family and mine had had neighboring estates with stables in upstate New York. We were the same age and had messed around as kids. Even the term fuck buddy was too kind for us, because we'd never been good friends. She'd been adventurous, I'd been a slut, and we were both accomplished equestrians. We'd done it just to see if we could. Nothing more to it than that, but I had a feeling Bianca wouldn't see it that way.

"It was. But it didn't mean anything. Please don't use her to keep me at a distance."

She tried to move off me, but I kept her flush against me, moving Devil into a brisk walk.

I started to move inside of her again, my cock growing inside of her. The conflict, our position, and my insatiable need for her saw to that.

She gasped, slapping at my shoulders. "You can't use sex to subdue me," she told me.

The hell I couldn't. "You can't withdraw from me every time you get mad or jealous. We need to talk this out. I'm not letting you go until we do."

She pulled my hair, but her body betrayed her. "You call this talking?"

"I call this making love, and yes, talking." I gave her a tense smile, and she yanked hard on my hair. I winced, and let her at it.

"Why do you keep calling it that? Why do you keep calling it making love?"

I shot her a heated look. "You know why. You keep trying to belittle what we have, but you need to understand that it's as new to me as it is to you. I have a past. A wildly sordid past. I can't change it. I would if I could.

I took a few deep breaths, feeling helpless and agitated. It was so hard to make her understand, when I was only still just figuring it out myself.

"You are going to run into a lot of my ex-lovers. That's an unfortunate fact. It will be a lot less painful for you if you can just get it into your head that none of them were anything but a fuck to me. And fucking was nothing to me before I met you. Sex was a bodily function to me before I met you. That's why I call this making love. It means something to me."

I kept moving as I spoke, "I've never even had a girlfriend before you, never even considered the idea. I'm sure it sounds callous, but no woman has ever been anything to me beyond a fuck, a sub, or a friend, occasionally all three, though never all of them for long. They all knew the score. I was brutally honest with every single one of them, without exception. You are the one that I want, the one that I need. So getting upset about my past, or feeling jealous of women I've been with, is unwarranted."

"Unwarranted?" she said bitterly, sounding nothing so much as *hurt*, which I affected me the most.

"I've years' worth of pictures of you going out with Jules," she continued. "How can you expect me to dismiss that out of hand?"

I thrust harder inside of her.

"Unfair," she accused. "And you are hardly one to talk. I was a virgin when I met you, but you're still jealous of every man I speak to. *That's* unwarranted."

She had a very good point, but that didn't make it easier to hear.

I was quiet, focused on moving inside of her for a few beats of charged silence.

"When I was about eighteen," I began, "the paparazzi were hounding me relentlessly, printing silly stories that drove me crazy. They were hiding in the bushes when I left school. It was out of control."

I couldn't even tell if she heard me, she was so worked up, but I continued, "You know how I need control."

I clicked Devil into a trot, thrusting harder, then moved into a canter.

This was unfamiliar to her, and she clutched my shoulders in panic.

I continued to move, fucking her in earnest now.

"Come," I ordered, and she did.

I slowed the horse to a walk, but I didn't stop moving inside of her.

"You know I need control," I repeated. "But the things they were doing were completely out of my control, and I realized one day that the press was like a garden hose."

She blinked at me, looking adequately confused by my vague explanation. "A garden hose?"

I smiled at her, my heart in my eyes. "A garden hose," I confirmed. "If you turn it on too lightly, you can't control the flow. It just drips where it will. But if you turn it to full force, you can control the flow, sending it wherever you want. So I began to court the paparazzi rather than ducking away. I encouraged their attention by charming them, and publicly, becoming an open book.

Or rather, making it appear that way. Jules was my best friend's sister, and occasionally, a very casual lover of mine, and we'd been friends for a while. We were seen out and about together, since we traveled in the same circles. I quickly noticed that she loved the attention, encouraging rumors about us shamelessly, even leaking lies to the press about us."

"I see now that it was stupid to let her take it so far, but at the time I couldn't see a problem with it. Other women thought she and I had an open relationship, so no one tried for anything more with me. It saved me from worse misunderstandings, for a time. I see that it looks bad, but I want you to trust me that that's all it was. Jules is not someone you need to worry about."

I lost control as I saw her softening toward me, fucking her with frenzied abandon, finally finishing inside of her.

It was so intense, the feelings between us so enormous, that I saw her eyes getting moist, and had to blink mine repeatedly to keep my heart from spilling out of them.

I leaned her back against my arm, looking down at the spot where we were still joined. Her wetness and my seed were intermingled on the base of my shaft. It was a drugging sight.

"You're so full of my semen right now. You're stuffed full of my cock and my cum. I want to keep you like this forever. I might have gotten you pregnant just now, if you weren't on the pill."

Why had I said that? I knew it would freak her out, knew I was farther along in the acceptance process of this thing we had than she was.

She stiffened, but didn't say anything about my slip. I figured her going into denial mode about it was probably bet case scenario for me anyway.

Because even though she was emphatically not ready to hear it, I'd meant it, every word of it.

TRISTAN

I'd come to hate my former friend, but that wasn't why I went after him.

I was angry, furious, so jealous I didn't know what to do with myself, but that wasn't why I rearranged his face.

I did it because it needed to be done, and though what I felt was a red-hot hatred for him, it was actually a cold move, calculated.

You see, I knew Milton. I knew how he was with women, had heard him talk about it, knew his philosophy. He didn't see women as people. He fucked around. Lied to them and bragged about it. Used them and walked away.

Just thinking about the things I'd heard him say about other women and thinking about him saying something like that about Danika.

Not fucking happening. No. Just no.

Over my dead body. Or his.

I broke things just thinking about it. Dishes, furniture, walls.

It should be noted that I did try a friendly warning first.

I was never close with Milton. He was friends with Kenny first and would show up to listen to us record our upcoming album. He was a fan of the band, a fan of me, and we were friendly, but I *always* thought he was a douche.

And yes, I kept tabs on Danika. I knew he'd started sniffing around, knew he flew to Vegas just to see her.

I cornered him the next time he swung by the studio. "You going out with Danika Markova?" I asked him bluntly.

He looked surprised, then his face split into a smile. "Trying. Been asking her out, think I'm wearing her down."

I shook my head, trying to look concerned. "You should really stay away from her."

He cocked his head. "Why is that? She's fucking hot, dude. I've got plans for that one."

Hated. Him.

I tried to smile, but he would have seen through it if he looked down at my clenched fists.

"She has a crazy ex-husband. He is *psycho*."

He didn't look fazed. "Good to know. Thanks for the heads up, but I can handle myself."

I stood up straighter, folding my arms across my chest. I was taller than he was, bigger. I wanted him to notice.

"You don't understand. This guy is huge. And he knows how to *fight*. He wouldn't take kindly to her going out with a player like you."

He shrugged. "He'll get over it. If he doesn't, he's welcome to come take it up with me."

He jumped when I swung my arms out, slapping them down on his shoulders. Hard. I grinned into his face. It was an effort, and it couldn't have been a pleasant sight. It *felt* unpleasant. "I'm telling you, *friend*, you don't want to mess with this guy. He'd chew you up and spit you out. He's really not right in the head. He might just do something insane, something homicidal, I don't know, maybe stab you in your sleep, or hell, take a bat to you, if you pushed the wrong button. You getting me here?"

The dense motherfucker didn't get me. Not at all. He just gave me wide eyes, made an excuse, and got the hell away.

Fuck.

Danika heard about that little conversation. The fucker had tattled on me?

She was so pissed about it that she actually came to see me. Sought me out in my dressing room before the show.

I met her at the door. She was livid, so pissed she couldn't contain herself.

So beautiful it made my chest hurt.

She barged into the room. I shut us in.

She whirled on me. "How dare you?" she hissed. She was shaking. She looked like she wanted to attack me.

I wished she would.

"I know why you're here," I said in my most fake calm tone. "I can explain."

"Oh please do. I would *love* to hear it."

God, I missed her. Even her temper I loved.

I took a step toward her, but she backed away fast. "Don't you dare try to touch me."

I looked down, taking deep breaths, trying to cope with the gaping hole just a few words could leave in my chest. I deserved this, deserved the one I loved most thinking I was *scum*.

"Of course, Danika," I said, trying not to sound bitter, trying not to sound as gutted as I was. "I know how you feel about that. I take it this is about Milton?"

She curled her lip at me, nodding. Even that I loved. Sharing this air with her, anything she did I would have taken, just to keep sharing it.

I was so fucked.

"Of course it is. Why else would I be here?"

Deep breaths. "Why else indeed? Listen, I told him that because—"

"I can't believe you told him I was divorced!" she burst out.

I looked at her, just looked, jaw clenched. Now *that* was a tough blow to take without fighting back. "You are divorced," I said softly.

"That marriage was a joke. It didn't even count."

I flinched. I'd been punched in the face, been knocked across the fucking room and not felt it like I felt those two sentences. *Jesus*, she knew how to rip me apart.

Didn't matter. Didn't change a thing. I couldn't let her go out with that creep.

"I told him that because he is not the guy for you." My voice was shaking. She didn't notice.

"How cute," she said scathingly. "You think you know what's good for me?"

I did not have the heart to fight her. I wanted to spread my arms out, lay myself in front of her, waving a white flag, because my heart was not in it, when it came to this fight. It had surrendered to her, years ago.

But I knew my Danika, knew how she felt about me now. If I'd handed her that flag, she was liable to just light it on fire and throw it back.

"He's a womanizer," I explained to her. If she had a clue about this guy, she wouldn't go near him. I wanted to give her that clue.

She laughed, a bitter laugh that scratched at my insides like nails on a chalkboard. "Look who's talking."

"And a liar."

She started looking around the room, eyes wild.

I watched her steadily, determined to take whatever she was about to dish out.

"That is beside the point," she said, voice low and mean. "None of this is your business. Nothing in my life is your business. Are we clear?"

"Please, Danika," I pleaded. "Stay clear of him. I know you have a right to do as you please, but understand that I wouldn't have interfered if I weren't concerned. This guy is bad news. He'll break your heart, and when he does, I may well break his neck."

She pointed a trembling finger at me. "You stop it. Quit acting like you give a damn, and stay the fuck out of my life. You and I . . . we are nothing to each other. Less than strangers."

I shook my head, trying not to sway on my feet, even though she'd just blown my chest open wide with those shots.

We stared at each other, both of us panting.

I saw things in her eyes that I *could not bear,* and God only knows what she told herself she saw in mine.

I knew one thing. She didn't see the truth, didn't see the love, the agonized remorse they held.

"Please," I mouthed.

She went out with him. Very publicly. There were pictures of them together. I didn't dare hope she'd done that for my benefit.

I sought him out and warned him again.

This warning involved more contact.

I'd just landed another solid blow to his stomach when he warded me off, gasping. "What the fuck, dude?"

"I told you to stay away from Danika. Fucking *warned* you."

"What the hell is your problem?"

"You're my fucking problem. *You.*"

I got a little carried away, bruised up his pretty boy face.

And still he kept seeing her.

And then I found out about his girlfriend, how he'd been playing them both, from Kenny.

Needless to say, I didn't handle that well.

I beat him bloody, the worst loss of temper I'd had in many years. So bad I started doubling up on therapy, going through anger management steps again.

I even checked myself back into rehab for a few days. I hadn't slipped, but my sobriety felt just a bit too fragile for a time. It was preemptive, and it helped.

And even with all of that, I wasn't sorry I'd messed up the motherfucker.

JARED

I would not recommend reading this if you have not read *BAD THINGS (TRISTAN & DANIKA #1)*

THE GIRL

JARED

It was too late by the time I met her. By then, she was already falling for my brother, even though she'd only met him that day.

Still, a guy had to try.

Tristan established at the start that they were only friends. I believed it for about two hours.

As soon as I said a few friendly words to her, he was pulling me aside, chastising me.

He clapped my shoulder and led me away from the group.

"Don't," he said quietly, with a look to tell me he meant it.

I raised my brows. We had a solid brother code and if he said she was off limits, that was as good as law. But . . . "You said she was just your friend."

He shook his head, "I'm not going there. She's off limits. End of story."

It was a fact that I didn't like to fight with my brother. He was the fighter.

I loved him, more than anyone on earth. He'd always taken care of me. He'd done more for me than my own dad, my own mom, and he was only a few years older than I was. If I had a problem, I went to Tristan. Big brother could fix it, I had absolute faith.

That being said, he was a stubborn cuss. Just then I found that to be annoying as hell.

"So you're just staking your claim on random women now, just in case you might want to fuck them later?" I asked, cringing at what came out of my mouth.

I was just frustrated, and if I was honest, jealous.

He gave me a look that shut me the hell up. He hadn't liked that.

"Don't, just don't. Don't talk about her like that, and get it out of your head if you're thinking you want to hook up with her. She doesn't hook up."

"What if I want to date *her*?" I asked quietly, testing him more than I normally did. I liked that girl, Danika, and I would have liked at least to feel her out.

"No. Knock it off. I'm done talking about it."

From the very start, the very *first* day they met, Tristan was incapable of being logical when it came to Danika.

THE DATE

I'd finally gotten Danika to go out with me.

I was crazy about this girl. We hadn't been able to spend much time together, but I felt like I knew her, felt like I got her.

She was smart, funny, nice, and gorgeous. She was the kind of girl I wanted to marry someday. She wouldn't put up with any shit, but that was okay, I wouldn't be dealing any, if I had her around.

And then I kissed her. It was a good kiss. Fucking great.

And she shot me down. She was falling for Tristan. My brother. Had fallen.

I tried to shrug it off and enjoy the rest of the night. I enjoyed her company, even if she didn't like me *that way*.

What could I do? If the feelings weren't there for her, they weren't there.

"I won't make this awkward," I told her.

We smiled at each other. She was so beautiful. "Good," she said. "Thank you. I hate awkward."

She loved my brother, I realized it that night.

And he'd fallen for her too. That was another thing I learned that night, though I didn't think he realized how far gone he was. Stubborn bastard.

He'd caught us on our date, and pulled me aside to rip me a new one.

"What did I fucking tell you?" he gritted out, getting in my face, finger jabbing at my chest. "You stay away from her."

I studied him. He was a scary motherfucker, but never to me. His fists went flying often, but not at me. I was his baby brother. He was there to protect me, not hurt me, and he'd always made sure I knew it.

Since I was five, I'd known it, when he got in front of a careless backhand from my dad that was aimed at me. It hadn't been an accident.

He'd stepped into that hit.

"Don't you lay a hand on him, you bastard!" he'd snarled, taken another hit, and gotten right back up, right back into my dad's face. "You touch him again, I will *end you*."

Another hit, curses, followed by my mom kicking Tristan out of the house, telling him to take a breather, not to come back until he'd calmed down.

He was ten.

My dad never tried to hit me again, that I could remember. He always went after Tristan, the bigger, easier target.

He might have been furious, snarling at me now, but I knew his heart. He loved me more than he loved himself, would and had inflicted pain on himself to prevent mine.

"You can't put dibs on girls you aren't even dating," I told him quietly. I could be stubborn too.

He shook his head, eyes wild. "This is not 'girls,' this is Danika. And I don't need to explain myself. Back the fuck off."

It was so crazy, his reaction so over the top, that I knew then. "You're falling for her," I told him, voice pitched low. "At least admit it to yourself."

He shook his head, not admitting a thing. "Don't change the fucking subject. You going to stay away from her, or are we going to have a fucking problem?"

Stubborn cuss. "I'll stay away."

THE LAST DAY

I was strung out in the extreme, had been for days, and the only cure for that seemed to be to further partake. Speaking of which.

I answered my phone. "What's up, Dean?"

"I've got a present for you. Where you at?"

"My apartment."

"Have you even gone outside this week? You're just sitting at home getting high right now, aren't you?"

I grinned. "Just pot, dude. What are you, my mother?"

He laughed, and he sounded a bit like the old Dean, from years ago. "Your mom is the one that handed me my first joint, Jared. You can do better."

"Okay, what are you, my brother?"

We both laughed at that one. It was accurate. He acted more like my parent than my actual parents.

"You up for a party?" he asked me.

"Always."

"I'm bringing it to you."

The upcoming high had me feeling instantly revived. I actually got out of bed, gave Tristan a call.

He was in a rough place, I knew. He didn't pick up the phone.

"Love you, brother," I said after the beep. "Don't you give up on her. She'll come around."

Dean showed up at my place a few hours later. It wasn't much of a party, just him, a bag full of something fun, two girls, and a bottle of vodka.

The girls were groupies.

I invited them in, but I didn't try to flirt with them. Dean could have them. I didn't like the girls Dean found. They always seemed far gone to the point that sleeping with them would just be exploitive.

I might have been covered in ink and in a band, but I liked nice girls. Ones that smiled with their eyes and wanted to fall in love. Until I found that, I could wait.

Dean went straight to the living room sofa and started mixing on the coffee table. Speedballs, I saw. Good shit.

The girls followed him like he was feeding them catnip.

I snagged his bottle of vodka, went into the kitchen, and poured us all a shot.

"Cheers," I said, and drank mine. No one even noticed what I was doing. The girls were watching Dean's activities with rapt attention. Junkies then.

One of them held out her arm for him to shoot her up.

He shrugged her off. "Don't be a bitch. Host first. Get over here, Jared."

I moved to sit by him on the couch, holding out my arm, jonesing hard for that first sweet high. This shit was the best high there was, when the rush from the coke met the bliss of the dope.

He shot me up.

I sat back and sighed as I felt it hit my bloodstream like a Mack truck.

"Fuck, that's good," I said softly, a head to toe rush sweeping me, shivers and pins and needles moving through me, all at the same time.

Dean shot me a sharp smile as he emptied another needle into one of the girl's arms. "The best, right? And you're gonna love me, because I brought plenty to go around. You can thank me later."

FRANKIE

The first time I met her I was positive we'd never be compatible. It took me no time at all to come to that conclusion. Her smile was too nice, too free of baggage.

I met her in a college bar across the street from UNLV, at the insistence of a well meaning Danika.

I *hated* college bars. They were always full of college guys, and college guys seemed to all live under the delusion that lesbians were just girls that liked to go that extra mile to turn them on. I wasn't crazy about that.

Estella was beautiful. I didn't have a type, but this girl was *everybody's* type. Of a height with me, she was shapely, with a body that wouldn't quit. She was showing a lot of that hot little body, in a skimpy black top that clung to her breasts, and a white mini skirt that barely covered her ass. Her skin was a creamy caramel that struck me as edible.

She'd recently moved to the states from Brazil, and had a sexy as hell accent.

Her hair was also a showstopper. It was a sun streaked brown, and there were wavy masses of it.

My mind ran a little wild with the things I'd like to do to that hair, but I put a stop to that pretty quickly.

She was an edible little distraction, to be sure, but not for me.

Not for me. Not for me. Not for me.

So what if I had to tell myself that several times within a few minutes of meeting her?

Didn't mean a thing.

"I'm Estella," she said with a blinding smile, holding her hand out to me.

Was I supposed to shake it?

I did, awkwardly.

"Frankie."

"Frankie," she rolled the name around in her mouth, somehow making it exotic. "I love that name. It's strong. It suits you."

I smiled neutrally. "Thank you. Estella's a beautiful name. Suits you." Nothing about my tone or my eyes was flirtatious. Just making conversation.

Estella's eyes, on the other hand, were running all over my bared, inked flesh. She wasn't even trying to hide the fact that she liked what she saw.

I glanced at the dance floor. One of their group was trying to get her attention.

I pointed. "I think you're wanted on the dance floor."

She glanced back, then shot me a blatantly seductive smile. "Join me?"

I shook my head. "No thanks. You have fun though."

She walked away, a sexy little shake to her stride.

Danika was giving me a look, and I leveled a rueful one back at her.

"It's hard to explain a preference like mine," I explained. I'm attracted to Estella. She's highly fuckable, but that is not the point. I couldn't be who I need to be with her, and I won't settle for less."

"How do you ever find anyone?" Danika asked, sympathy in her voice. "It's hard enough finding decent people to date and then throwing something like that in the mix . . ."

"It's not easy. Not at all. But I'll tell you what, I won't ever be finding that somebody at a college bar. I'd rather be celibate for life than try vanilla again. Does nothing for me."

"So you have tried it?"

I grimaced. I had, with disastrous results, to the point where I'd thought something was broken inside of me, with no remedy to fix it. "Not with a lot of success, and not since I was too young to know better. A preference like mine . . . It's a dark thing, in a way, but when I get it right, God, there's nothing like it. Regular sex could never compare. Has all the excitement of a board game to me."

Eventually Estella came back, handing me a martini, flashing me a big smile.

"I love tattoos," she said, eyes all over my skin.

"Oh yeah?" I questioned, thinking she didn't mean it, since she had none of her own. "I have a tattoo parlor. If you're ever thinking of about getting ink, you should come to me."

She looked interested.

I didn't know how it happened, but the little vixen talked me into taking her home that night.

We made out for hours, and I got her off. Repeatedly. She was a hot little piece.

She slept over at my house, and nosily interrogated me about anything remotely fetish related that she found there.

The whipping post by my bed was a little hard to overlook, so I couldn't really blame her on that one.

She was completely new to it all, even though she said she was interested, so I didn't really let myself hope.

But even being new to it, she didn't seem put off by much. In spite of myself, I started to hope.

Keep an eye out on my site for more of Frankie and Estella's story:)

Www.rklilley.com

JAMES & BIANCA'S WEDDING

RECEPTION

AKIRA

I hated wearing a tux. Fucking hated it. Suits were bad enough. Tuxedos were man torture.

I tugged at my collar.

James, who I'd been chatting with, laughed. "Feel free to go change, if you want. All of the wedding party pictures have been taken. No one here will care if you dress down. Hell, run around in your boxers, for all I care."

Someone giggled to our left. It was so loud that we both turned to look. A little blonde thing, who I assumed was drunk, had found that very funny.

"I would pay to see that!" she told us with no shame. "Hell, I'll go find some ones, to tuck into your G-string, stud muffin!"

I glared at the loud mouthed little pixie. Her name was either Marnie or Judith. I couldn't remember which one was which and likely never would.

The dark haired one, again, either Marnie or Judith, added, "Fuck ones, I'll find twenties to see that fine ass."

"What the fu—" I started to rip into them.

Lana took pity on me, or them, or both. She brought her lovely self to my side, tutted at the girls, and started to lead them both away, murmuring something about coffee.

"Sorry, Lana, we meant no harm. Your husband is fucking *hot*," one of them said as they walked away.

"Those girls are a nuisance," I told James.

He laughed. "No, no they aren't. They're actually the opposite of that. Completely harmless. And very drunk."

I made a face. "Well, they've distracted my wife, when I was just going to distract her myself, so they're a nuisance to me."

Luckily, she wasn't gone for long, came back to me smiling, taking my breath away.

She was just too perfect, elegant and beautiful, strong and capable. And mine. I still couldn't believe it.

It was her own fault when she got into arm's reach of me, and I plucked her up and started to carry her away from the party. She was too damned irresistible.

There were some cheers from the partygoers as they caught the spectacle. Whatever. Let them look. She was mine. No matter how far out of my league she was. Mine.

She was strangely quiet, not teasing me for once.

"Something wrong?" I asked her as we neared the house.

She sighed against me.

"You want me to put you down?" I asked her.

"Never," she said softly.

I smiled.

She broke the news to me at the strangest moment.

We were both naked. Sweating. I had my face buried in her

pussy, about a second away from replacing it with my cock.

Her hands were in my hair and she was crying out, crying out.

I moved up her body, lingering on her flat belly.

"I'm pregnant," she panted, clutching me to her.

I lost my mind after that, took her like a man possessed, jolting into her again and again.

"I love you," I panted into her lovely face.

"I love you," she said back. It was about the tenth time we'd both said it, repeating it back and forth as we made love, like we couldn't say it enough, couldn't hear it enough.

Afterward I laid my head gently on her taut belly, hands running over it tenderly.

My baby in her belly. I shuddered, my entire massive self shaking with pleasure. It was all I'd ever wanted.

R.K. LILLEY

BOOKS BY R.K. LILLEY

THE WILD SIDE SERIES

THE WILD SIDE

IRIS

DAIR

TYRANT - COMING SOON

THE OTHER MAN - COMING SOON

THE UP IN THE AIR SERIES

IN FLIGHT

MILE HIGH

GROUNDED

MR. BEAUTIFUL

LANA (AN UP IN THE AIR COMPANION NOVELLA)

AUTHORITY - COMING SOON

THE TRISTAN & DANIKA SERIES

BAD THINGS

ROCK BOTTOM

LOVELY TRIGGER

THE HERETIC DAUGHTERS SERIES

BREATHING FIRE

CROSSING FIRE - COMING SOON

TEXT LILLEY + YOUR EMAIL ADDRESS TO 16782493375 TO JOIN MY EMAIL NEWSLETTER.

Visit my website for news and new releases here.

R.K. LILLEY